JEFFERSON McGRAW

Also by Weldon Hill

Lonesome Traveler
A Man Could Get Killed That Way
Rafe
One of the Casualties
The Long Summer of George Adams
Onionhead

JEFFERSON McGRAW
by Weldon Hill

a novel

William Morrow & Company, Inc., New York, 1972

To my kids, Randy, Mike, Susan, Steve and David

JEFFERSON McGRAW

1

It was another Friday afternoon and time for what used to be group singing before skinny Alice Brubaker gradually took it over. She finished rendering "Little Rosewood Casket," her second long dirge of the half hour, and stood with eyes modestly downcast while everybody but Jeff and his swarthy nemesis Chester Stone applauded with a solemn reverence suitable to the mournful occasion. Jeff abstained because he hated gloomy songs, couldn't stand her twangy nasal voice and resented the way she'd turned the weekly songfests into her own personal concerts. Hard-faced Chesty was too darn mean ever to show approval of anything but himself.

Hud Yancy put in a request for "The Death of Floyd Collins" and Jeff groaned, looking imploringly toward Miss Evans, but she just kept grading papers at her desk. It beat him how she could concentrate with such gruesome sounds in the room, dreary old songs about death and coffins. . . .

Lanky, shingle-bobbed Alice cleared her throat and strummed her Christmas guitar *plunk plink thunnnk* and said gravely: "Here goes 'The Death of Floyd Collins.'" And there it went.

Next year Jeff would escape from Alice by migrating upstairs to the seventh- and eighth-grade room. He'd leave mean Chester behind, too. That was the good part. The bad part was he'd be in the same room with his brother Mutt again.

Alice would be a sixth-grader next year, but Chester would most likely still be in the fifth—he wouldn't even be that far along if Slapper Hallet hadn't passed him last year just to get him out of her room. Chester was no dunce, he just hated school. Maybe that's what made him so ornery. He said he already knew all he needed to know, all about farming, breaking horses, working mule teams, casterating hogs, etc., and although the law could make him attend, it couldn't force him to study. He slept a lot, when he wasn't deciding which of his victims to chase home at four o'clock. Today Jeff figured it was about his turn again.

Miss Evans was good-natured and seldom whipped anyone, but next year he'd have Doris Ewbanks, a tall, freckled, hefty redhead who wore specs. According to Mutt, she was easy to get along with unless you happened to be a lazy useless dummy like you-know-who. Meaning Jeff, in *his* opinion.

There were many sad verses about poor Floyd Collins trapped deep in a Kentucky cave, his leg pinned by a boulder, and Alice threw in some fancy guitar frills between verses, dragging it out. Jeff remembered that tragedy, a couple of years ago; it was in the paper for nearly three weeks. The whole world prayed for poor Floyd, but he died in the cave, and they sealed it off. (If millions of prayers couldn't move a boulder, what good would *one* person's praying do? Like asking God to sprain Chester's ankle.)

It was funny about Chester Stone, in a way. Except for chasing guys home after school, his awesome reputation was based on his own boastful stories and one savage fight he had over a year ago with much bigger and older Lumpy Jackson, a sophomore who used to be quite a bully himself. That fight was legend now. How Lumpy cuffed Chester a few times, then wrestled him down on the cinders and started to strut away—only Chester jumped up and grabbed a baseball bat from Jake Ballew and chased Lumpy all over creation for about ten minutes, flailing away like a maniac

2

every chance he got. They ran into the highschool building, across the basketball court and out the side door, around the gradeschool and all over the baseball diamond for a while (somebody said they crossed home plate five times) with bloody-headed Lumpy hollering for help. Supt. Virgil Glass and some highschoolers finally subdued crazy Chester, ending the massacre. With Lumpy's reputation ruined and Chester's made.

This year Lumpy had gradually been reverting to his old overbearing personality, but he hadn't demanded a rematch. Losing to a bigger guy was no disgrace, but if you got licked by a smaller guy it made you a kind of social outcast. Even though Jeff was taller and heavier, he was durn glad he could outrun Chester, who was a year older. So far he managed to think of the extra-curricular activity as simply a footrace he'd always won, but each time it got harder to pretend he wasn't buffaloed by that mean-eyed, dangerous sonofagun.

Jeff had enough worries just being the son of an ex-schoolteacher and the brother of a straight-A student who was also a scrapper, ambitious and eternally sarcastic. Jeff had trouble even making B's, except in English and Spelling—one of his prized possessions was a pocket dictionary won in a spelling bee in December.

To alleviate the gray monotony of Alice's interminable song and the tension of Chester's ominous glances, he started whipping up a poem in his head.

> Old Alice can sure fill a room
> with the worst singing I ever heard
> about dying and misery and doom
> and I wish the janitor, Mr. Bird,
> would hit her in the mouth with his broom . . .

But instead Mr. Bird rang the big bell on top of the building, interrupting poet and singer alike, and Alice's fickle audience immediately bolted for the exits. She looked hurt, but doggedly finished the legend of Floyd Collins, with only Jeff and Hud and Miss Evans there at the end. Jeff felt kind of sorry for her as he went through his usual four o'clock stalling, suddenly dry-mouthed and flutter-gutted, in no big hurry to start home. "Enjoyed it, Allie," he lied, and she gave him a grateful toothy grin as she put her guitar in its canvas case.

He glanced at his long-time buddy Hud Yancy in the sheepish way he'd been doing since February when for no particular reason Chester had picked him as one of the rabbits in the hare-and-hound sport. Before that Jeff and Hud always walked home together, and Hud couldn't seem to adjust to the new arrangement. With two big ornery brothers in highschool who would kill anyone that hurt him, Hud could amble homeward at a leisurely pace. Jeff's only brother would, he suspected, enjoy *watching* him get beat up almost as much as doing it himself.

Hudson Yancy, the town cow drover, was rusty-haired, buck-toothed, did his homework at school and never had to take books home like Jeff. Hud never had a fight, or made eyes at a girl. Few people realized how comical he was sometimes.

"Maybe next week she'll sing faster," he remarked as Alice went out of the room. "How you goin' home today, Jiffer— walkin', trottin', or gallopin'?" He didn't crack a smile. He hardly ever did.

Neither did Jeff. "I dunno yet. It ain't up to me."

"Guess not," Hud agreed. "Any chance of you goin' to the pasture with me?"

"Nope, but maybe after supper we could roll hoops or play Annie-over or something," he suggested. Okeydokey, Hud said, starting to leave, and Jeff felt very lonesome, and asked quickly: "How many cows you herdin' now?" Seventeen, Hud said, and Jeff whistled enviously. A dollar a month per cow for six months of grazing season came to—lessee, now, six tens was sixty, six sevens was forty-two, a hundred

4

and two dollars old Hud would earn by October. Some guys just had the gift of making money, but Jefferson McGraw had been so broke all of his life he was used to it by now.

Hud went on out, and Jeff strolled north along the hall. Miss Burns was in the east room tacking Crayola drawings along the top of the blackboard. She was youngest and prettiest of the teachers and he had a secret crush on her. Slapper Hallet was keeping a couple guys in after school as usual. He moved on to look out the door and Chester wasn't going to the school barn to get his horse, so he was out front, waiting.

Sitting on the top step to untie and retie his tennis shoes, he considered sneaking around the highschool to the alley that went all the way home. But that would be cowardly, and darn hard to live down.

Blowing out his breath resignedly, he went on to the front corner of the building, and Chester was by the slippery slide, not looking at anyone but watching everybody with his dark beady eyes. All his other regular customers were lined up against the front of the schoolhouse, which was King's X—while they stayed there they were safe. The problem was how long could they stay there, versus how long would Chester hang around? They all had chores to do.

The other rabbits were Spotty Higgins, Oggy Arlen, Dick Spitzer and Elmer Hoffman. The first three had to go north past the school barn, which was convenient for Chester. Elmer and Jeff had to go straight east.

It wasn't just the chasing Chester got a pleasure out of, Jeff realized, it was also keeping a herd of scared guys hemmed in after school, proving how feared and respected he was. Jeff had wondered what would happen if all five of them stood up together against the bully, but concluded it just wasn't possible. Each rabbit was all alone with his private fear and humiliation, aware that nobody would lift a finger to help him. The only possible way they might ever get together on it would be to all start running at once.

5

He was amazed once more about how few people knew what went on here nearly every day after school. He'd kept hoping some other guy would complain to his parents or the superintendent, but they all probably felt the same way he did. Ashamed to confess their yellowness, but also leery of making Chester really *sore*. My lord! Imagine if he ever got *mad* at you! At first Jeff thought of telling his father, but then he'd imagined his dad showing up after school and saying sternly: "Okay, point out this bully to me, son, and I'll have words with the jasper." Then after one look at deceptively lean, average Chester he would say disgustedly: "You mean to tell me you run from a kid *smaller* than you are? By God, if you ever run from him again I'll skin you alive! Now you just march up to him and call his bluff!"

So the way it was, Jeff worried that Mutt or Jody would blab to his parents and he'd have to choose between fighting Chester or leaving home in disgrace. Where could he go? Calling people's bluff was a lot more important to the other McGraws than it was to peaceful Jeff. Especially Slim McGraw, who although six feet tall had never weighed over one-fifty in his life, but had never backed down from a fight no matter how big the guy was. And never lost a fight, either, if his memory was accurate.

Oddly enough, along with the clammy dread, Jeff felt an exhilarating sense of adventure. "Who's that foolin' with your horse, Chester?" he asked, and when his nemesis turned toward the school barn he bolted for the street. But Chester was only fooled for a second and came galloping right after him.

The wide sidewalk made a T left and right and he hit the dirt street at full speed, not looking back. That was a mistake some guys made, trying to run and look back at the same time. He could hear clodhoppers thumping behind him. Halfway to the corner he realized there were no sounds of pursuit, and violated his rule about looking back. Tricky Chester had merely used him to decoy the other rabbits

6

away from their safe haven, and was now chasing north-bound victims. Probably poor old flat-footed Spotty Higgins, who always had skinned elbows and knees—and therefore the best reason to tell his dad or Supt. Glass or Miss Evans or *somebody*. But maybe he also had the most pride or shame, or whatever kept him silent.

Elmer Hoffman was coming east looking north, and Jeff felt sympathy for him because he had farther to go than the others, and got home later oftener, and therefore needed more alibis. Elmer slowed to a panting walk. "Much obliged. I wish someone would kill that guy, so long."

He went loping on and was passing the McGraw place when Mutt suddenly appeared, coming off the porch, going to deliver the *Times*. He was about the same size as Chester, and almost as mean, but the only fight he'd had lately was with loud-mouthed Lige Bowzer back in the fall. Lige peddled the *Tulsa Tribune* and was always trying to sign up Mutt's *Oklahoman* and *Times* customers. The fistfight had ended in a draw, and Lige kept offering to let their dogs settle it, his mean part-bulldog Bozo against Mutt's duke's mixture Ranger. But Ranger was too valuable a hunting dog for that kind of stuff.

Mutt looked back to make sure Ranger didn't follow him, but he needn't have worried. With his old hunting buddy due home from school, Ranger wasn't going anywhere. As Mutt and Elmer went loping companionably toward the depot, Mutt's dog came up the street to greet his favorite McGraw.

"Howdy, ol' pardner," Jeff said fondly, when Ranger reared up on him to be scratched and petted. "Hey, tomorrow it's Saturday. We'll take off somewhere an' do sumpin', if it don't rain, boy."

Ranger made querulous deep-throated sounds and nasal whines, trying to hold up his end of the conversation. Jeff figured he was probably saying: "Heck, why wait 'til tomorrow when there's so much *today* left?" He didn't understand

7

about Jeff being the family servant. Jeff didn't really understand it himself, doggonnit. All he knew was, every day when he came home from school he got the uneasy feeling a whole pile of tedious chores had been saved up for him to do—and he was practically always right.

2

Jewel McGraw was ironing clothes; he could smell the scorched waxed bread wrappers and cedar branches she rubbed her hot irons on for some reason he didn't clearly comprehend, except that the cedar made things smell nice. She seemed to be forever ironing or washing or patching or darning or scrubbing or mopping, and usually humming to herself, mostly church music like "Bringing in the Sheaves" or "Shall We Gather at the River?"

A plump corseted woman with brown hair pinned in a knot in back, even in repose her expression was rather stern —or so it seemed to Jeff. As if, in his case, she was always comparing him to Mutt, who ran home from school, grabbed a quick bite, and went galloping off to earn money and make something of himself, instead of frittering away his life like Jeff. He suspected that she was eternally vexed because her two sons were so different.

But all she said was: "Did you see Jody anywhere?"

"Nope," he said. "Ain't he home yet?"

She sighed. "Would I ask if you'd seen him?"

Heading for the kitchen, he thought: Well, heck, what kind of answer did she *expect* from the family dunce? She called after him: "And how many times have I told you not to say ain't?"

"About eighty-six," he said, well aware that she didn't appreciate his brand of humor, especially at this cranky time of day. Sure enough, she said: "Don't be a smart aleck."

That's how it went. If Mutt joked with her, she'd chuckle or smile. A job and money in the bank automatically made a guy witty, but a penniless loafer wasn't ever funny. If you made mostly A's you were a scream, but with just average grades you were only silly. Little Jody was often funny without meaning to be, and they all laughed at things he said and did. So around the McGraw ranch you had to be a scholar and businessman or a six-year-old kid to get a laugh out of Jewel McGraw.

He brooded about that while spreading wild grape jelly on homemade bread—for an ex-schoolteacher she could sure bake bread. Being lazy was more natural for a guy his age than trying to get rich. After highschool you *had* to earn a living, so a guy oughta just enjoy life while he could. Besides, there were only three paper routes in town and Mutt had two of them.

While he ate, his mother reminded him of all the chores, as if he didn't know the long list by heart. Carry out the ashes; bring in a bucket of cobs and some cookstove wood. She said it was still nippy enough mornings so a fire felt good. "Anyway, until hot weather I prefer the wood range for baking," she added in a sociable tone he really appreciated. Any small sign of friendliness always eased the tension. Around home he kept expecting to get bawled out—for something he'd done or failed to do, should or shouldn't have done, ought to begin doing or quit doing, etc. "Besides," she said, "wood and cobs are cheaper than coal oil."

She was thrifty, she appreciated a bargain—like a free hired hand who did all the chores for just his board and room and clothes. Mutt was like a guest around there. Right now he was probably sitting on a baggage truck at the depot reading the funnies in the *Times,* but Jeff couldn't even read the *morning* paper until he did all the work Mutt got out of. Something rotten in Denmark there, boy.

"Gather the eggs," she said. Jody liked to gather eggs but she wouldn't let him, he broke a couple once. "Feed the

10

chickens," she said needlessly. "Put more oats to soak—give them that pan of potato peelings." Potatoes—he wondered what was for supper, hoping it wouldn't be potato soup. (Hud would have said "pretater" or "pertatie" or "patooties," because he mispronounced words just to be comical.) "Clean the water pans before you fill them. See if the hens need fresh hay in the nests, but don't disturb the setting biddies," she said. Boy, she must think he was a regular sap. "Fetch a fresh bucket of water," she said. He was lucky she wasn't his teacher, he'd get all C's and D's, even some F's, because she sure thought he was stupid.

"What's for supper?" he asked, and she said, "Bacon and eggs and fried potatoes and biscuits—and gravy, naturally."

He grinned to himself. Naturally. With biscuits his dad always wanted gravy. And with fried spuds he wanted onions, although it gave him heartburn so he had to eat chalk of magnesia. Jeff had dozens of favorite meals. In spring he started looking forward to fried chicken and garden stuff. And fish he'd catch himself. Fishing was one of the few time-frittering things his mother approved of because it put free food on the table.

Doing chores required several trips to the barn, which also served as chicken house and for storing coal, cobs, stovewood and kindling. Hud's dad, Earl Yancy, hauled the coal and cobs in his dray wagon, and they bought chunkwood from various farmers. Splitting chunks into cookstove wood was one winter job he really enjoyed. Someday he'd have an axe of his own. And a rifle, traps, a snug log cabin away off down the creek somewhere . . .

Most people with barns kept milk cows, but Jewel McGraw said it would be more bother than benefit when you could buy milk delivered for two bits a gallon. The only advantage of owning a cow would be all that manure to put on the garden, and heck, you could get it free from neighborhood cowsheds. Horse manure was better, maybe because it was scarcer, but you couldn't milk a horse and needed a

11

better reason for owning one than just riding it or being able to grow bigger cucumbers and cabbages and so forth.

Every trip along the bridge-plank walk leading out to the barn and toilet he had to pass Mutt's sleeping tent, a square of canvas stretched over clothesline (telegraph wire) tied between two maple trees. It had a board floor, Army cot, homemade table, apple box cupboard, and a coal-oil lantern. Mutt had been sleeping out there for a couple weeks, claiming it was much healthier. In winter he slept on the dining-room couch, with Jeff and Jody sharing the duofold in the front parlor, which Jeff now had all to himself, and Jody the couch. Jewel McGraw slept in the one downstairs bedroom, Slim McGraw in the small upstairs bedroom. Jeff would soon move to the big bed on the screened-and-latticed back porch, as close to sleeping outdoors as he cared to get.

While pumping water he noticed old gawky, pigeon-toed, hoity-toity Caroline Riley watching him across the fence in her scornful way. She did that a lot. Nothing better to do, he supposed. She wasn't so much, just because her dad was mayor and owned a Model T flivver and managed the lumberyard. Who needed a tin lizzie if you could get railroad passes for traveling? Kerosene was always trying to get his goat, but he just ignored her. Hud stuck that moniker on Caroline. She was a gangling, clumsy fourth-grader, silly and dumb. Their dads were good friends and their mothers were friendly most of the time, so let the poor thing gawk if she enjoyed it.

This town could sure use a few *new* girls. The only new one lately was Goldie Strode, a sort of outcast because her dad was in jail and her mother had to take in washing. Besides, she was a ninth-grader. All the *pretty* girls were in high school.

He was nearly finished choring when Jody came slinking around the house with a guilty lopsided grin. "Did Mama notice I'm not here yet?" he asked worriedly. His real mother had died when he was three months old, so naturally he thought his aunt Jewel was his true mama, and Slim McGraw was his father—and didn't quite understand about having another in Kansas called Daddy Tobe he only saw about once a year. He seemed like a brother to Jeff, after nearly seven years, a real pest, an ornery little dickens. Spoiled rotten, if you looked at it a certain way—and Jeff did.

"She noticed," he growled. "Where the devil you been?"

"Stopped off to play with Woody awhile," Jody said. Woody Higgins lived two blocks north of the school barn, which wasn't exactly on the way home for Jody. "Is she mad?" the jug-eared culprit asked uneasily.

"Mad as a wet hen," Jeff said. "You're gonna get it."

Jody registered alarm. "She fixin' to switch me?"

"Probably use the razor strap," Jeff said ominously. But the sight of Jody's scared face made him feel sudden remorse. He often resented the little wart's privileged, favored family status, but he couldn't ever be mean to the little guy. He didn't have a cruel streak like some people, he had a kind streak. "Aw, heck," he said, "just tell 'er you played on the slippery slide or somethin', dummy. Don't say you went to Woody's house."

Jody nodded anxiously. Like anybody else he remembered the few times he'd been punished instead of the million times he'd only been scolded. He went reluctantly inside, and Jeff waited for sounds of scolding, but it stayed quiet in there. Shrugging, he went about his unpaid services, wishing he was either the oldest or youngest, instead of the middle kid in the family.

The unwanted second kid. Born when Mutt was a puny thirteen months old and needing all the milk and attention. One day last summer he'd overheard that awful conversation through the open dining-room window. Mrs. Riley said: Oh, if only men had to suffer a tenth of the pain, they'd be more considerate. And his mother said: Yes, how true, personally she'd only wanted *one* child, and certainly *never* two babies so close together, God forbid. But, as long as she *had* to endure that agony and humiliation twice, with Doc Schuman making crude jokes in his foreign accent, she'd hoped the second one would be a girl. Mrs. Riley said: Of course the war was on when Caroline was born, and John had got that doctor from Blackthorn, not wanting to trust a *German,* naturally. Then his mother said: Well, in any case, a girl or no girl, Matt (that was his real name and nobody called him Mutt until after Jeff was born) had been sickly and not weaned yet, and needed all her nourishment and attention, so the second baby picked the worst possible time to come along. She was so run-down and overworked, and had to put Matt on the bottle and take care of two at once, dear Lord, the diapers! ("I don't mind telling you, Ethel," she said, "there were times when I almost wished that second baby had been stillborn, God forgive me.")

At that point Jeff had fled to the barn loft and cried like a baby. He knew what stillborn meant. She'd wished he'd been born *dead*! Ever since that day he'd always felt kind of unnecessary, even a little guilty. Probably he was to blame for Mutt growing up leaner and shorter and meaner, deprived of his ninny too soon. But maybe cow milk made you smarter and spunkier and more ambitious—and human milk caused laziness and dumbness along with biggerness.

Sometimes he wondered whether his dad had wanted him to be a girl, too. Holy Moses! Never to hunt, fish, climb trees, shoot marbles, spin tops, make slingshots and bows and arrows, play baseball, have spear fights with dry weeds, smoke cornsilk and grapevine, chew tobacco, play tin-can shinny, ride stick horses, steal watermelons and all that! The only advantage in being a girl, they didn't have to fight or run from anybody.

There were three hens setting and two with broods of chicks. It was going to be a good summer for fried chicken, one of his favorite foods. Another was oatmeal cookies like Jody was eating when he went in the house. "You didn't tell *me* you made cookies," he said indignantly.

14

She stopped slicing spuds and gave him a look that always made him wince. "Now wasn't that thoughtless of me, you poor emaciated, undernourished thing?" Once a teacher, always a big word user. "If you can't survive until supper, help yourself, chubby," she said tartly.

Oh, yeah, he thought, stung. At least I don't hafta wear corsets. If I'm chubby, how come I'm so fast? And if it's too near suppertime for me, why not for the pest?

But in the dining room with the *Daily Oklahoman* he thought sheepishly, all I hadda do was look in the cookie jar like I usually do after school. With a half hour until supper, and a mother who couldn't abide idleness, he decided to go over and walk home with his dad. Ranger was on the front porch, keeping a sharp eye on his street, and didn't need any written invitation to go along.

Jeff hurdled the wicket fence and sprinted fifty yards, then slowed to a gallop as he passed the Yancy place. Now that it was cow-herding and planting time he wouldn't get much use out of Hud for a while. Earl Yancy, the town drayman, also did commercial truck-gardening on various plots around town (horse fertilized) and Hud had to help him. The older boys, Von and Lex, did odd jobs around the elevator, produce house and cotton gin—and spent the rest of their time playing elaborate practical jokes on people, mainly involving electrified chairs, fences, swings, gates, door handles, etc. All three Yancy boys called their father Earl, and he didn't mind. Jeff couldn't even imagine calling his dad Slim, or Gabe.

Passing the two-story Depot Hotel, Jeff went zooming up the steep cinder path where the street dead-ended against the railroad embankment, and across the tracks to the long brick platform. Cutting north toward Main Street, he was startled to see his father coming down the skinny iron ladder on the big black watertank.

Jeff had never thought whether his dad was handsome or homely, and it wouldn't have mattered either way, he just liked him as he was: a father any kid would be proud to have. Muscular, and by his own account (which Jeff accepted as gospel truth), ever ready to fight any man at the drop of an insult. When angered, Gabriel McGraw's angular face would harden, his friendly green eyes would blaze. So far Jeff had only witnessed that temper in cases where the cause of the hot Scotch-Irish wrath was luckily absent, safe from punishment richly deserved. Actually his dad hadn't needed to chastise a bully for so long that Jeff only knew of famous battles in retrospect, as history, from his dad's mellow reminiscing accounts of dandy scraps in the good old days, which Jeff sure wished he'd seen.

Aside from being brave and unwhippable, Slim McGraw was also wise, self-sufficient and skilled at his trade. He could have been a locomotive engineer or fireman, boiler-maker or master mechanic—instead of all four on a basis limited by the tools, equipment and job requirements of a layover town like Cottonwood. Blackie Arthur, Jeff's favorite engineer, once remarked that Slim McGraw was a one-man roundhouse and could probably take a locomotive apart and put her back together again, given the necessary jacks, hoists, wrenches, and a gallon of moonshine to keep his liver healthy. All the overnighting train crews respected him and liked him.

Besides admiring his dad, and being a little awed by him in a comfortable way, Jeff appreciated his attitude about fatherhood and discipline, etc. He left all the whipping up to his wife, and usually gave the subtle impression he sided with Jeff when trouble cropped up. Also he wasn't a tight-wad, frequently giving his poorest son a dime for nothing, or two bits for a couple hours of screening sand. And last but not least he liked dogs.

"What were you doin' up there?" Jeff asked curiously, and the jocular engine watchman replied: "I was looking for whales."

He was kidding, of course, and went on to explain. There

16

had been complaints from engine crews taking on water at Cottonwood about finding fish in their tenders, like Mack Gilmore saying he found a nine-pound mudcat clogging a steam pipe, and Blackie claiming that lately Number Nine's exhaust often spewed chowder instead of steam—he wasn't complaining except it needed more seasoning and henceforth he aimed to throw some onions, taters and salt in the tender when he took on Cottonwood water. But all kidding aside, sometimes small fish *did* come down the spout into the tenders, so Jeff's dad had climbed up there to take a look. The water was still muddy from the creek's last rise, and he hadn't spotted any fish—but the tank hadn't been cleaned out in about six years, so there might be some big fish in it now, pumped through the intake screen as minnows and growing a pound or so a year on a diet of wiggle-tails, insects and bugs, and eventually other minnows when they got big enough to turn cannibal. Squinting up at the vast mystery of the huge reservoir, Slim McGraw said: "By golly, there might be some whopper bass and catfish and perch in there by now."

"Boy, howdy!" Jeff exclaimed.

His dad gave him a thoughtful frown. "Hold 'er, Newt!" he admonished. "Don't get any big ideas. Go right on doing your fishing in the creek—and don't repeat that information to anyone, either. Some fool kid might get ambitious and fall off that ladder and break his neck. Understand me?"

Jeff nodded obediently. "How'd you get up to the ladder?" he asked. It was ten feet to the bottom rung.

"Took a run and a jump"—his dad grinned—"and made it the first try. Didn't think I had it in me, but I reckon there's life in the old boy yet. You suppose supper's about ready?"

Jeff nodded. "She was commencin' to fry taters."

"In that case we better start ambling homeward," his dad said, taking time to scratch Ranger's ears and ask him how he was getting along.

Nearing the cinder path, Jeff saw the oldest Strode boy,

Vernon, delivering a big bundle of laundry for someone at the Depot Hotel, probably one of the teachers, and mainly just to make conversation he said, "There's the convict's kid."

"I'm inclined to admire that boy," his father said. "Just because his dad's incarcerated for making and selling whiskey is no reason for you to look down on him. He's not accountable for what his daddy did—anyway, there's something wrong with laws that give a man free board and room while his destitute wife and kids hafta fend for themselves. That's punishing Dallas Strode's family for his crime. Anyway, goddammit, to my mind Prohibition is the worst law ever dreamed up, and I'd say that even if I didn't like a little snort now and then myself. It goes against human nature—and shows what happens when you let women vote. Next thing, they'll outlaw tobacco like they did whiskey, you watch!"

Jeff just shrugged. He was willing to go along with the prevailing public opinion that a jailbird's son was beyond the pale as far as nice people were concerned, although he didn't go along with the anonymous gradeschool poet who had composed the slanderous sonnet: *Old Vernon Strode he et a warty toad an' up he throwed right in the road.* That was a lousy thing to holler at anybody.

3

A bustling young railroad town east of the poor Pawnees and south of the oil-rich Osages, Cottonwood had no resident Indians of its own. Also no Negroes, Mexicans, Orientals or Hebrews. There was only one Catholic, Mayor Riley, and two Germans, Doc Schuman and his wife. Nobody had anything against Catholics except their religion, but there were still people nursing a postwar grudge against Germans. Doc Schuman, one of the town's first settlers, had delivered most of the population under twenty-one years of age, and he managed to survive the anti-Teutonic fad of hauling broken bones and pregnant wives to *American* doctors in Blackthorn and Bear Creek. His drugstore sold a lot of ice cream and sodas, as well as medicines, and since Prohibition he was the main dispenser of "blood tonics," preventive snakebite remedies, and even prescription wines and cordials. He drove a 1926 Cleveland and offered sick or injured kids all-day suckers or jawbreakers if they wouldn't bawl. Old Doc gave Jeff his first spanking, one of many.

Cottonwood was a shipping point for farm products hauled in from as far away as a dozen miles in horse-drawn conveyances—a number of farmers owned autos, but hardly any owned trucks. The wheat, oats and corn were brought in to the grain elevator; the cotton to the gin on south of the elevator; poultry, eggs and cream to the produce house across Main Street from the elevator. All managed and partly owned by rotund Claude Calvert. Cattle, sheep and pigs were shipped from the railroad's loading pens north of the produce house and east of Slim McGraw's ex-boxcar office and storehouse, known as The Shack to the McGraws.

Claude Calvert's silent partner was a reclusive gentleman named George Rose who dwelt in baronial splendor eight miles from town in a hilltop mansion overlooking the Arkansas River valley and eight hundred acres of cotton, corn, alfalfa, sorghum cane, orchards, pecan groves, horses, cattle, pigs, sheep and No TRESPASSING signs. He was also president and main stockholder of the bank, and owned rental properties in town, all wired for electricity. The McGraws wished he was their landlord; the skinflint they rented from said if he wired the house he'd have to raise them five a month.

Seldom seen and little known, George Rose was fair game for rumors and conjecture. Jeff and Hud favored the rumor that Ol' George had gotten his wealth by marrying an Osage princess and skinning her feckless family and kin out of their oil royalties. Everybody knew that kind of stuff happened all the time, white slickers cheating the Indians—but unfortunately no one in Cottonwood ever got a real chance to gyp a gullible Red Man. The Osages seldom came south of the river to barter, except for an occasional blanketed, braided, portly, impassive old buck in his touring car driven by a usually rather shifty-looking white chauffeur, shopping for vanilla extract or bay rum.

Besides the elevator-gin-produce complex east of the tracks and the bank on a corner of the main intersection, Cottonwood had the usual essential establishments. Two grocery stores, the drugstore, two filling-station-garages, two barbershops, a shoe shop, a large blacksmith shop with a sociable smithy who liked kids, two hotels catering to railroad men, salesmen, bachelor workers, teachers and pensioners; a dry goods store, a carpentry and plumbing business, post office, telephone office, a beauty parlor, furniture store, electrical supply and service place, and two cafés across the street from one another.

The Kaw and Washita Railroad supplied Cottonwood with life-sustaining commerce, and paychecks for a dozen resident employees plus extra revenue for feeding and sheltering the train crews that laid over seven nights a week.

The younger firemen and brakemen lodged at the Osage Inn on West Main, handy to the cafés, the drugstore and Slick Melton's barbershop, all of which stayed open until around ten at night. The conductors and engineers, observing an ancient caste system, stayed at the Depot Hotel, whose permanent guests included three lady schoolteachers. This nocturnal juxtaposition of single women and married men under one roof caused some gossip, but sensible people ignored it. The engineers and conductors were elderly products of a slow seniority system, and men of unquestioned honor and character. Furthermore, Lizzie Horn, Doris Ewbanks and Clara Conners were a far cry from flappers or jazz babies. As Slim McGraw remarked, hell, you only had to look at them to know they were nice, virtuous girls, whether they liked it or not.

If there was an official tally of Cottonwood's regular denizens, nobody had bothered to notify Jeff or Hud, so one late April evening while loafing at the depot they took their own mental census. Faster at figuring, Hud said: "Three hunderid an' thirty-six souls, an' soon be five more when the new people move into the old rest-your-rump building." If he'd said café, he'd of made it rhyme with safe.

Unless there'd been a birth or death the past couple hours, Hud was probably right. "Okay, how about dogs?" Jeff suggested, although it wasn't quite the same. If dogs died or had pups the news didn't spread very fast. There were a couple dogs he wished would either get bad teeth or leave town. Lige Bowzer's part bulldog Bozo, and Chink Britton's slobbering crazy Killer. Lige was always trying to promote a fight between Bozo and other dogs, and Chink's big shaggy mongrel was so vicious it had to be kept in a high-fenced yard. Just walk past in the street, minding your own busi-

21

ness, and Killer would chew on the wire making blood-curdling sounds of fury.

"Not countin' recent pups," Hud reported, "I can think of twenty-eight dogs, which I wish five or six of would either perish or quit chasin' cows, ever which is quickest." He didn't have a dog of his own, since Earl didn't believe in keeping any animals you couldn't harness, milk or sugar cure.

Jeff was still thinking about Killer. Squinty, strutting Chink, who had arrived last autumn to stay with his uncle Ralph after his aunt died, claimed his brute had killed so many dogs and cats and chawed up so many people, mostly Negroes, that a fifty-dollar reward had been offered to any-one who killed old Killer. Hud said in his opinion Chink would murder his own dog for that kind of money. Even when his wife was alive Ralph Britton had been a sour, un-sociable recluse, disfigured and crippled by the war, people said, and since his cocky fifteen-year-old nephew from Sa-pulpa moved in with his bloodthirsty dog, nobody tried to visit the shut-in vet anymore, not even the preacher. Chink claimed the government paid him fifty dollars a month to stay with his uncle, and did seem to have plenty of spending money. There was something sly and sinister about that guy.

"Seven head of horse an' two of mule," Hud announced, causing Jeff to chuckle. "Cows, you say? Twenty-one, not counting calfs. Just as well to skip pigs as they flucturate somewhatly, either gittin' butchered or havin' pups so you can't keep track."

Jeff grinned at "flucturate somewhatly." In winter his mother bought whole sides from hog raisers who butchered and peddled, and they got their fill of fresh pork for a while. She also bought hog heads to make headcheese and souse. Pork liver fried with bacon and onions was one of their favorite feasts, although it gave his dad the onion regrets. Boiled fresh ham with dumplings, spareribs and sauerkraut, side meat and porkchops, oh, man! That was living. Sausage and pancakes . . .

The McGraws would feed out a couple of pigs every fall and winter except for a town ordinance that prohibited raising, keeping, penning, breeding or. otherwise harboring swine along or near Main Street or in residential areas where said swine would be a nuisance or aggravation to adjacent citizens. Cantankerous Granny Hicks said she'd kept a cow, chickens and pigs for fifty years and was too old to change her style. Besides, pigs across the alley didn't smell as bad as your own chicken pen after a rain.

"Cats are a horse of a different color," Hud said. "I'll bet even cats don't know how many cats there are."

The McGraws' scarred old tomcat wasn't home much this time of year, just when he felt like a saucer of milk, or when he needed to sharpen his claws on Jewel McGraw's corset. Old Fred liked to lie in her lap purring and flexing his talons, causing her to yelp now and then and scold him fondly for gouging her. She liked cats better than dogs.

"Automobubbles," Hud said. "Countin' the gas truck, seven." Inner tubes for slingshot rubbers were scarce.

"Brings us to bathrooms," Hud said. "Around ten, countin' two yonder at the hotel, the downstairs one bein' on the west side." He slid Jeff a wary glance. "Ever see a naked woman?"

Jeff was startled. "Heck, no. Did you?"

"A few, here an' there." Hud shrugged, poker-faced.

Oh, yeah? Jeff thought. "Like who, for example?"

Hud glanced surreptitiously over both shoulders. "Three schoolmarms." He nodded toward the hotel, and Jeff was astounded. Lizzie Horn, Doris Ewbanks and Clara Conners? All three? Naked? Hud must be joshing.

"All at the same time?" he asked skeptically.

Hud shook his head. "One at a time, takin' baths." He gave Jeff a guilty, skid-away glance. "That downstairs bathroom, the winder's eight feet from the ground with curtains acrost the bottom, but you can climb a tree an' look right into the durn tub, practically."

My lord! Jeff thought. "Well. How'd they look?"

23

"Priddy dang unusural," Hud declared. "Man, I can't describe it, you'd hafta shinny up there an' see for yourself—some night between nine and ten."

"They all take baths *every* night?" Jeff asked incredulously, and Hud said well, hell no, of *course* not. They took turns. Like Lizzie on Monday night, Doris on Tuesday, Clara on Wednesday, then Liz again on Thursday, an' so on.

Jeff made a joke. "Reckon that's why Miss Ewbanks looks so rusty? All them baths?" But Hud never would crack a smile when Jeff said something comical.

"I'll tell ya one thing," Hud said. "Clara Conners ain't near as skinny as she lets on to be. But Lizzie is the other way, fatter than she acts like she is. Doris looks about the way you'd expect."

Somehow the idea repelled more than attracted Jeff. He wouldn't mind seeing *a* naked woman, but three was overdoing it. He just wasn't up with the latest craze. Old Chink claimed he had a platform high in a tree, from which he could see all over town with his uncle's binoculars, and into certain bedroom windows at night. But everyone agreed Chink was the biggest liar in town, whereas Hud was an honest man, and a generous friend, saying: "Any night you wanta use that roost, it's all yours, Jifferson."

Well, shoot. Jeff liked to climb trees as much as the next guy, but he'd never played Tarzan after dark. Be just his luck to fall out and break a leg and they'd come out there and ask what was he doing in a tree that time of night? What could he say? Trying to catch a hoot owl? Oh, they'd figure it out, all right, and he'd be disgraced forever. If it was Miss Ewbanks' night to bathe, every time she graded his report card next year she'd remember he'd seen her bare naked.

It wasn't worth the risks, but he still kind of envied Hud. Feature that, all *three* of them!

4

He awoke in the ruddy glow of sunrise needing to go to the barn, but reluctant to leave his snug bed, too comfortable otherwise and knowing it was Saturday. The weather in May had taken a turn for the better, and Chester had gone hurrying home after school all week because of urgent farm chores, and life was nice and peaceful. So he yawned and shut his eyes, thinking another hour of slumber wouldn't stunt his growth. But just as he was sinking into blissful numbness he got a sudden prickly feeling of alarm and twitched wide awake.

She'd been saying the first *nice* Saturday she was going to take up the parlor rug, and this was it. Shivering in the cool morning, he got dressed in a fumbling, yawning hurry. She might have expected this sunny day and set her alarm for the usual schoolday summons, rug-beating uppermost in her mind. And of all the miserable dusty wearying jobs, that one took the cake.

He checked his pockets to see if he had the Saturday necessities. Barlow knife, ball of all-purpose string, spare slingshot rubbers, fishhooks stuck in a cork, sinkers, matches, a hunk of plug tobacco. He emptied out the unneeded marbles and went tiptoeing past her open bedroom door to the kitchen, still shivering in his dank tennis shoes, night-chilled shirt and overalls, and limp-billed baseball cap. The dining-room couch was vacant—Jody was already up and gone again, sneaking away before anyone else was awake. He

25

could sleep until noon if he wanted to, so it didn't make much sense.

After eating a bowl of cornflakes, he made a bean sandwich and an egg sandwich, with sliced onion on both, putting all of the food in a paper sack. He filled a pint jar with cold coffee, milked and sugared, and added two hard biscuits to his sack. Then he eased across the creaky dining-room floor, carefully unhooked the twangy front screen-door spring so it wouldn't betray him and froze in his tracks when she suddenly cleared her throat. But she didn't speak, and he made it out onto the porch.

He wasn't safe yet. Down the street, he would be in plain view in case she got up and glanced out the door. Up the street, if she looked out her west window she could holler him back without even getting out of bed. The quickest, most sensible route was straight across the street and around Hallets' house to the alley behind the drugstore, then east, but old Slapper had bawled him out twice for using her yard as a shortcut. Still, any teacher in her right mind would surely sleep late on Saturday.

Ordinarily Jeff would whistle, or wait for Ranger's sensitive nose to discover his presence, but he couldn't risk waiting. He loped across the street, cat-footing along on his toes, not worried about encountering henpecked, mild-mannered Mr. Hallet, and made it safely around the house and halfway along the path to the alley when suddenly to his consternation the toilet door opened and there was Slapper in her nightgown and carpet slippers. And no place he could hide.

The big glowering woman came along the path clutching the flannel gown in front, angry and embarrassed. "This is your last warning, Jeff McGraw, my yard is not a public road. Is that perfectly clear?"

He nodded sheepishly, sidling out of the path to let her go sailing past, still yammering over her shoulder. People

26

were entitled to *some* privacy even in a town full of backward yahoos and ignoramuses, she said.

Main Street was empty except for a bunch of sparrows breakfasting on horse manure, a Jersey cow ambling lazily around the bank corner and two bluejays quarreling on the horse trough in the center of the main intersection. Hud must be in the north part of town gathering the cows and starting them on their way, riding Blackie, a tall horse with a sharp backbone. If Hud let you ride old Blackie he sure wasn't doing you a favor.

Feeling pursued, Jeff headed on east. In passing he squinted through the dusty window of the ex-café that Hud said soon would be a grocery. A man named Dexter had leased the building and hired Earl to plow up the adjoining vacant lot for a garden. Four kids, Hud said Earl said the man told him, the oldest a girl. Cottonwood didn't much need another grocery store, but it could sure use a few new girls.

He loped northeast across the sidetracks to the locomotives hiding the engine watchman's shack, going around the cowcatcher of the northbound engine and the tender of the southbound, and Dolittle was at the north end of the shack shoveling screened sand into the high funnel-shaped, coal-burning dryer.

Dewey Little was an erstwhile doughboy who had got to France in time for some combat before the war ended. Dolittle was a real friendly and likable guy, not big but well-built from his years on the section gang before getting promoted about a year ago. He gave Jeff an amiable welcoming grin.

"Let me guess," he said, leaning on the shovel. "It's Saturday, so you're goin' fishin' an' need worms."

Behind the shack was a spade, Prince Albert cans, and long cane poles racked on nails in the wall, all for the convenience of overnighting train crews. But most of them

27

seemed to prefer pitching horseshoes, playing dominoes, hanging around the barbershops and cafés, or just sitting on the hotel porches gabbing.

The stock pens back of the shack contained years of accumulated manure that had spilled or washed out along the sides to make a strip of enriched ground which produced bumper crops of fishworms, especially at the northwest corner where a leaky spigot caused a water trough to run over. Two turns of the spade in that rich juicy loam filled Jeff's flat can with big red worms. When he went back across the stockyard track, Dolittle asked if he wanted one of the cane poles.

"I prefer a willow pole," Jeff said. "Anyway, I need both hands free to use my slingshot in case I see a woodpecker or something."

"We didn't have slingshots when I was your age," Dolittle said. "There was no such animal as a used inner tube in those days."

"They're *still* plenty scarce," Jeff informed him.

"When I get my automobile you can have dibs on all my old inner tubes," Dolittle said, and grinned at Jeff's dubious expression. "You probably wonder when that'll be." He shrugged. "I got the big eye, Jeff. Originally I only wanted a Model T, but then I suddenly wanted something niftier, a coopay or roadster, maybe even a big sedan. It'll most likely be the only one I'll ever have, so I might as well get a good one while I'm at it. Longer I wait, the longer it'll last. Meanwhile my money earns interest in the bank."

Over eleven hundred dollars, Jeff's dad said. Dolittle lived with his parents, paying twenty a month room and board, leaving him seventy to save or spend. Slim McGraw had to support five people on his hundred-and-twenty-a-month wages. No wonder Dolittle wasn't in any hurry to start wife-hunting.

"How far will one of those rubber catapults shoot?" Dolittle inquired, and Jeff said it depended on how thick the rubbers were, and whether you used chat, stones, marbles or slugs made of melted babbitt, like Mutt.

"Let's simple it down," Dolittle said. "How far can you fire yours right now, usin' whatever you're usin'?"

Unwinding the slingshot, Jeff got a piece of chat, looking up at the chute. "How far away are them pigeons?"

"A hundred feet away, ninety feet high—so let's call it long shotgun range. Fire when ready, Gridley."

Jeff reared back and cut loose, and the unpredictable chat went humming in a beeline to rattle off a corner of the steep roof peak. The birds erupted in startled flight, and Dolittle said: "Well I'll be slightly doggonned!"

Acting casual, Jeff hung the slingshot around his neck and adjusted the sack of grub inside his overalls bib. "That's the general idea. Well, I better get goin'."

Dolittle looked at his watch. "Same here, pard. The crews are smellin' the coffee and flapjacks, so I better cook up some steam pressure in these jessies. Good luck."

Jeff started across the siding, looking back toward Main Street, feeling exposed to view in case his mother had discovered his escape and sent Mutt to look for him. That thought made him hurry and glance back frequently. The railroad ran level, but the town west of the built-up right-of-way sloped down to the creek, so he could see off across the northwest part of town. Before he reached the narrow steel bridge the double mainline tracks became a single track and the roadbed dropped off steeply on both sides. At the south end of the high black span a worn path went down the sharp incline and across a willow-thicketed swale to the south end of the dam, fifty yards upstream. From the bridge in winter you could see up and down the creek, but now most of the trees were leafed out, restricting the view. But nobody was fishing at the dam yet—he'd have it all to himself for a while, at least.

In late summer the path would be a narrow trench descending through rank weeds higher than his head, but now there were only burnt-off stobs studding a green carpet of grass and wildflowers. Before starting down he took a final wary look along his backtrail and saw a figure under the coal chute. As the guy disappeared behind the chute, he decided it wasn't Mutt. Too tall.

The morning paper route was more important to Mutt than hunting an escaped rug-beater—unless there was a reward, which wasn't likely. She might pay Mutt to perform that dreary annual chore, but she wouldn't spend money trying to locate old lazy Jeff. She might tan his hide when he went home, and his best hope for justice tempered with mercy was to take her a big mess of free fish. Anyway, he'd developed the ability to not worry about a crime while doing it, otherwise it wasn't any fun. Meanwhile, he owned the beautiful balmy fragrant morning, and even if the creek was still a bit murky, the fish oughta be starved for worms.

The dam was eight feet high and sixty feet across, with an overflow trough along the base. From the dam to the bridge huge boulders and rock slabs had been dumped in the creek bed to control floodwaters, but the force of the bigger floods over the years had rearranged the boulders just below the dam in a fan-shaped pattern, with a fairly deep hole in the middle and smaller ones flanking it. After the spring rises these pools usually held a variety of fish that had been washed over the dam, and although the water was foamy and yellow he decided to try his luck there before moving on above the dam.

The silvery curtain of water pouring over the dam made a splashing roar that muted the music of red-winged black-birds and cardinals in the willows. Putting his lunch on a flat rock, he cut a long limber willow pole, eager and exhilarated. Boy, this was the way to spend a Saturday.

He was tying line to the pole when a disturbance in the middle pool required his immediate attention. Carrying the pole, he went hopping nimbly from rock to boulder to slab across the burbling rivulets, then nearly fell in from sheer amazement when he saw what it was. A big fish swimming around with its dorsal fin and part of its broad greenish back out of water—an enormous bass!

While he tied his biggest hook to the tip of the pole with hands made clumsy by excited urgency, the fish continued its drunken circling. He extended the pole cautiously, worried that he might scare that booger into diving deep and staying there, losing him the biggest fish he'd ever had a crack at. Holding his breath, he made two shaky unsuccessful attempts, muttering anguished cuss words. Then on the third try he felt the hook grab hold, and the bass came violently alive, splashing and rolling. Scared of losing the sonofagun, he towed the fish into a pocket between the rocks and got a firm grip on its gills, his heart thumping like a drum. Carrying the potbellied old whopper to the safety of the shore, he estimated its weight at ten pounds. Then allowing for inaccuracy caused by excitement, he scaled it down, say between eight and nine pounds—but still the biggest bass he'd ever caught.

Except for scrapes and bruises it wasn't visibly damaged, and sure wasn't sick or lame—just addled, dazed from banging into concrete or rocks. He was glad no one had been there to witness his bodacious capture of the Moby Dick of bassdom. Dried, shellacked and nailed to a board, that head would be a prize souvenir to keep forever.

Not trusting just a mere stringer, he built a rock pen in the shallows, with slabs of slate on top to prevent anything happening to that sonofagun. Boy! Maybe when *she* saw it she'd forget what she was so mad about.

Rigged for ordinary fishing, he went back out to the middle hole and sat cross-legged on a flat boulder, the pole anchored under a haunch, his slingshot draped across his lap in case a careless turtle showed its head. He was at peace with the world, serene in the morning sun, lulled by the drumming water and trilling redwings, all his senses attuned to the smell and feel and look of the May morning.

It didn't much matter if he caught more fish or not, that dude would make a meal by itself. He was content to just sit there whistling under his breath the way he usually did when alone.

His cork bobbed in the foam-flecked current, but it wasn't a fish biting, just undertow. He probably oughta go up above the dam where it would be clearer, but he was just too comfortable, mesmerized by the sound and movement of the familiar creek. He wondered if Alice Brubaker went around humming or whistling her favorite songs about caskets and letters edged in black. Death was a subject he tried not to think about. It could happen anytime to someone you knew, and you could worry yourself sick thinking about it.

Two things happened simultaneously to divert his mind from the macabre—the cork sank like a rock, and he realized that greenish piece of driftwood bumping gently against the boulder across the pool was a big old bullfrog! The frog had first call, and he slowly raised the slingshot, ignoring the urgent tremor of the pole. A dozen feet away, the broad gray-green back was a perfect target. Easy, boy, take real careful aim, he cautioned himself.

Flap! went the taut rubbers, *whap!* went the rock as it struck the frog on what might be called the nape of its neck. It gave a convulsive lunge against the slab—and slowly vanished into the murky depths. He sighed and reached for the pole. That usually happened. Even when you shot a frog on the bank, unless you broke its back it would make that final jack-in-the-box jump and you had to retrieve it from the bottom. If it wasn't too deep.

The mudcat had snagged itself and was a dandy, a good foot long. Letting it dangle between the boulders, he went dubiously to try to salvage the konked frog, pessimistic because of all the deep fissures and crevices in the rocky pool. But his crazy luck continued to amaze him; the durn thing had lodged on a narrow shelf just elbow deep. What tickled him most was thinking how pleased his dad would be. Slim McGraw liked frog legs even better than fish—and he was welcome to this baby. Something about frogs Jeff couldn't quite stomach, mainly a strong horse-urine smell that was hard to wash off your hands.

Adding the frog and catfish to his stringer, he thought: I already caught enough stuff for a feast! Maybe when she takes a squint at these jessies she'll just bawl me out and let it go at that.

Feeling shivery good, thinking the summer was really starting out swell, he was getting ready to go back out to his lucky hole when he got the itchy sensation of no longer being alone, and took a quick nervous look around.

Vernon Strode and his flop-eared hound were up on the south end of the dam studying him with a wary curiosity, neither friendly nor hostile. After a long sober scrutiny the hound lost interest. Or let on it had, anyway.

Jeff sighed to himself. Vernon Strode was the last person he would have wanted to see up there at the moment—well, except for Mutt. Or Chester Stone. Or Chink Britton. In fact, on second thought, Vernon was only about the *fifth*-to-last person he'd want to see up there at the moment.

5

Vernon Strode was twelve, lean but sturdy-looking, with untrimmed yellow hair curling around his ears, dark eyes cautious, his manner slightly defensive. His shirt and Levi's, though faded and worn, were clean, but his bare feet were muddy. Jeff's eyesight was myopic due to a certain pious prejudice—the shadow of imprisoned Dallas Strode lay across all the members of his family. Vernon was tarnished with his father's outlaw taint, the son of a convicted moonshiner and bootlegger. There were two kinds of people, good and bad, Christian and sinner, pure and wicked, and never the twain should socialize openly. Vernon was by ancient boyhood rules beyond the pale, a sort of outcast.

"Good shootin'," the outcast said. "Your name's McGraw, ain't it?"

Jeff nodded curtly, wanting nothing to do with the guy but feeling a stir of unbidden sympathy for him just the same. Life must be pretty darn lonesome for the Strode kids, and Vernon probably went around feeling itchy embarrassed and ashamed, and in a way it wasn't fair.

"Nice catfish," Vernon said. "An' a jim-dandy bass."

Jeff stared at him. "How long you been here, anyway?"

Vernon shrugged. "Since before you showed up."

"Then how come I never saw you?"

"I was behind that cottonwood snag, catchin' perch an' mindin' my own business," Vernon said.

"Yeah," Jeff snorted. "An' spyin' on me, huh?"

"Nope," Vernon said, "wasn't payin' you no helluva lot of mind. But I seen you gill-snag that ol' bass."

That's what was the matter. An eyewitness was the difference between letting on he'd caught the lunker. fair and square and having to admit he'd merely taken advantage of an accident victim with the blind staggers.

"If it was me," Vernon remarked, "I'd make out I caught it on a crawdad. Who'd ever know better?"

Jeff eyed him uncertainly. "*You* would, for one."

"Who, *me?*" Vernon grinned. "Never saw a thing."

Jeff was beginning to take a mild liking to the outcast. "Be a good joke on everybody," he said, like it was all Vernon's idea. "By gollies, I might just do that."

Vernon grinned like a conspirator. "Say, the perch are bitin' good up here."

"Wouldn't wanta crowd you," Jeff told him.

"Already caught all I wanta hafta clean."

Jeff shrugged. He only needed a few fat perch to round out the fish-fry, so he went up there and dropped in his hook, and right away the cork began dancing. But the durn perch stole the bait. Vernon asked if he ever tried tight-lining, fishing without the cork. Jeff tried it, and by George it worked—as the hook disappeared in the murky green water he felt a tug on the line, and was suddenly battling a scrappy punkinseed perch. And wondered how come *he'd* never thought of such a simple method of catching worm-swiping perch? You didn't need a cork.

"You need another stringer," Vernon said, and whipped out a big pocketknife. "This old string I found oughta hold ten or twelve pounds of perch."

Jeff grinned—it would take about sixty perch that size to make twelve pounds of fish.

"Quite a knife you got there," he said admiringly.

"Paw's stock knife," Vernon told him. "Wish I had a nickel for ever' pig an' bull calf this thing altered in its day. I use it to clean fish an' so forth, but mainly for skinnin' possum, mushrats, squirrels . . ."

He had aroused Jeff's avid curiosity. "You trap 'em?"

Vernon nodded. "Use to trap an' hunt both, when we had a rifle. Ol' Milton there, he's the best tree dog I ever seen."

"What breed of hound is—what's-his-name?"

"Milton, named for my uncle in East Texas. He's a crossbreed, Blue Tick an' Walker, Paw says." He was silent for a moment. "Wasn't for trappin' an' Milton, we'd been short on meat this winter." He strung another punkinseed for Jeff. "Yessiree, without all the possums, groundhogs an' rabbits me an' Milton furnished, we'd a got sick of beans an' taters an' canned stuff."

He caught more perch, keeping only the bigger ones, and Vernon went on talking like he'd been long hungry for some conversation, reminiscing about the good times on the farm when his dad used to butcher hogs and milk-fed steers, and they had ducks and guineas and chickens galore. Now all they had was fourteen Plymouth Rock hens, three with chicks already and three more setting.

Him and his paw used to keep trotlines in the river and bait with chicken gut or small perch, Vernon recalled fondly, and they'd caught a heap of channel cats and big flatheads, including a twenty-pounder once. "Well," Vernon finally reminded himself, "time to git on home and clean my fish, and help Maw and Sis with the washing."

Feeling a humane impulse to say something nice about the disgraced Strodes, Jeff remarked that Goldie sure was smart for a girl.

"She studies a lot," Vernon said. "Aims to be a teacher— an' by Nellies we aim to see she goes to college. Me an' Milton can start puttin' fur money in her college fund once I git me a rifle an' lantern—you hafta hunt nights to really sack up coons an' possums." He hesitated. "Say, McGraw, you know where I could git some rubber? I sure need me a slingshot."

"That stuff's mighty scarce," Jeff said. Where rubber was concerned he was a miser, but he had a small hoard buried in the cob pile, and knew of an old tube hanging on a certain garage wall begging to be swiped, and he could imagine the frustration of being a slingshotless newcomer with no pull anywhere, no friends. Well, heck, he thought, and got his spares out of his pocket. "Might loan you these here 'til you can get hold of some."

Vernon was tickled pink. He said he already had a good fork cut, and an old shoe tongue for the pocket. He wondered if all those pigeons around the elevator belonged to anyone, and Jeff said whoever was able to kill or catch them. Pigeons nesting in barns sorta belonged to the barn owner, but you couldn't beat fried squab, taken from the nest just before they learned to fly. That was justifiable larceny.

Vernon lifted his stringer of fish out of a clump of cattails and Jeff forgot about pigeons. Besides perch, the stringer held four or five nice catfish, which Vernon explained had come from throwlines he kept set upstream, baiting and running them mornings and evenings. If he had a lantern he could run them around bedtime. Figured he lost a good catfish now and then from it having all night to work itself loose, and sometimes turtles messed up a good fish. "You happen to have a lantern, McGraw?" he asked, and Jeff said well, a little red-globed railroad lantern he'd got for Christmas. "Maybe after I git some trotlines set," Vernon said, "you might be interested in heppin' run 'em nights for part of the fish."

"Sumpin' to think about," Jeff replied noncommittally.

Vernon said so long and went up the creek, turning south up the street, taking the easier, longer route home.

Running trotlines at night might be fun—but going down to the Strode place and back by himself at night was a horse of a different color. He wasn't too crazy about the idea. Anyway, bumping into Vernon accidentally was one thing, but meeting him on purpose was something else entirely. Some of his disgrace might rub off on you and sorta ruin your reputation. Anyway, Jewel McGraw wouldn't want one of her sons hobnobbing with that kind of kid.

With eight nice perch strung he decided to go down below the bridge and load up with smooth slingshot rocks. He stuck the pole in the bank, hid his perch in the cattails and headed downstream under the bridge, breathing "Yes, We Have No Bananas," and wishing he had some. Below the bridge the creek curved to the north, the high banks and the woods hiding the dam and bridge, so he could pretend he was miles from the haunts of men, following an uncharted stream where any second he might see a big buck drinking, or maybe a bear. He was half convinced there *were* bears away on down the creek—or, anyway, out in the tall-timbered Arkansas River bottoms. But all he saw were big frogs that croaked and jumped before he got in slingshot range, smaller ones he missed, and a water snake he almost hit. After stopping at a gravel bar to fill both hip pockets with selected rocks, he suddenly began to feel uneasy and started back upstream. If the frog and the bass got to flopping, they might jar the slate loose and somehow get out of that suddenly undependable rock enclosure . . .

The fish pen was just as he'd left it, but he checked it anyhow—and it was empty! Jeff realized he had been robbed —and the logical suspect was that jailbird's son! He took off upstream thinking furiously: I'll whip me a toad-eating thief, or know the reason why!

When he reached the foot of the street he got another nasty surprise. There went old Chink Britton swaggering south, half a block away, carrying a frog, a catfish and a bass. Clearing Vernon, but presenting an even bigger problem. Jeff couldn't jump Chink—he was too big, too much older. So instead of pursuing the scoundrel he turned back down the creek, hurrying past the dam, across the swampy low place and up the steep path to the tracks. Already winded, he loped south beside the tracks, spotting Chink over on the street strutting along nonchalantly. When a house hid him from view, Jeff poured on the steam, thinking all that running after school was paying off now—only that had been sprinting and this was a long-distance race. But Chink didn't know it was a race, and presently Jeff passed him and slowed to catch his breath. The rocks in his back pockets were chafing his bottom, and by the time he loped under the coal chute he was pretty tired, gasping for breath. Crossing Main Street, he looked at all the wagons up there and slowed to a walk, thinking: He'll stop to show off that bass and brag about how he caught it, probably.

Passing the watertank, he wondered if there were any bass as big as his in there. When he hit the long brick platform he started running again. It would take a while for his dad to get up and get dressed and everything. Veering across the tracks, he went chugging down the cinder path and was at the bottom before he noticed the shampooed teachers on the hotel porch drying their hair in the sun, the Misses Horn and Ewbanks. Self-conscious even at a time like that, he pretended not to see them, or hear Lizzie ask amusedly, "Why the mad rush, Jeffy?" Little did she know how serious his hurry was.

He was passing the Yancy yard when the small miracle happened. His dad appeared up ahead as if by magic, coming through the gate and turning up the street. Early for him to be up, but there he was.

"Hey! . . . Dad! . . . Wait!" Jeff hollered breathlessly, and his father stopped, looking alarmed. "What now?" he called out, like he thought it was bad news.

"Chink Britton—stold my—big bass—an' frog!" Jeff puffed, holding his pockets so they wouldn't rub him any rawer. His dad looked relieved but aggravated.

"Well, hell," he growled, "the way you acted I thought it must be a calamity. Catch your breath and elucidate." A reassuring tower of strength, he listened gravely to Jeff's

39

tale of woe, nodded and said firmly, "Let's see if we can head that gentleman off."

Jeff followed him up the street, puffing and panting but greatly relieved now that Slim McGraw was taking charge, and as they turned the corner by Bradman's hedge his dad gave a snort. "There he comes now, as cocky as all get out."

There he came, all right. Strutting along with Jeff's stringer, Chink was passing the alley between Ballew's grocery and the hardware store when he saw the McGraws, and he broke step, plainly astonished, looking as if tempted to bolt west into the alley. But then he came swaggering on, his right eyebrow raised and his left eye squinted as usual, cocky as ever.

They headed him off at the lumberyard gate by the hardware store and Jeff's dad said, "What did you catch 'em on, Britton?"

"Never caught 'em, bought 'em," Chink said. "From a kid." He didn't turn a hair.

"I'll be durn," Slim McGraw said. "How much?"

"Four bits for the bass. He throwed the rest in for boot, Slim," brassy Chink said. Most men resented him calling them by their first names or nicknames, like he was a man himself, or never learned to say mister. He considered himself a good-looker, and almost was, despite the greasy high rooster-comb pompadour, but his natural beauty was spoiled by a kind of gnarled, shifty-eyed insolence, and a touch of slink in his arrogant strut. "Uncle Ralph's been hungerin' for a fish dinner," he said. To hear him tell it he was always thinking of his poor uncle. Trapped in dinky Cottonwood by his pity and family duty when he could be in Tulsa earning thirty-five a week managing a big café, or even more selling automobiles, and so on. You had to give him one thing though, he was always neat and clean—if that was in a guy's favor . . .

"You got a bargain. What's that kid's name?" Jeff's dad asked mildly. "I'm partial to frog legs myself."

"Can't help you there, Slim," Chink regretted. "Wasn't anybody I know—a few people here I don't know yet. Mighta been one of that jailbird tribe for all I know."

Vernon! Jeff thought. After me giving him slingshot rubbers! That's gratitude for you, boy!

Slim McGraw's fingers rasped on his unshaven chin. "A feller doesn't catch a prize bass like that often, Britton, and when he does he hates to have it end up in someone else's skillet. I regret giving you bad news, but Jeff here caught that bass and mudcat, and bagged that frog with his slingshot. Then when he wasn't looking somebody sorta borrowed his stringer without removing the contents, and he wants his property back."

Chink got a little red-faced. "Whoa, now, Slim! Before I just hand anything over, I'd like some goddanged proof it ever belonged to your boy. He got any witnesses?"

"Darn right," Jeff said. "Vernon Strode seen me catch the bass an' catfish an' shoot the frog." Then *swiped* them, he thought bitterly.

Chink seemed taken aback, but recovered. "He'd make you a dandy witness in court, seein' he's probably the kid *sold* me this bass. Who'd believe *him*? And possession is nine-tenths of the law, in case you didn't know it."

Scratching his stubble, Jeff's dad said, "Since you think you've got an airtight case, let's give 'er a test. Mayor Riley, the local Solomon, is right handy there in the hardware store . . ."

He was interrupted by a voice from the lumber shed. "Solomon ain't in the store, Gabe—I'm in here taking inventory and eavesdropping. Hold the fort." And Mr. Riley came out of the long two-story shed and through the gate, a portly, potbellied man with thick gray-speckled hair, a knobby nose, bushy brows, shrewd blue eyes and a small mouth that was always curled in a kind of rueful smile. He wore a seersucker suit, a string tie, high-topped shoes with slits cut to accommodate his corns, and had a corncob

41

pipe clamped in his teeth. He was the only Catholic in town and had been mayor and justice of the peace as long as Jeff could remember. The only thing wrong with him was being the father of Caroline Riley.

"You heard the powwow, Mayor," Slim McGraw said. "What's your official verdict in this open-and-shut robbery case?"

The mayor rubbed his pocked nose judiciously. "I know Jeff is an honest upright citizen incapable of serious prevarication," he said. "But my skimpy knowledge of legal procedure gives Britton the best of the argument so far. Proof of original ownership is the crux, here." He passed judgment on the bass, calling it a dandy, and said he might have to remand the evidence into the court's custody, unless the complainant could offer some proof of prior ownership of the contested fish. Jeff's dad said goddammit, to prove his son wasn't a liar he'd take it to the county courts, etc. Cost money for a lawyer and meanwhile the bone of contention would rot and develop an offensive stench, John Riley said smilingly, adding, "Why don't we settle it by having me eat the evidence?"

Jeff didn't much like the sweetish flavor of bass, but he wanted that head for a trophy. Angry and unhappy, he rubbed a hand across his sweaty face—and thought: *Hey!* He tried the other hand and gave his dad a startled grin. "Smell my hands," he said.

Slim McGraw smelled the extended hands and nodded. "Your honor, at this time I would like to introduce evidence. Smell Jeff's hands."

Looking mystified, Mr. Riley sniffed Jeff's pudgy hands while Chink fidgeted uneasily. "Yep," the mayor said, looking puzzled.

"Left hand smells like frog, right hand smells like bass," Jeff's dad said. "Would that convince a jury?"

"Well, it convinces me," the mayor said, and gave Chink his little apologetic smile. " 'Fraid I must find your current possession of the fish and frog null and void, Britton. You want to smell the evidence?"

Chink gave a nervous laugh. "I'll take your word for it, John. I was swindled—but don't worry, I'll get my four bits back." He let Jeff's dad take the stringer. "Well, I better go see if Uncle Ralph needs anything." He cut a swift evil look at Jeff and went swaggering on south like nothing much had happened.

They watched him for a minute, then the mayor gave his wheezy soft laugh. "Cheekiest bird I ever knew, all gall, strut and blow—spends most of his time either talking through his hat or laughing up his sleeve. Don't act like an exposed thief atall, does he?"

That's who I saw at the coal chute! Jeff thought suddenly. I bet he was up on the bridge when I was looking at those babies . . . heck, I knew Vernon wasn't a crook.

"Let's take that bass inside and weigh it," Mr. Riley suggested, and Slim McGraw agreed, so Jeff was outvoted. He preferred not to know exactly how much it weighed— just call it about seven pounds and let it go at that. "Betcha it won't exceed four and a half pounds, Gabe. Two bits says it won't," the mayor said.

"You got yourself a bet," Jeff's dad agreed, and they went into the hardware store. He followed the men along an aisle between glass showcases and bins and counters full of riches and treasures and daydreams. Saws and hammers, hatchets and axes, big spools of rope of all sizes, coal oil and gasoline lanterns, flashlights and batteries, pocket-knives and sheath knives, baseballs and bats and gloves (boy, to be rich like Mutt and walk in here and buy a new finger mitt!), and roller skates (only $2.75. *Only!*), and racked shotguns and rifles, including a peachy single-shot bolt-action .22 that cost a mere four dollars. He didn't come in here very often because it made him wistful sad, reminding him how bad he needed so many things he'd never be able to afford, especially a rifle to hunt squirrels

43

and pigeons with, skates, a belt hatchet, sheath knife, and on down the long list. Rope, lanterns, etc. Mutt the miser could afford a rifle and skates and about anything else he wanted, but he'd rather *save* his money.

"Well, now, if it wasn't my own scales I'd quarrel with you," Mr. Riley remarked. Then instead of telling how much it weighed he said: "By the way, Gabe, what was all that hand-smelling business? Sure, I smelled *fish*, but mainly I just took your *word* . . ."

"Simple," Gabe McGraw said. "Frogs smell like horse pee and bass have a sweetish smell. You want another whack at it?"

Mr. Riley waved the thought away. "That's exactly how it smelled, come to think of it. Well, you win. It runs a mite over five pounds."

Five pounds, heck! Jeff thought indignantly. But if the scales were dishonest they'd be in the store's favor, weigh heavier instead of lighter. What it was, fish out of water dried fast and lost a lot of their heaviness.

Mr. Riley paid off the bet and Slim McGraw gave the quarter to his son, then added a dime. "That's for the frog. Better go clean 'em before they turn blinky."

Jeff nodded dazedly. Thirty-five cents! The most money he'd had since picking cotton last fall. Enough for an agate —or a lot of jawbreakers, licorice, pop. But his joy was dampened by the prospect of going home now and getting stuck with the rug job. He dawdled, yearning over all the stuff he couldn't afford, half-listening as his dad said, "You wanta tell me what's so damn important you had Mutt get me up an hour early, John?"

"Firstly, our wives went to Blackthorn in my flivver bargain hunting, and likely won't be home before sundown. And I've got some chock back yonder."

Chock. Choctaw beer. Homebrew, and illegal, but if you were the mayor—hey! She wasn't home! No rug-beating. He could clean the fish and go back to the creek.

"Secondly," Mr. Riley said, "us merchants decided to sponsor a Junior Legion team this summer." If I put a quarter down payment on that rifle, Jeff reflected, that'd be a sixteenth—I'd only need fifteen more quarters. "Supply the bats and balls, and each of us furnish a cap, and a shirt with the name of our store on it." Or skates, two bits would be nearly a tenth.

"I doubt if the Kaw and Washita would kick in, John."

Aw, heck, even thirty-five cents wouldn't begin to buy that rifle, or skates, a new glove or anything else in there. He drifted on out the door as Mr. Riley said, "Thing is, we'll need a manager."

Feeling solvent but not affluent, Jeff went home in the warm May sunshine whistling "Sweet Evelina." One reason Jeff didn't frog hunt more was because skinning them was even worse than catfish. He was durn glad when he finally finished the repulsive job. Behind the barn, he poured out the fish cleanings unhurriedly, rich in time, and something banged loudly against the barn wall, causing him to jump with surprise. What the heck? he asked himself, startled and confused. Another rock buzzed past his ear like an angry hornet, whacking against the weathered boards, and he *knew* what the heck and fled around the building, his spine tingling icily. Someone was taking potshots at him, and Chink's yard was in slingshot range.

That dirty skunk! Jeff thought. He's mad because I foiled his attempt to steal my prize bass and exposed him as a liar and a thief in front of the mayor.

Dammit, anyway! he thought, with consternation. He'd been looking forward to a peaceful Chesterless summer, and now all of a sudden he had an even worse enemy right here in town, in slingshot range. A sneaky bushwhacker.

While washing out the dishpan he thought, by gollies, *two* could play that game, boys. Leaving the fish and frog in the pan, he headed for the alley, removing his slingshot from around his neck and getting a smooth creek rock out

45

of his pocket. From the corner of the barn he fired four rocks in rapid succession over Granny's orchard toward the Britton yard, retaliating twofold, declaring war right back at that skunk of a Chink. How you like *them* apples, you dirty lying bushwhacking crook? he silently asked his new enemy.

He felt good about it all the way back to the well, but then he started kind of wishing he hadn't done it. Probably just make old Chink madder and meaner.

6

No matter how eagerly a guy looked forward to the last day of school, it was a pretty sad occasion because of saying good-bye to country kids you might not see again all summer. It was also a dangerous occasion if sentiment caused a guy to forget to be careful.

After final tests on Tuesday they went back for a half day on Wednesday to attend a last assembly and get their report cards. Around eleven they got their cards and cleaned out their desks. Most people had carried home their books and stuff Tuesday, but some, like Jeff, were loaded down with ink bottles, pen staffs, paste pots, Crayolas, pencils, tablets and four or five books. He was relieved that he'd got all B's and C's, no D's or F's. Loitering and lingering over the farewells until the last of his rural chums were leaving, he sighed and looked around at the schoolhouse that already seemed deserted and lonely—and abruptly sentiment fled, leaving only chagrin and alarm.

Chester leaned patiently against the northeast corner of the gradeschool, barefooted, wearing an ominous sly grin, waiting for Jeff, determined to win this last footrace of the year.

Jeff sighed morosely. Loaded down, he'd surely get caught, but there was no one to carry his stuff. If he left his stuff here and won the race, he'd still have to come back after it and Chester would just wait and chase him again, or take Jeff's valuable stuff and dump it somewhere west of town. So his only chance was to outsmart his nemesis, and the one chink in Chester's armor was his winter-softened feet.

"Forgot to say good-bye to Miss Evans," Jeff said loudly, moving toward the south door. But when he reached the steps he cut out onto the cinders between the buildings and remarked: "I'll just holler through the window." When he reached the windows he kept going, glancing back. Chester was trying to follow, but cinders were murder on tender feet and he was limping and wincing, scowling. Chester was catching on to Jeff's cunning, and waiting to see which way he would go back there. He was still between Jeff and home sweet home, still had him bottled up, and Chester was sly enough to figure whichever direction Jeff went would be just another trick. Jeff gave him credit for being that smart, so he suddenly took off south behind the highschool, then stopped and peeked back between the buildings as Chester limped around the front of the highschool. Now it really got tricky. He sprinted across the exposed interval, hoping Chester was peeking, stopped again, and peered around the corner in time to see Chester going north in front of the gradeschool, falling for the trick. But all the way south around behind the highschool, and east along the south side, realizing how much all his stuff slowed him down, he kept expecting his enemy to suddenly pop out in front of him. In which case he'd just hafta plow into Chester and try to knock him down, and keep going. Veering away from the building to aim for the alley, he passed the front corner and saw Chester coming back south, but too late to keep him from reaching the alley. And safety, because that alley was no place for a barefooted runner. Not even wagon tracks in it, just last year's dry weed stobs, broken glass, rusty tin, sandburs and bull nettles, and after about ten feet Chester gave up the chase and hollered threats after him.

"I'll git you next year, you dirty cheat!" he hollered.

I know you will, you ornery sap, Jeff thought, continuing briskly because Chester might try racing around by the street to head him off. Before next year Chester might break a leg or get religion—or Jeff might get tougher, develop more courage, give up running for pugilistics. Or his dad might get transferred to another town.

I could take boxing lessons this summer, he thought. But not from Mutt. Two years back their dad had bought some pillowy gloves, to teach his sons the manly art by having them spar with each other. But Mutt tried to kill a guy instead of sparring, throwing haymakers and uppercuts. The best self-defense was never to spar with Mutt.

When he reached the east end of the alley with no sign of Chester, he slowed to a walk, and was warily looking north as he crossed the street when the first rock spanged off the ground in front of him, causing his neck hairs to bristle and tardily reminding him that he was in enemy territory. Old Chink had been laying for him, right out in the street half a block away, coming toward him now, shooting too fast for real accuracy. Bolting into his own familiar alley, Jeff started zigzagging, his exposed back side puckering and flinching as Chink kept sending rocks after him. For a city dude he could sure reload fast.

Even fleeing for his life, Jeff noticed the sunbonneted women down behind the major's place and recognized his chubby mother and thin Mrs. Riley, picking greens to can—poke, dock, calf's-tongue, lamb's-quarters, etc.

As he skidded around the corner of the barn, Chink's last rock hit the ground and skipped over the Riley hen house and clanged loudly against the mayor's galvanized tin toilet, causing its occupant to utter a startled squawk. After peeking cautiously up the alley, where Chink was turning homeward, Jeff leaned against the barn, suddenly grinning about Caroline being in the toilet when it got hit—her ears

49

would probably ring for a week. Mrs. Riley complained about that metal closet being hotter in summer and colder in winter than any outhouse in town.

Caroline suddenly appeared from behind the hen house, marching along with outraged dignity. "I'm going to tell my father the mayor what you did an' have him put you in jail, you dumb ignorant thing!" she said furiously.

"Oh yeah?" he retorted, being on pretty good terms with the mayor.

As Jeff neared the house Mutt came out the back door smearing oil in the pocket of his new catcher's mitt. "Did you flunk, knothead?"

"Yep, like I always do," Jeff answered.

"Ask me how I done," Mutt suggested.

"I don't wanta know," Jeff told him from the kitchen, where he discovered a big kettle of beef and vegetable soup still hot and redolent of garlic and suet. Judging from her location in the alley, his mother wouldn't be home for quite a while; he could eat slow, then beat it. Baseball practice was scheduled for one-thirty, excuse enough not to hang around home after lunch.

He was dipping a hunk of bread in the delicious soup when Jody came in wearing a kind of sly grin. "Where's Mama?" he asked, and Jeff said she was picking greens, adding, "I suppose you made all A's, huh?"

"Priddy neardy," Jody said. "She oughta be here."

"She's just down the alley," Jeff said. "Eat some soup." He filled a bowl and poured some milk.

"I git a dime for every A," Jody said. A dime for A's— for B's, nothing. "How much is five dimes?"

"Fifty cents," Jeff said glumly. "Half a buck."

He was busted again already. That thirty-five cents hadn't lasted very long. No willpower at all. So today Mutt would get sixty cents and Jody four bits, and old Jeff would get scolded for lowering the family reputation for brains. And maybe a few jobs to do before baseball practice if she came home before he beat it, a possibility that made him eat faster. He just couldn't relax around here.

Jeff changed clothes, got his finger mitt, and lit out for town, feeling swell because the summer stretched endlessly ahead of him. Halfway to town, Ranger overtook him, eager to go wherever Jeff went. One reason Mutt was so insulting and antagonistic was because his dog preferred the company of a lazy, bankrupt dumbbell. Money and grades didn't impress a dog much.

Main Street was somnolent and deserted in the golden noon, except for a truck backed up to the high sidewalk down past the drugstore. As he sauntered aimlessly down the broad empty sidewalk, well-fed and lazy and kind of lonesome, he daydreamed of sudden wealth, like finding a ten-dollar bill. Boy howdy, that would buy an agate, a .22 rifle, roller skates *and* a new finger mitt! But not much else. The trouble was if a guy went in the drugstore aiming to buy an agate, the tantalizing smells of the soda fountain would sap his character and cause him to put off buying the agate awhile longer.

He held his breath passing the drugstore, then expelled it noisily as he got his first look at Alma Dexter. Her family was moving into the ex-café, and she glanced his way as she came out to the truck, and the impact of her brief curious gaze caused a pleasurable shock to his nervous system. She took a chair inside and he advanced past the ex-barbershop to lean against the big Bull Durham sign and wait for a closer look. A smallish dark woman came out and got a box of stuff without noticing him, and a boy of nine or ten gave Jeff a shy sidelong grin as he took in a box of kitchen things. Then a short, black-haired man came out and got some bedsprings, seeing Jeff but ignoring him. Then *she* came out again and gave him a tentative smile. She had dark eyes, a pretty mouth, bobbed brownish-black hair and an olive complexion. She was small but kind of filled out, with shapely arms and calves and everything else. Compared to the local crop of females, she was very pretty, neat and cute.

On a sudden brash impulse he said, "Need any help?"

"No thanks," she said. "We're about finished." Her voice was low and melodious, and she had a dimple when she smiled. Despite her small size she seemed quick and strong; not your average weak, sissified girl, but not a tomboy, either. He walked on past the door with Ranger, thinking they could be part Indian or Mexican, or maybe Italian or Greek or something. He turned around and backed east, and the boy came out and said, "Nice-lookin' dog you got there. German police?"

"American police," Jeff said, and the boy laughed and went inside and *she* came out again, although it wasn't her turn. He said, "Gonna open a grocery store, I hear."

"You heard right," she said. "Grocery and butcher shop, cure our own hams and bacon, specialize in chili. Dexter's Chili." She was gone again and the boy was back—the parents were probably putting a bed together or something. This time the boy said, "What's your name? Mine's Roy."

"Jeff McGraw," Jeff said. "What's your sister's?"

"Alma." Roy took a coal-oil lamp inside. Wouldn't need it, Jeff thought; they had electricity in the café.

When she reappeared he said: "Howdy, Alma." And she came right back at him with: "Howdy yourself, Jess." Close enough, he thought, and went loping east grinning like a durn idiot. Straighten that out later. Main thing was, he had the honor of being the first guy in town to meet Alma the enchantress. Also the distinction of being the first to get a crush on her, but he didn't kid himself about that, being neither a sheik nor a jelly bean. There were several guys around town better looking, richer, wittier and bolder —guys like Mutt and Lige Bowzer, who'd soon be swarming around her like mud daubers around a busted watermelon. So count him out, let them settle it among themselves.

But the old town suddenly looked and felt different, a

more exciting place to live, more romantic. He used to wonder what age a guy began to really get interested in girls, and now he knew. Twelve, give or take a few days. Going across the tracks toward the shack, he found himself humming "Yes, Sir, That's My Baby," and changed it to "Somebody Stole My Gal." Shortest romance in history.

The erstwhile boxcar that served as office and storehouse for his dad and Dolittle was his favorite all-season refuge and loafing place. The office part had a coal stove, a one-legged worktable built into the southeast corner with pigeonholes on the wall over it, a straight-backed chair, and a sort of homemade, padded barber chair in the southwest corner, a great place to read or take a nap. By the west door there was a washstand with water bucket, washpan, mirror, soap shelf and a keg of iced drinking water. A loafer's bench ran along the wall behind the stove, for chilled train crews waiting on winter mornings to start the day's run. A shaded bulb hung over the table, and there was a stack of magazines under it, and a wealth of tablets and scratch pads, ink, pens and indelible pencils in its capacious drawer. The smaller storage room contained all sorts of interesting stuff, sticks of journal grease, flares and fuses and explosive signaling caps, kegs of bolts, pins and stuff for patching and repairing steam lines. Because of all that stuff, the storeroom was kept locked when neither engine watchman was there, and it was locked now.

His dad might be down at the pump house halfway to the creek, or on his way home to eat lunch. He could be at the depot, gabbing with the agent-telegrapher, or somewhere on Main Street, socializing. He was like that.

Jeff was glad for the chance to requisition some chewing tobacco, having shared his last piece with Vernon Strode down at the dam yesterday. This was sure the place to stock up, because most of the thirty square pigeonholes over the table contained some kind of tobacco or pipes. He took inventory, and at the moment there were eight brands of chewing tobacco—four plugs, three packages and one twist—and three of pipe tobacco, along with five pipes. One of Jeff's great temptations was to try a pipe, see what real smoking was like. So far he'd only tried cornsilks, coffee and grapevine.

He decided to chew some Beech-Nut, a moist shredded brand he'd never really tested yet. Ranger followed him out and across the tracks and up onto the loading platform; he could nap anywhere there was some shade.

Chewing tobacco gave him a kind of relaxed numb, dizzy feeling for a while, so he was content to just sit still and look at the sunny green day, the tufts of white clouds in the deep blue sky, the empty pens with pigweeds and sour dock growing in the old manure. Hot sun and noonday silence suited him fine—it sure didn't take long to get used to school being out.

It was depressing how baseball, which was supposed to be fun, caused so much hard feelings and resentment, straining friendships. If he got to be right fielder as usual, guys would say naturally, his dad was manager. He wished his dad wasn't manager, knowing in advance how clumsy and self-conscious he'd feel with his dad watching, and Mutt criticizing . . .

Presently he worked the cud out of his cheek and went around to the water keg to rinse his mouth and drink the tooth-aching ice water and headed for the old ball park. Needing a cookie or something, he stopped off at home and found his mother in the hot kitchen surrounded by scalded fruit jars and about a ton of wild greens, preparing to can all that free nourishing food for the winter. She was glad to see him. "Go pump me some more water. Did Jody eat anything before he vanished? That is the most elusive child I ever knew, here one minute, gone the next."

"He ate," Jeff said, and fetched the water before getting an oatmeal cookie, and she said, "Your grades were better than I expected, but still not as good as you ought to do."

It was a familiar refrain; she wasn't scolding, merely pointing out he could do much better if he'd apply himself. He'd noticed she was always cheerful and more tolerant when preserving stuff for the winter, even though it was uncomfortable and tedious work.

"The new family's movin' into Archer's Café," he told her. "Gonna open a butcher shop. Dexter's their name."

She nodded absently. "Matt was telling me. He signed them up for the morning paper. He says they have a cute daughter who is twelve and plays the banjo, which seems a peculiar choice of instrument for a girl."

It seemed so to Jeff, too. Alma plucking a banjo! He asked what was for supper, and found out. Meatloaf, mashed potatoes and all the boiled greens he could eat. She made a great meatloaf. He'd thought of running away from home a few times, but knew her cooking would keep him from ever becoming a hobo. She had her faults, but she sure knew how to feed people. . . .

There were about twenty guys at the school diamond, including Mutt, who as catcher was team captain and filled in for the absent manager, bossing things. He was having infield practice, with Dock on first, Jake on second, Windy Mills at shortstop, and Max Gillis at third. Pitcher Jelly Wurtz would fire the ball to Mutt, who would flip it to Charley Clovis, a highschooler too old for Junior Legion, and Charley would knock a grounder to someone and they'd peg it to first base and Dock would throw it back to Jelly. Jeff noticed that Jake Ballew was having trouble with his stiff new glove. The ball kept bouncing off the thick padding.

"How's about someone knockin' flies to us outfielders?" he asked, and Mutt said, "We only got one ball, Dummy."

That seemed reasonable, so Jeff sat cross-legged on the sideline with the other outfielders, second-string infielders, hopeful substitutes, or just spectators.

When Mutt kept bawling Jake out for dropping everything, Dock stood up for his brother, saying, "I thought your *dad* was the manager, not you." And Mutt said, "I'm the captain, an' if you don't like the way I run the team, get another catcher. I could be earnin' me some wampum instead of doin' this, so less git it settled right now. Either I'm catcher an' captain, or I ain't."

Whereupon everybody but Jake looked at Dock disgustedly, and Jake said apologetically, "It's just this new glove ain't broke in yet, Mutt."

That was another advantage Mutt had—he could get away with being bossy because catching was a dangerous job nobody else wanted. In Jeff's opinion, *any* infield job was dangerous because of ground-skinners and bad-hoppers. At least a catcher had a mask and belly pad.

Mutt kept nagging the pitcher, too, because he couldn't get it over the plate worth a darn, and Jelly said resentfully: "You expect me to git my arm in shape in six minutes, for crobly sakes?" He had a habit of inventing new words when he was sore, or maybe just getting his tongue tangled. "Crobly sakes" was a new one. "Anyways, I'll settle down when we git a batter in there, don't worry."

"I'm not worryin'," Mutt said, but he probably was, Jelly being the only pitcher they had. "Less try havin' Charley stand here like a batter an' fake swingin'—only for horse sakes *don't* swing, I ain't wearin' no protection."

So Charley got in the box and waved the bat like Babe Ruth, but it didn't help—Jelly was still scatter-armed. Between pitches he rubbed his arm and shook it, but he kept throwing high, wide or in the dirt. Jeff was beginning to worry—without a pitcher you'd have no team—when Conrad Coonrod muttered, "Well, look who's comin' up the road."

Jeff looked, and it was his fishing chum, Vernon Strode. Ambling up the street with his hands in his pockets. Jeff felt uneasy, alarmed—he wasn't eager to acknowledge their friendship in front of all these guys. But not to would be kind of shameful and cowardly. So he compromised by

56

pretending he hadn't seen Vernon, hoping he'd just walk on by and disappear.

"Got his nerve," Lefty Gronstetter muttered. "Lookit 'im strut, like butter wouldn't melt in his mouth." Jeff had never understood that expression—if you were cocky, you had a cold mouth?

"Free country, Grinstutter," Jug Hazlitt said. "He ain't hurtin' you, is he?"

"Well, it makes me sick, a crimnal's kid goin' around actin' like he's as good as you an' me," Lefty growled, and easygoing, portly Jug said: "Hell, he may be *better* than us." And in some ways no truer words were ever spoken, but you notice it was Jug that defended Vernon, not his friend and fishing buddy Jeff McGraw. Old Jiffy was just scared itchy that Vernon would try to join the crowd and impose on what was a casual acquaintance.

Out of the corner of his eye he saw Vernon stop across the road and sit on the low bank with his bare feet in the ditch, chewing grass and watching. He looked kind of lonely and left out, and Jeff felt shame and guilt. If he wasn't a false friend he would at least go chin with him awhile, even if that sorta made him an outcast, too. Feeling gutless, not liking himself much, he went on pretending he didn't have the slightest notion old Vern was within miles of the ball diamond.

Then something happened. Jelly threw a pitch high and wide, and Charley stuck the end of the bat out, nicking the ball just enough to send it over the screen and bouncing straight at Vernon. Who just sat there calmly until the last split second before reaching out to stab it barehanded. Mutt went to the end of the backstop, after a disgusted look at Jelly, and Vern stood up lazily, studying the ball like he'd never seen one up close before, and Mutt said impatiently, "Okay, less have it, huh?"

Vernon Strode rared back and fired the ball across the street and it popped loudly in the mitt, and that should have been that. But Mutt stood there with a tough frown, like maybe he resented Vern's attitude or something. But all he did was lob the ball back to Vern and say curtly: "Do that again." Vern did it again and the ball hit Mutt's new pood with a loud WHAP! that echoed off the schoolhouse. Mutt kept pounding the ball into the mitt for a while, frowning at Vern, and it was so quiet you could hear the meadowlarks. Something was fixing to happen, maybe a fight, and everybody watched except Jelly, who was rubbing his arm and making painful faces. Finally Mutt said: "Wanta throw a few from the pitcher's box, Strode?"

From the team captain it was an official invite, but Vernon hesitated like he wasn't sure he was altogether welcome, so Jeff decided the heck with his social standing, and hollered: "Come on, Vern, it's tryout day." Vern shrugged and nodded, accepting the double McGraw invitation.

With the natural authority that set him apart from his fellow men, Mutt said, "Give your ol' soupbone a rest, Jello. No sense takin' a chance on hurtin' it. We'll play work-up and have battin' practice." He put on mask and chest protector. "Charley, you bat first since you got the hickory."

"Be a pleasure," Charley said humorously, "after lettin' alla those fat strikes go by." Jeff grinned as he got up to head for right field—only to see Jelly loping out there, sore arm and all. Like maybe he figured he'd better learn a new position, if his control was gone. To atone a little for his unfaithfulness, Jeff sailed his glove out to Vern, saying: "You never told me you pitch." And Vern grinned. "You never ast me," he said.

Although no Babe Ruth, during the short highschool season Charley had hit around three hundred against pitchers bigger and older than Vern, plus being a basketball star. But the best he could do against Vernon was a feeble pop-up to third base that brought Max Gillis in to bat. Max fouled a couple, then fanned. In regular work-up he would have taken over the pitching, but Mutt wanted Vern to keep

58

throwing and said, "You bat, Weary." So Jeff took the bat, figuring friend or not, J. McGraw always tried to knock that apple into the next county. The first pitch looked perfect, and he took a hefty swing and missed. Happened sometimes in the best of families. He missed the next fat pitch, too, and blamed it on the old heavily taped bat. The third pitch came in like a ripe peach on a low limb, and he knocked an easy fly to Jelly—which was one way to get him out of right field.

Jelly was a fair hitter, but with his sore arm he couldn't bring the bat around, he explained after striking out. Vern struck out Lefty Gronstetter, but anybody could do that. Lefty relieved Dock; Dock popped up to second; Jake managed to catch it and went running in to show what a woodchopper he was. He nicked the ball, so it hit Mutt on the knee and he had to limp around in a circle, but he also whiffed. Jeff could see that most of the pitches were right over the plate and couldn't understand why people kept fouling them, popping up, or missing altogether. Even Windy Mills, who busted more bats than all the rest of the team put together.

Manager McGraw showed up with two new balls and a bat, and shin guards for the catcher. Which didn't help the batters, but kept old Mutton from getting crippled up by all those deflected fouls. Jeff was tickled about Vern, knowing his pitching skill would change his social standing—at least during the baseball season. People could forgive a good pitcher for being the son of a notorious jailbird. Anyway, *most* people could.

Slim McGraw stood behind the backstop watching with grinning pleasure, a good pitcher being even more important than good hitters. Vern complained good-naturedly about not getting his turn at bat, and Charley volunteered to pitch to him and paid one in there that looked high and outside to Jeff, but Vern knocked it into left field. The next one he hit a clean line drive over shortstop. Then he laid down a bunt. "One more, then I got to beat it," he said, and smacked a ground-skinner straight at Jeff that scared him silly. But somehow he got Jake's fat glove in front of it, pinned it to the ground and threw it to Dock. And heard his dad say: "By golly, maybe we also found us another second baseman!"

"I doubt that," Mutt said, and was right for once.

"Take care of that arm, Strode," the manager called as his new pitcher headed homeward, and Vern grinned and said: "I keep it in shape pumpin' water, Mr. McGraw." He was polite for a pitcher, compared to Jelly.

After Vern's departure practice wasn't much fun. Around three o'clock, when the southbound local whistled up north, the manager left and Mutt started bossing again, making the players restless, and when he finally said it oughta be enough for the first day, nobody argued with him.

Another disadvantage in being the manager's son was having to carry the equipment home after practice and risk being stuck with chores, but at least Mutt was in a rare good mood, gloating about getting to catch a *real* pitcher for a change. Jeff asked what kind of stuff Vern had been throwing, in-curves, out-curves, drops or what? No curves or drops, Mutt said without sarcasm, just straight stuff, but at different speeds, all with the same delivery—fast as a blue streak, fast as greased lightning, or not fast at all. It fooled heck out of the batters.

"Took nerve, showin' up like he did," Jeff reflected.

Mutt shrugged. "He knew he was good an' hoped for a chance to show it. Anyway, *he* ain't to blame for his dad."

"I ain't ashamed of bein' his friend," Jeff said, since Mutt felt that way. "Tell you somethin' else," Jeff added defiantly, "if I was gonna have a party of some kind, like maybe on my birthday next week, I'd invite ol' Vern. An' anyone didn't like it could lump it, by gollies."

"I know someone that might not lump it so durn fast," Mutt said. "Or wasn't you plannin' on invitin' Mama?"

Yeah, Jeff thought, sighing. She wouldn't exactly cotton to having Vern for a guest, and some other guys might not like socializing with a Strode. But maybe Vern wouldn't come. The main thing was just *inviting* him.

But he didn't have to worry about the problem very long. Thursday night Dallas Strode escaped from the county jail in Blackthorn, making the Strodes famous all over again, their name in the paper and everything.

Besides, nobody decided to throw a birthday party.

:

7

One of the best things about summer was being able to sleep much later and wake up to the smell of coffee and bacon. Now that he was twelve he was allowed to drink coffee. Up to twelve, Postum, cocoa or tea. After twelve coffee wouldn't stunt your growth, although smoking still would. His mother was full of notions like that. No going barefooted until the middle of May. Sulphur and molasses in the spring to clean your blood, castor oil for stomach-ache, turpentine for cuts, flaxseed poultices for boils, warm skunk oil for earaches, hot mustard poultices for chest colds —and plenty of exercise at all times, especially on washdays.

During the school year she always got up extra early on Mondays unless it was raining or snowing, and woke him to pump and tote water to fill the big copper boiler on the stove and the rinse tubs. Mutt's only washday job was to bring in the benches and tubs and fasten on the wringer, then go peddle his papers. Sometimes in real cold weather Jeff's wet cotton gloves would freeze to the pump handle, and any winter washday was pure misery, stumbling around shivering, yawning, wishing it would hurry up and be time to head for the cozy steam-heated schoolroom. But a winter Monday was only a before-school ordeal, whereas in summer his washdays lasted until noon.

But in summer she heated water in the big iron kettle in the backyard, with her tubs near the well, and he spent more time resting between jobs than working. But he felt so durn tied-down, fidgety restless, wishing she'd get finished and emancipate him. Fill the darn tub, put more cobs under the kettle, add water to the kettle, sliver more brown lye soap in it, bring the clothespin bag, help hang up sheets and stuff, turn the wringer, bring more dirty clothes from the back porch, empty the dirty lukewarm water in the potato rows, go see if the beans needed more water, and so on. But even while feeling sour about his slavery he realized how much harder *she* worked, leaning over her scrubboard with sweat dripping from her pointy nose and round stubborn chin, wearing a fierce expression like dirty garments were her bitter enemies—and they sure as heck weren't her friends. Now and then she would straighten up with a sigh and press her wet hands against the small of her back and gaze into the distance kind of wistfully, as if wishing she'd taken up some other line of work. But she didn't waste much time resting. Her motto was: The sooner it's done the quicker it ends.

On this sunny mild May morning, he watched her scrubbing dauntlessly, all flushed and sweat-beaded and enduring, and felt such a sudden sentimental compassion seasoned with old guilt that he darn near made the fatal mistake of offering to take a turn at the scrubboard himself. *Here, madame, go set down awhile and let me fight that dirt . . .* if a woman could do it, a strong boy surely could.

Well, he squelched that notion in nothing flat. Boy, if she found out he could operate a scrubboard he'd really be in a pickle. She'd at least make him do his own clothes. Anyway, it was her own fault she had to use that raw-knuckle scrubboard. Last fall his dad brought home a secondhand gas-engine washing machine for a trial, a dirt-fighting son-ofagun with a big flywheel and pulley belt that did a batch of laundry in no time at all. But she was scared of machinery, afraid that noisy popping thing might blow up any minute, and the fumes gave her a headache—and, besides, it would be putting on airs since very few women in town had machines.

Also, he was still miffed because his twelfth birthday had caused such a small commotion, although it was surely a pretty special age, halfway between six and eighteen, halfway through school, old enough to drink coffee. No party, no cake with candles on it, no guests bearing gifts. No roller skates or .22 rifle or Benjamin BB gun, and no agate shooting taw. All he got was a new pair of Sunday school knickers, a dress-up shirt, a bow tie, handkerchiefs and a passbook showing he had two dollars in the bank—for his college fund, and his mother said she hoped it would inspire him to start saving up a nest egg.

Nest eggs were glass balls for dumb hens that didn't know where they were supposed to lay real eggs, and he wasn't a Rhode Island red, or a Plymouth Rock.

While straightening the kink out of her plump back, she interrupted his brooding. "Where do you suppose that little dickens goes when he slips off before breakfast?"

Jeff shrugged. He hadn't the slightest idea.

"Sometimes he comes home with candy on his breath," she said, meaning she kissed the little wart occasionally. She'd never detect anything on his breath, not that he craved any kissing. He would settle for a simple thanks for all this slaving, a pat on the back, a friendly handshake. "Not that I think he's up to any mischief"—she frowned—"but it's high time we settled that nagging little mystery of where he goes and with whom."

Jeff wondered how many women in town knew they were supposed to say *with whom?* Off of whom was Jody mooching breakfast—possibly the Higginses, he suggested. "I'll ask 'em. I'll be goin' right by there after we've finished."

She gave him a stern look and said: "Now listen, I don't want you going swimming this early. Not until June."

Who said anything about swimming? "Dad asked me to go ask Vern Strode to come back to baseball practice, is how come I'll be passin' the Higgins place," he said, and she frowned and said she wasn't crazy about having him seen visiting the home of a notorious escaped criminal, and he blinked at her and asked whom would see him?

She nearly grinned. "I'll tell you whom, smarty-pants. The sheriff, or one of his deputies. I imagine the proper authorities are keeping an eye on the Strode place in case that man should try to see his family. Anyway, I'm surprised your father would want that boy on the team."

Jeff explained that to her with weary patience. Vern just happened to be one heck of a good pitcher. Furthermore, a kid wasn't to blame for stuff his dad did, for gosh sakes.

She agreed Vern was innocent, and the Strodes were more to be pitied than censured, but just the same—and besides, was baseball that important? Your typical woman's point of view, there; they thought it was just a game you played for fun, and it would be nice if it was, but of course the main thing was to beat the other team even if you had to use a convict's son to do it. "Someday," Jeff predicted, "ol' Vern will be a famous big leaguer an' people around here'll be braggin' how he use to live in Cottonwood. . . ."

Accompanied by Ranger, another bum who didn't do any work around the McGraw ranch, he headed for Strodes' by a roundabout way, down through Yancys' yard and over to Main Street. He sort of dreaded facing Vern, or maybe having to ask his mother where he was. His visit might seem more like an intrusion to the embarrassed Strode family.

Freckled Lex Yancy told him Hud was helping Earl plant cowpeas and stuff, which Jeff had expected somehow, and he went on out along the narrow lane and found the new meat-market family also planting garden stuff in what used to be a weed-grown vacant lot in summer. Mrs. Dexter, Alma and Roy were working close to the raised sidewalk he had to go west on, but he would have gone bashfully on past if Roy hadn't hailed him, saying, "Hi, Jeff." So he

stopped and asked what they were planting, and Alma said
okra at the moment, and her mother gave him a squinty
smile as if trying to sort him out and put a name on him.

Mrs. Dexter said: "Your brother is the paper boy—a polite,
mannerly boy, always so neat."

Suddenly squirmy self-conscious about his clothes, groom-
ing and personality, Jeff sauntered on up the sidewalk with
faithful Ranger, who didn't give a dang if you weren't
neat and mannerly, or the answer to a maiden's prayer.
Doggonnit, there were only so many paper routes and cow-
herding jobs in a town like Cottonwood. Who did you go
see about a job, anyway? Guys like Dock and Jake had it
easy, helping out in their dad's store for weekly allowances
—plus all they could swipe, mainly tobacco, candy, sardines,
etc. Clarence Olive delivered the *Saturday Evening Post*
and *Grit* and peddled sachets, salve and what not, and had
won his bicycle as a prize. He was one of the guys that
hung around Alma, but who'd want a guy that wore glasses
and played the violin?

Passing the Bull Durham sign that walled off Dexters'
side yard, he remembered vividly the only time he'd been
alone with Alma so far. Last Friday he'd been passing the
side yard and she'd been swinging by herself. She gave him
a nice smile, so he stopped to visit, and one thing led to
another, and the first thing he knew he was sharing the
swing with her—standing up, stomach to stomach, pumping.
It wasn't the first time he'd pumped with a girl, but it
was different, a dizzying, exciting experience. Their bellies
bumped each time they pumped, and her flushed face and
sparkling eyes would be smiling down at him, then up at
him, and his senses reeled with every straining contact. She
had smelled nice, except for a slight oniony hamburger
fragrance he didn't mind at all—mainly of soap, starched
clothes and the indescribable aroma of *girl*, which was very
different from even a clean boy smell.

But it hadn't lasted long. Her dad hollered out the window: "Here now, none of that! One customer at a time!" So they quit, and Alma leaned against the wall out of her dad's sight and gave Jeff a sparkly grin. "Fun while it lasted, Jess," she said. Couldn't seem to get his name right, but what the heck, he wasn't in the running anyway.

It was three houses, two alleys and one street from Main to the Higgins place, then another street and house and alley to Strodes'. Mrs. Higgins and little Woodrow were in their garden, so he stopped and asked if Spotty was home, only he said Fillmore because she might not like her son's nickname—although personally he'd rather be called Spotty than Fillmore any day. She said Fillmore had gone to the hardware store for some window screen and asked how Jeff's mother was.

"Pretty tired, I guess," he said. "From scrubbin' clothes." Mrs. Higgins washed on Saturdays, at least during the school year, which sure ruined Spotty's weekends. "That reminds me," he said casually. "She wanted me to ask Woody if he knows where Jody gets up and goes off to without any breakfasts."

"Maybe I do," Woody said, "but I ain't tellin'."

"Oh, yes you are," his mother said.

"Well, gee whiz," Woody said, "I promised 'im." But when she frowned, he readily spilled the beans. He said Jody helped old man Ketchup deliver milk and got breakfast plus a nickel a day, thirty-five cents a week plus all the durn waffles he could eat. It made Jeff green with envy, listening. Thirty-five cents a week to blow in, plus waffles. The little wart took after Mutt, and the reason for his sneaky secrecy was easy to understand—he was afraid frugal-minded Jewel McGraw would make him bank some of his earnings.

"Old man Ketchup" was Mr. Ketcham, who owned the cornfield, the big barn and the alfalfa field you cut across going to the swimming hole. He sold milk, hay and pigs,

67

and bragged that he hadn't missed church or prayer meeting in forty years, even when he had smallpox. And his wife was noted for her cooking. That darn Jody.

How do people locate these great jobs? Jeff wondered as he walked on down the road. He saw white smoke rising above the shed that hid the Strode yard, and noticed that the old house had some new shingles on the roof to patch the leaks. Glancing west to Mr. Ketcham's big barn, he wondered uneasily if the sheriff or somebody could be in the hayloft right now, watching the Strode place.

Vern was pumping water. Mrs. Strode, a slender, dark-haired woman, and Goldie were both leaning over scrub-boards, and the two younger boys were carrying water and tending fires under two big iron kettles. None of them noticed Jeff until Vern's hound bawled a challenge to Ranger. Old Milton knew Ranger fairly well by now, but they went through the routine of circling each other stiff-legged and bristling—that was how dogs did business. All of the other Strodes looked up and then went on about their business, but Vern stopped pumping, his expression neither welcoming nor hostile, and it struck Jeff that *every* day was washday for the Strodes, and a lot worse than, say, a McGraw washday. All of them, even Mrs. Strode, who seemed rather pretty from a distance, were barefoot, indicating how hard up they were for shoe money. That sort of embarrassed Jeff, somehow.

"Hi," he said. "Haven't seen you around lately."

"Haven't *been* around much lately." Vern shrugged.

Jeff explained the reason for his visit, and Vern was visibly surprised. He said he hadn't figured he'd be missed, and Jeff assured him he had, and Vern studied about it for a moment, then said, well, if they got finished by two o'clock he'd probably show up for practice.

"Fine an' dandy," Jeff said, and headed south, feeling pretty good. He tried to imagine how Vern would feel about his dad being an escaped jailbird with a price on his head.

That brought up an interesting question. How many people around town would turn Dallas Strode in if they knew where he was and collect that thirty-five-dollar reward? Jeff McGraw sure wouldn't. He wasn't any lousy bounty hunter. Maybe someone like Chink would do it for the money, or Jelly Wurtz for spite because Vern was a better pitcher . . .

After passing the Higgins place, he turned east into the alley, free to do as he pleased for the next hour or so. He liked alleys. A guy could travel all over town in privacy and seclusion, except for having to cross an occasional street, because alleys were walled off by sheds, barns, chicken houses, toilets, board fences, etc.

But suddenly he didn't have this particular alley all to himself anymore. Spotty was coming from the other end carrying his little dog in his arms. Duffy was a rat terrier, and so small that other dogs were ashamed to pick on him, but it looked rather silly for a guy to carry his dog like it was a doll or something, and Jeff was getting ready to say something derisive when he saw that Spotty was crying. His grin muscles went slack, watching Spotty come stumbling down the alley carrying Duffy and crying, and he felt alarmed.

"Hey, wot's the matter?" he called out, and Spotty said with bitter grief: "He's d-dead, is wot's the mu-matter."

Duffy *dead*? That friendly wriggly yapping little sonafagun *dead*? He looked like he was grinning in his sleep, or like he knew the joke was on him this time. Jeff saw no blood, no sign of injury from getting run over or anything, and thought: Well, he was awful old for a dog. . . .

"How'd it happen?" he asked, uneasy in the presence of death, and Spotty gave a retching moan and said: "Puh-poisoned. He nuh-never bothered no one, huh-he never chased cats or nuh-nuthin'." He wiped tears on Duffy's short clean fur, like a caress. "Suh-some dirty buh-bas-tard thowed poisoned muh-meat in the ditch right uh-uh-up yonder. I even seen 'im chuh-chuh-chewin' it, on our way to the huh-hardware store, but I never thought nuh-nuthin' about it." He cuddled the small dead dog like a baby and rocked back and forth, weeping unashamedly in the bright May noonday. Ranger walked around him in a wary circle, looking up at the still Duffy curiously, until Jeff gruffly called him away, afraid the poison might somehow be contagious, feeling a chilling worry.

Whoever *does* it is doing it *again*! he thought.

It had been nearly a year since the unknown, heartless dog poisoner had struck last, and you kind of forgot about it between times—how the sinister, mysterious madman (or woman) was at it again and nobody's dog was safe.

"Oh, gee, I hate to guh-go home," Spotty said miserably. "He's two years older'n I was—they had 'im goin' on thuh-thirteen." He used Duffy's coat to swab tears again. "Whuh-when I come out of the hardware store he was huh-havin' a kinda fit, layin' there . . ." He gave a sobbing groan. "Nuthin' I could do, or nuh-nobody else. Gee, I hate to go home."

But he went, stumbling, blinded by his tears, and Jeff watched him go, feeling pity and a growing fear, gripping Ranger by his loose neck skin, thinking worriedly: Who's doing it? Some people always thought Doc Schuman, because he had plenty of strychnine in his drugstore and was German, and dogs didn't much like him. But lots of people kept strychnine, a nerve tonic if you only used a little dab, used to treat horses and cows for certain things. But an overdose was fatal. Smear it on a soupbone or weenie and drop it anywhere, and suddenly every dog in town was in terrible danger. Like, right now, Ranger. Keeping his grip on the dog's neck skin, he headed for home, unnerved, confounded, scared. Earl Yancy kept strychnine and threw cobs and things at dogs that nipped at his team of drayhorses, and wouldn't let Hud have a dog—but you could name half a dozen cat-lovers around town who hated dogs . . .

He just wanted to get Ranger safely home—if anyplace was safe. The murdering devil could go anywhere in town and drop poisoned bait, even in the McGraw front yard. They ought to have that reward on the rotten poisoner instead of Dallas Strode.

As he was passing the scene of Duffy's death Mr. Riley hailed him. "Give you a dime to take this roll of screen wire to Mrs. Higgins, Jefferson." No sirree! Jeff thought. Not even for two bits. He wasn't going back into poisoned meat territory while Ranger was with him. He needed the dime, but just shook his head and said: "Wisht I could, Mr. Riley, but I got to get home."

As soon as Mutt heard the bad news he said, "You keep 'im right here until I git back." And he left home at a dead run. But then he got delayed and didn't return for about fifteen minutes. Had to go all the way to Higginses' and back on a ten-cent delivery job. But when he got home he had a dog collar and chain that cost a lot more than he'd earned.

"Now, lissen, lummox," he said grimly, "from now on, unless he's with me, Ranger stays home, izzat clear?" He got no argument from Jeff about that but ran into difficulties with his mother when he snapped the chain to one of her clotheslines. "I don't want any dog poot where I have to walk," she said, and her word was final. Mutt had to stretch a wire between two trees so Ranger would have a little freedom of movement.

A local tragedy like Duffy's death didn't interfere with the workings of Jewel McGraw's practical mind, like remembering potato bugs needed picking and mulberries carried out to the alley. Having seniority, Mutt took the bug job and left Jeff the harder work. From mid-May to late June that tree rained ripe berries on the backyard, making a splattery messiness that attracted flies and had to be swept into piles, shoveled into tubs and dumped in the alley. The inky mess stained bare feet and wouldn't wash off—you had to just wear it off. Despite many mulberry pies and cobblers, tons of berries just went to waste and had to be removed. And he was the remover.

He was dragging the tub to the alley when an idea suddenly hit him. "Hey," he said, "if you had like a catcher's mask for Ranger, he couldn't eat anything, probly."

Mutt paused in his tater bug picking, started to say something sarcastic, then he looked surprised. "Well, hot dang! How come I never thought of that?" He set down the can he was putting bugs in. "If she asks where I'm at, I went to see if ol' John's got any dog muzzles." And he lit out for the hardware store again.

When they went to baseball practice Mutt said comically, "I like you guys to meet the new substitute catcher." Meaning Ranger with the wire muzzle over his face. After telling the guys about poor little Duffy, he said casually, "If any you guys innerested, I happen to have two more muzzles like Ranger's, an' a couple that are just straps so a dog can't open his mouth wide enough to eat somethin' poison." Having bought Mr. Riley's entire supply on a gambler's impulse, he was now the only dog-muzzle dealer in town. And the alarmed dog-owning baseball players committed their parents to buy Mutt's extra muzzles at a nice profit. Whereupon Mutt suddenly pulled out his dollar Ingersoll watch and said, "Thirty minutes' battin' practice, then I hafta leave an' you guys can have infield practice an' knock flies."

Vernon Strode came up the street warily, but the McGraws and some others welcomed him warmly enough to ease his nervousness. When Jeff told him about poor Duffy, Vern said he always kept Milton tied up when he left him at home, and he started warming up his arm, making that old apple pop in Mutt's glove.

They had a regular batting practice, with each guy taking his turn and getting six strikes instead of three, but most of them were so upset about the dog poisoning (as they

72

explained it) that nobody was hitting well. Or else Vern was pitching great, take your pick.

Slim McGraw hadn't done much managing yet, being tied up with the schedule, equipment, transportation problems, etc. He'd named Dolittle infield-outfield-batting-and-pitching coach, but Dolittle left batting practice up to the captain, and Jeff got tired of Mutt's sarcastic remarks about a chicken-livered second baseman who backed up on grounders instead of charging in on them. It was a relief when Mutt checked his watch again and said he had to leave.

Infield practice was the part Jeff hated, so he hollered, "Hey, Jake, take over second, I'm tard." Then on a sudden conciliatory impulse he added: "Here, try my glove for a change." They swapped and he went to sit on the grass and study Jake's new glove, which was like a big fat hand with an inch of numb callus in the palm.

Dock Ballew had cut his foot and couldn't practice, and he limped over to sit beside Jeff and remarked in a kind of casual fashion, "You people quit eatin' meat?"

"We been eatin' a lotta fish," Jeff said lamely. The truth was, they got their meat from the new butcher shop now. Mr. Dexter bought hogs and steers and did his own butchering, instead of buying sides of beef and pork from the slaughterhouse like Mr. Ballew did, so naturally he could sell it cheaper. Wasn't any of Dock's business anyway. That old stuff was aggravating—storekeepers acted sore if you didn't give them all your business, but never gave you a darn thing in return.

Jake was snagging grounders and stabbing line drives one-handed with Jeff's glove, and presently he hollered: "What'll you take for this ol' rag, Jiffy?" Annoyed at the whole Ballew family, Jeff said it wasn't no rag and wasn't for sale. Pretty soon Jake hollered: "How much boot'll ya give an' trade gloves?"

Jeff hooted. "Boot my eye!" he said scornfully.

After a while Jake hollered: "Trade ya even?"

"Heck, no!" Jeff replied, feeling excited. "Take a *year* to break this stiff booger in." It wouldn't, though; all it needed was some padding removed from the palm.

"Speakin' of dog poisonin'," Dock remarked, "some *people* are liable to git poisoned on that Dexter meat. Know what I heard? Somebody's cow dies, he buys it, even swelled up an' stinkin', to grind up for hamburger an' his durn chili. Ol' fly-blown sick carcasses."

Jeff grinned. "An' he puts cats in the sausage, huh?"

"Okay," Jake hollered, "I'll give you a dime to boot, an' that's my final offer." And Jeff hollered back, "Well—okay then, it's a deal, I guess."

Dock argued with his dumb brother for trading a new glove for an old one, but Jake said, "Shut your big yap. It's my glove an' I don't need no damn advice from you." So Jeff called everybody to witness the transaction, and just like that he was the proud owner of a practically new finger mitt and a slightly tarnished dime.

"Well, I jist hope you live long enough to git some use out of that glove," Dock growled, probably meaning he hoped Jeff would die from eating cheap Dexter meat. He added slyly, "Seems kinda peculiar—certain people move here an' right away dogs start dyin' . . ." He didn't have the sap to come right out and say Mr. Dexter was the dog poisoner, but the hint was clear. Try looking at it another way, Jeff thought. Maybe the Higginses quit buying meat from a certain store, so a certain person put strychnine on a piece of high-priced meat for spite, etc.

Jelly Wurtz yelled to ask where Mutt was in such a hurry to go to, and Jeff shrugged and said, "I dunno, maybe he went to locate some more dog muzzles to sell."

The amazing part was, that's exactly where Mutt had gone. He caught the afternoon freight train to Blackthorn (the county seat, with what used to be an escape-proof jail), bought all the muzzles he could find, returned to

74

Cottonwood on the passenger train carrying his evening papers, and sold seven muzzles to *Oklahoma City Times* customers who owned dogs. All told, he made a clear profit of around fifteen dollars in one day, causing sour Dock to kind of hint that a certain person might have put out strychnine just to drum up customers for dog muzzles—but he had the sense not to say it to Mutt. Anyway, the buyers were satisfied—especially after two more dogs died in the north part of town and one in the south part before the poisoning epidemic finally petered out.

Probably what caused the inhuman devil to quit was the twenty-buck reward the merchants and citizens put up for information about who was doing it. Everybody in town started keeping an eye on everybody in town, especially the half-dozen *known* dog haters. That was twenty dollars Jeff would dearly love to claim, but the sinister mystery continued to hang over the town for a long time, until other things crowded it into the back of people's minds.

Spotty Higgins stayed away from baseball practice a few days, in mourning for his dog, and Jody quit going down there to play with Woody because he was scared of getting poisoned from associating with anyone connected with the grisly affair.

"Just stay away from where they buried Duffy," Jeff said, "an' you got nothing to worry about."

"I won't," Jody said earnestly. Which, if you knew him as well as Jeff did, made sense.

8

A strong wind during the night had flailed a bumper crop of mulberries onto the ground, and during the ordeal of sweeping and shoveling the pernicious berries—a waste of pies and cobblers and jelly—Jeff was wishing the darn tree would get through producing. There were places he needed to go, things he needed to do, a thousand better ways to spend his time. And he was thinking of some of them when he dragged the tub out to the alley, and a rock bounced whining and ricocheted off the barn wall.

He beat it around the corner and removed his slingshot from his hip pocket. Unfurling it, he said grimly, "Okay, boy, you're askin' for it." He'd thought, or hoped anyway, that Chink was through being sore, but he'd made provisions just in case he wasn't. See how that sneaky buzzard liked some of Mutt's babbitt slugs whizzing around him.

He had swiped four of the slugs from Mutt, and he fired them one after the other in the general direction of Chink's invisible tree roost, and had the satisfaction of hearing a yelp of alarm, or indignation, or maybe pain, over there beyond Granny Hanks' orchard. Maybe I hit 'im, he thought triumphantly. But then he thought: My lord, maybe I *hit* him! One of those slugs could do a lot of damage to a guy. And make him crazy mad and vengeful. Oh boy.

Feeling rather remorseful, he headed for the house and safety, his mind picturing Chink skinning down out of his tree and coming after a certain dumbly reckless kid. Then he saw his mother and Mrs. Riley on their way downtown, and thought: If he comes here now there won't be anybody here but me. But then he corrected himself, there won't be *anybody* here, and took off around the house.

Halfway down the street Ranger overtook him. As they were loping past the Yancy place, Hud came chugging out to join them. "Goin' for a little trot?" he asked, and Jeff said yep without breaking stride. He said he was scooting for safety, mainly, but was also going by the shack to borrow some chewing tobacco.

"Oh brethern an' sisterns, that filthy weed it'll destroy your mind an' soul," Hud said like a preacher, and Jeff said: "Amen!" "Wotta you aim to do after the burgulary?" Hud inquired, and Jeff slowed, looking back up the street and seeing no enraged pursuer. "I dunno," he said. "Wotta you gonna be doin', Huddleson?"

They zoomed up the cinder path to the right-of-way and cut across the tracks, and Hud said some of his customers were complaining that their cows weren't giving as much milk as they should lately, and all he could figure out was that maybe dogs were pestering the cows during the day, and he was going over there to check into it. Jeff said that suited him, he had nothing better to do. So they were wincing along the hot brick platform companionably, and Hud said, "You ever git a bean stuck in your nose?"

"Not lately," Jeff replied. "Why?"

"Alamo's little kid brother did this mornin'," Hud told him. "I knew a kid once that poked a watermelon seed in his ear."

His dad was planning to drain the watertank in July, and Jeff couldn't tell Hud about it. "Zat so?" he asked.

"They tried to flush it outa there with warm water, but it was stuck fast," Hud said. "An' you know what? The durn thing sprouted. Here was this watermelon vine growing out his dadblamed ear." His deadpan solemnity caused Jeff to feel wary about asking questions; he'd been taken in before.

77

Testing a rail with his still sensitive feet, he found it as hot as he'd figured it would be. "Zat a fact?" he said.

It was rooted too tight to pull it out, Hud soberly explained, without damaging the kid's ear. So it kept on growing, and his parents got kinda proud of that watermelon vine and instead of trimming or pruning it they just let it grow. Kid had to drape it over his shoulders and wrap it around his neck, Hud said, and Jeff had to laugh at the mental picture he got of that, but he also remembered to look back toward enemy territory. "Then wot?"

"Durn thing bloomed an' started growin' melons," Hud said mildly. "They knowed he couldn't perduce a whole durn patch, so they picked off all but one melon." That made his audience laugh, so he threw in another item. "They tried to rent 'im to a circus, but it already had a woman with punkin vines growin' outa both ears."

Giggling helplessly, Jeff said, "Aw, cut it out!"

They went on to the shack in silence and drank ice water from the keg, and Ranger tried to rub his muzzle off against the stove, but it wouldn't come off. Jeff pilfered some Day's Work and decided it was high time he tried smoking a pipe. He took one that was dusty, like it hadn't been used in a long time, and swiped one of three half-empty cans of Prince Albert and a book of papers—it was time he learned to roll his own cigarettes, too. And all this time Hud remained silent, waiting for Jeff to ask him what else happened to the kid with the watermelon.

Beyond the stock pens there were only scattered houses on the left, and then no houses at all, and the street became a grass-grown road that took a long swing west around the rim of a shallow, timbered hollow, but there was a shortcut path the cows had made down across the hollow. "You take a durn cow," Hud remarked, "they perfer goin' straight ahead, except when passin' someone's garden or front yard. Hey, Jiffo, if we had some top cord we could make us some bows."

Jeff never went anywhere without his ball of stout cord, so they were in business. And while cutting limbs for bows, Hud acted like he'd forgot all about the kid with the earache. "Whilst we're stealin' timber," he said, "I haven't rode a persimmon mustang in a coon's age, how 'bout it?"

"Okay by me," Jeff said. He still liked to ride stick horses, although Mutt would razz him if he found out. There were some kiddish things a guy hated to give up, and making believe was one of them. As for Hud, riding a sapling pony should be a lot more comfortable than his real horse. So after gathering dried weeds for arrows, they became for the time being a couple of well-mounted Kiowa braves hunting buffalo or antelope, but ready for a quick switch to the warpath. On their prancing, skittish steeds, they reached the bouldered, sprout-grown, rugged vastness of the town pasture, called Buffalo Wallows because up on its flatter middle there actually were eight or ten round depressions made by buffalo forty or more years ago. This time of year they were shallow ponds inhabited by spotted cowfrogs. From the pasture gate cow trails fanned out like spokes in a wheel, and they followed one northeast, with old Ranger scouting up ahead, and presently Jeff sighed and gave in.

"Okay, wot happened to that kid, durn ya?"

"Wot kid?" Hud asked. "Oh, him. Lessee now." He had to gentle his half-wild pinto for a minute. "Well, that was a real dry summer an' they hadda keep waterin' his ear, an' they poked cow minyoor an' hen hocky in there to fertilize it, an' the durn melon got so big he couldn't carry it anymore. Hadda push it around in an old baby buggy."

Jeff nearly fell off his horse, laughing.

"At night it slept on a rug beside the kid's bed."

Jeff went ahead and fell off, picking a patch of soft-looking grass, and he lay on his back chuckling, squinting up at the deep blue sky, feeling tickled and happy. But Hud's pony bolted, and he had to remount and give chase all the way to the first wallow. They fired a few arrows at small frogs without inflicting injury, and Ranger got a drink, although hampered in even that by the durn muzzle. Hud was stalling again, so Jeff said, "I know, someone stole it."

"You're close," Hud said. "The kid woke up one night on account of the earache, an' a guy was thumpin' his melon to see was it ripe yet. It wasn't, an' the guy snuck out the back door. After that they locked all the doors after sundown." He swung his impatient mount around and galloped toward the creek, flushing out a cottontail that took out for the timbered creek bottom with Ranger in hot pursuit. When Jeff caught up, Hud said, "If he catches it, wearin' that muzzle, it'll whup him."

Several arrow flights later they reached the bouldered rim of the wide valley and sprawled on a big slab, looking down at the shady woods where the town herd was loafing, lying around chewing its collective cud. Hud said they didn't act like any dogs had been pestering them today; they didn't seem at all edgy.

"I've heard of snakes suckin' cows," Jeff said, getting out the tobacco and papers. Bull snakes, no doubt, Hud remarked, and they chuckled while rolling cigarettes, neither of them quite ready to swallow that snake yarn. They lit up and puffed like old hands, and Hud trickled smoke out of his nostrils. Jeff couldn't do that yet.

"If I hadda be an animule," Hud said, "I druther be a milk cow. A horse hasta work all its life. You know wot happens to *pigs*. An' take dogs, now . . ." He shrugged, and Jeff nodded. Life was very hazardous for dogs. They were always in danger of being poisoned, run over, having distemper or hydrophobia, and they suffered from worms, fleas, mange and other dogs. "I figger cats has the most fun, prowlin' nights, gorgin' on mice an' birds, an' people give 'em milk an' let 'em stay in their houses. But dogs chase 'em an' they git caught in traps an' run over, an' people use catgut for violins an' tennis rackets—hey, ain't you spose to practice baseball today?"

80

Jeff shrugged. That would be the second place Chink would look for him, doggonnit.

"The worst thing in bein' a cat," Hud expounded, "an awful lot of 'em are drowned before they even git their eyes open. Or else their own daddy comes around an' kills all the boy kittens later on." He oozed smoke out his nose and looked reflective. "But your milk cow lives a life of ease. Snug shed an' plenty hay an' bran in the winter, an' summers they spend every day over here eatin' grass an' layin' in the shade, an' all they hafta do is give milk—which they'd do *anyway*." He stood up and flipped his cigarette away. "Well, by the time we ride these here buckin' broncos back to town an' see wots goin' on along both sides of Main Street, it'll be time for me to come back over here an' take them ol' gals home for the night."

Main Street was a good place to run into old Chink, so Jeff said he'd better go see about Ranger; he might have got his muzzle snagged on something, or something.

Hud mounted his sapling. "Okeydokey, I'll explain to Alamo why you didn't make it," he joshed, knowing perfectly well that Jeff wasn't entered in that race. Then as he went galloping away his unsatisfied audience hollered: "Hey, what happened to the kid with the watermelon in his ear?"

Hud yanked his obstreperous mustang in a high-stepping circle. "They entered him in the county fair," he said, and took out again.

Jeff hadn't been this far down the creek since October, and it was different now, all grown-up and closed in with lush greenery, shady and sort of mysterious. The spongy leaf mold was balm to his feet, but the brooding silence under the canopy of elms and oaks and cottonwoods kind of set his nerves on edge. No birds singing, just a rather stealthy hush, and when a nervous frog cronked and splashed into the creek his scalp twitched and tingled for about a minute. He whistled softly for Ranger but didn't feel like shattering the brittle silence by calling him. Were

81

the birds taking a nap or had something scared them? Funny how a guy alone in the woods could get all spooked up by the lack of noise. . . .

A sudden furtive cough nearby raised the hackles on his neck, and he froze, holding his breath and listening tensely. Then a muffled, impatient bark made him feel relieved and sheepish. He angled off through the undergrowth and located old never-fail Ranger by a patch of buckbrush with a fat young male rabbit he'd managed to catch and kill, but couldn't carry. Jeff was glad it wasn't a bitch rabbit with nursing babies, or about to hatch some. He never hunted rabbits in nesting season, but a summer-fat unmarried cottontail of either gender was prime eating in case of a fortuitous accident like this.

"Dunno about you, boy, but I'm thirsty for some good ol' cold spring water," he said, patting Ranger approvingly.

As he headed on down the creek a funny thing happened. Suddenly he became aware of normal woodsy sounds, crows fussing in the distance, a woodpecker drumming on a hollow tree, redbirds singing and quail calling, and abruptly all of the vague menace was gone from the sunny afternoon.

The sweet cold spring bubbled out of the rocky bluff and spilled down a winding mossy rill over shale and sandstone shelves and ledges, forming small pools and potholes and miniature rapids before emptying into the creek. Jeff galloped the last few yards and reined in at the high edge of the bush-fringed branch, feeling thirsty. "Whoa!" he said. And then he noticed the shirt, pants and BVDs draped on a bush on the other side. But he didn't see the man until he said, "That's quite a hoss you got there, cowboy."

Jeff was startled at first and then embarrassed at being caught playing like a stick was a horse, and because the man sitting on a rock was stark naked. A lean man with a growth of reddish whiskers and uncombed yellowish hair, and a certain resemblance that caused Jeff's embarrassment to change into uneasy surprise. "Well," he said self-consciously, "it don't cost much to feed 'im, at least."

The man squinted at him awhile. "Don't suppose you'd trade that rabbit for a three-pound catfish," he said. "I'm tired of a steady diet of fish, an' don't have any string for rabbit snares." He kept gazing at Jeff with a kind of rueful intentness. "There's lot's of things I don't have, like tobacco, flour, salt, coffee, soap, a razor, a skillet, you name it. Us hoboes live skimpy sometimes."

He was too far from the railroad tracks to be a real hobo, and besides, the resemblance was unmistakable. Wanting to get along with what's-his-name, Jeff said he had some string he could spare, also tobacco, matches and cigarette papers. But none of that other stuff.

"I'd sure be much obliged for a smoke," the apparition said. "And any matches you can spare. I got me a fire banked off yonder, but I'm plumb outa lucifers."

Jeff was about to go down across the branch when he saw the butcher knife on the ground beside the man and quickly changed his mind, just tossing the Prince Albert can and the twine to the naked stranger, suddenly plenty worried about being so far down the creek with a probable escaped convict armed with a butcher knife. And with only a muzzled dog for protection—wherever Ranger had got off to. Trying to conceal his uneasiness, he said, "Were you serious about swappin' me a big catfish for this rabbit?"

"Dang tootin' I was," the man said, rolling a cigarette. "Fish cooked on a stick gets old. I can noodle all the fish I need, but I can't noodle rabbits or birds. Go see if you think the biggest cat in that chughole is worth a rabbit."

Jeff went to the indicated tub-sized pothole up the branch a few feet and was amazed to find that it contained seven fish in all, four cats, two carp and a drum. He was impressed because he'd tried noodling a few times himself and didn't much care for it, groping around up under rocks and logs, feeling barehanded for fish. Every time he had touched something he'd yanked his hand back, convinced it was a snake or snapping turtle or something.

"Tell you what," the noodler said, "take any two of those jessies an' leave me this tobacco."

Even if it wasn't such a good deal Jeff would have assented, not wanting to cross a desperate escapee with a big butcher knife. "Okay," he said, "only I'd like to put just a smidgen in my pipe first if it's all the same to you."

The probable Dallas Strode laughed, then apologized. "It just struck me funny, buddy—you ride a stick horse but you smoke a pipe."

Embarrassed, Jeff explained he'd never actually smoked a pipe yet, and this was the first time in about a year that he'd played stick horse—and possibly the last.

"You enjoy pretendin' that stick was a hoss?"

Jeff shrugged. "Long as nobody *seen* me I did."

"Take some free advice," the naked man said. "Don't quit somethin' you like just because someone might razz you for doin' it—an' don't smoke your first pipe when you're a long ways from home. If you are."

"I am, sort of," Jeff said, putting the pipe away. What the heck, he had all summer. No big rush about it.

"Bein' camped out here waitin' for the wheat harvest to start, I haven't seen a newspaper lately," the noodler said. "Any big news events been happenin' lately?"

"Not much," Jeff said, "except a man named Lindbergh, he flew across the Atlantic Ocean to Paris, all alone."

"In a plane, or just flappin' his arms?" the probable jailbreaker asked, and Jeff grinned nervously. Another kidder here—but with a butcher knife. "I miss the baseball news," the kidder said. "How's Babe Ruth an' Goose Goslin doin'?"

"Okay, I guess," Jeff said, and they discussed baseball awhile, and he mentioned his own connection with the great American pastime as a fair-hitting right fielder currently playing second base against his private wishes. He said his brother was catcher on the Junior Legion team—and then before he realized what he was saying he blurted: "An' Vernon is our pitcher." Oh lord! he thought. Now I did it.

The man stared at him bleakly. "I git the odd feelin' you think you got a notion who I'm liable to be, buddy."

Jeff swallowed nervously, nodding. "Sort of."

"I ain't admittin' a thing, but in case I was who you think I might be, how's his family makin' out?"

It was him, all right: Vern's father, the escaped convict. Jeff told him the Strodes were all well, lived about a block south of the creek at the west edge of town, had a big garden and a lot of young chickens, and Mrs. Strode seemed to have plenty of washing customers. And all the time he was talking the man kept eyeing him like he hadn't made up his mind what he had to do about a town kid sneaking up on him, discovering his whereabouts. "Vern's about my best friend," Jeff threw in, "an' the best pitcher we ever had." A man wouldn't hurt his son's pal, would he?

"If I see that feller I'll tell 'im all that," the ex-prisoner said gravely. "But if he's a down-an'-out hobo like me he wouldn't want his folks seein' him that way, or even knowin' he was livin' thisaway. His woman, now, likely she is still purty mad at him for the shame an' disgrace that ol' boy brought down on her an' the kids—I mean, if I'm thinkin' of the same feller you had in mind."

"All I know," Jeff said earnestly, "is if I did happen to see anyone like whoever you thought I mighta had in mind, he wouldn't need to worry about me blabbin' it to anybody." Dallas Strode just scratched and gazed at him glumly, so he added anxiously: "Besides keepin' it a secret, I could bring him stuff he needed, food an' tobacco an' like that."

The man smiled. "You're talkin' to a feller that about all he owns is a borrowed blanket an' kitchen knife, the clothes on his back, an' a couple pork-an'-bean cans to cook in." He gazed off down the creek for a moment. "Do people come here much this time of year?"

"Well . . . ol' Turkey Dobbs, he fishes away off down here somewheres, I guess," Jeff said. "He don't have nothin' to do with anybody, but I always figured he cuts east across the pasture. Takes a beeline route. Outside of him nobody comes down here much until Clem Parker's watermelon patch starts gettin' ripe." Tossing the plump young rabbit across the narrow branch, he said, "I could bring stuff down here an' leave it on that rock if you weren't around at the time."

The man nodded and scratched some more, pondering. "Well, there'll be some fish in that chughole tomorrow, an' in case you showed up with some salt, coffee, flour, or purt near anything I'm fresh out of, you could help yourself to them fish. All right?"

"Darn tootin'!" Jeff said with relief. "I'll be here." He cut a limb to string the two biggest catfish on. "Well, I better head tords town, I guess."

"Don't forgit your hoss," the man said. "Save you all that long walk." He sure had a sense of humor.

Laughing nervously, Jeff mounted up and took off at a gallop. How many guys ever had the privilege of being friends with an escaped convict? The only trouble was, you couldn't brag about it. But he could bug a few eyes with his catfish, and they ought to please his mother—and make old Mutt sick with envy.

Passing through the grazing cow herd halfway to the pasture gate, he had a sudden suspicion as to why some of them hadn't been giving as much milk as they should, and thought: Boy, imagine a steady diet of fish and warm milk!

He discarded his stick horse and archery equipment where he'd got them, and entered Cottonwood encumbered with nothing but ten pounds of prime catfish he aimed to display proudly on Main Street—only it didn't work out that way. As he was passing the elevator Claude Calvert hailed him, saying, "By George, I was just wishing I could have me a mess of catfish for supper. What'll you take for one, Jeff?"

Money being much scarcer than fish in Jeff's life, he shrugged and said, "I dunno, wot'll you give?"

"Forty cents for the big 'un, or fifty for the little 'un," Mr. Calvert said. He was always confusing people with crazy offers like that. Grinning, Jeff slid the smaller cat off the stick, thinking: Four bits, for gosh sakes!

And he still had the big one left—but not for long. As he sauntered on west feeling well-to-do he was accosted by banker Bradman, who stopped his car on the main-line tracks and expressed a desire to acquire the big fish, and shelled out six bits without batting an eyelash. So Jeff was suddenly fishless and a little sad about not getting to show off that baby uptown, but mainly he was dazed by his abrupt rise from rags to riches. Pow! Just like that from flat broke to a buck twenty-five. Which he didn't deserve, he thought with a twinge of guilt. He'd traded Ranger's rabbit and his dad's tobacco for the fish. All he'd done was take a walk down the creek. But what the heck, he'd use some of the money to buy stuff for old what's-his-name—and tomorrow there'd be more fish, and maybe more customers. Holy smoke! he thought with a wide grin, looks like I'm in the fish business, probably.

Alma Dexter was bouncing a tennis ball on the sidewalk and Hud was coming out along the lane on old Blackie, and he thought how amazed they would of been if they'd seen those dadgummed fish—and how astonished Hud would be if he knew where they came from. But instead, Hud was grouchy, saying, "Thought you's gonna wait over there."

"Too durn lonesome," Jeff said, fondling his money.

"Chink was lookin' for you while ago," Hud remarked. "He was limpin'—hit his knee with a hammer, he claimed. Said he had sumpin' that belonged to you. Reckon wot it is?"

"I dunno," Jeff said, "but if you see 'im again, tell 'im it belongs to Mutt, not me." He suddenly remembered, and said, "Hey, finish that nutty story, the watermelon kid."

Hud eased his bottom on Blackie's inhospitable spine and

squinted into space. "Lessee—well, they was all fixin' to git in the wagon when the durn boob went an' tripped over his own vine an' busted the melon, so they et it, an' his paw said next year they'll try cucumbers."

He kicked his reluctant nag into motion and left Jeff giggling and snuffling and eyeing Alma nervously. Had to pass her going to the drugstore. What could he say to her? *Bouncing a tennis ball, hey?* Or something dumb like that. *Well, how you like Cottonwood by now?* Mutt would probably start telling her all about tennis, including who invented it. Lige would probably tell her she was cuter than a bug's ear—which she was, all right. But Jeff didn't have nerve enough to come out with stuff like that.

She said howdy Jess, and he said howdy Alma, and then he surprised himself by asking if she'd care for an ice-cream soda, and she said she sure would. "Go on ahead an' I'll be along in a minute," she told him. But she never showed up. She gave him the old runaround—but it saved him a dime. What the heck.

9

Mutt brought the letter while their dad was having his morning coffee and toast, then went out back to melt some babbitt for slingshot slugs. Jeff was in the kitchen having his mid-morning coffee and toast, and he cocked an ear toward the dining room. He figured it was just the regular monthly letter from Uncle Tobe until he heard his dad give a snort and exclaim: "My kid brother has up an' went crazy! He says here he's fixing to get married, he thinks."

Jeff heard his mother sort of catch her breath. "Oh, no," she said protestingly. "After all this time? When?"

"Doesn't say. Just says he found a dream girl, a real tootsie-wootsie with a sunny disposish—must be serious, he never wrote mush like that about a woman before."

"Oh dear," she said in a peculiar tone. "I thought by now . . . does he say anything about . . ." She interrupted herself and came to look in the kitchen. "You're supposed to be hoeing the garden," she told Jeff. Meaning she didn't want him eavesdropping on the conversation. So he shrugged and went outside and told Mutt that Uncle Tobe was fixing to get married again, and Mutt said: "Holy cow! At his age?" He seemed kind of horrified about it, but it didn't bother Jeff. Uncle Tobe probably needed a housekeeper, what the heck.

While hoeing the garden he stopped occasionally to feel the spare change in his pocket, gloating a little. It sure was nice to have dough. He could be even richer, but his partner said selling too many fish too often might arouse suspicion and curiosity, and somebody might try to find out where his catfish mine was. Which made good sense, probably.

The noodler still didn't know there was a reward on him, but then he hadn't even admitted he was Dallas Strode. Anyway, after all this time it wouldn't matter if he knew— they were friends and trusted each other. In fact Jeff felt so easy around the erstwhile jailbird that during their last conversation he had impulsively offered some free advice, saying: "If *I* was that guy I thought you might of been for a while there at first, I'd ease up the crick some night an' visit my family, so they'd know I was okay, an' so forth."

Noodler rolled a cigarette before answering. "I dunno, buddy. That feller might figure no matter how bad he yearned to see his wife after all this time, she's got a hard enough row to hoe without the risk of havin' another mouth to feed later on, if you see what I mean."

Jeff didn't see what he meant. Over his head.

"Right now I'd reckon that ol' boy just appreciates bein' on the loose, free as a bird. After six months in jail he'd be satisfied to live like *I'm* doin' —which, if he is, he might stay put all summer, long as he knew his family was okay, an' close by in case they needed him some way."

All summer! Hot doggies! Jeff thought. By fall he'd be a rich man at the rate he was going. He figured he was saving around two bucks a week. That chance meeting had been a lucky day for him—and it was working out pretty good for Dallas Strode, too. His secret hideaway must be pretty homey by now, with all the stuff Jeff had brought him. Food, camping gear, a tarp, etc. At first he'd been uneasy about buying stuff for his partner, but nobody had ever been curious about it. When he got the tarp and skillet and coffeepot he'd told Mr. Riley he was buying camping stuff for himself. Which, in a way, was practically the truth. He was buying it for the Strode and McGraw company, wasn't he?

When he finished hoeing his mother had retired to her bedroom with a splitting headache, so he ate a couple baloney sandwiches and read the funnies, wishing he looked like Captain Easy—but durn glad he didn't look like Andy Gump or Uncle Bim, who had no chins.

Muzzled Ranger was sitting on the porch steps moodily watching the street for unauthorized cats and dogs he was in no condition to tangle with, and Jeff said, like old Easy: "Blazes, podnuh, less go find out wot's happenin'." Having nothing much better to do, Ranger followed him down across the street to the Bell place, vacant since the end of school and grown up in grass and weeds, but a better shortcut to Main Street than Slapper's yard, being right across the alley from the Dexter garden. At the sagged alley gate, he froze in his tracks with a shock of pleasure and alarm. There across the alley, near the corner of the shed that hid the meat market from Jeff and vice versa, Alma was straddling a radish row facing away from him, wearing a faded sleeveless dress, barefoot, hands on her curvy hips, looking trim and cute, unattainable and generally swell. All alone, too, causing him to falter, bashful, but sort of trapped. No escape.

He said quietly, "Howdy, Alamo."

She wasn't startled. "Stay outa sight," she said, beginning to turn slowly, "or she'll call me inside." Completing her graceful pivot, she knelt and plucked a small weed. "I saw you coming," she said, and the significance of that casual remark gave him a big thrill. Since the day she didn't show up at the drugstore for the ice-cream soda, he'd stayed away from her, but he'd seen her from afar with yearning. He crossed the alley and leaned against the shed, and Ranger sighed and lay down.

"I never had a chance to explain about that ice-cream soda," she said. "They called me inside—they're always calling me inside for some darn reason, especially at a time like that, it seems like."

91

"Well, the offer's still good," he said.

"Much obliged." She sighed loudly. "You realize how lucky you are, bein' a boy? A girl is like a darn prisoner, her parents watch her like jailers alla time . . ."

As if to illustrate, her mother called from the store. "*Al*-muhhh? Watta you *do*-ing?" *Doo*-wing, she said.

"I'm pullin' *wee*-yeeds outa the *reddy*-shiz!" Alma hollered, and scowled at Jeff. "See what I meant? You can go anywhere you please, fishin', huntin', play baseball, hang around gas stations or the lumberyard—I see you guys climbin' on boxcars over yonder, and Roy told me about playin' tag on the stockyards. Gee whiz, even your little brother can run around all over town all day."

"Cousin," Jeff corrected her. "His mama died when he was a baby. He's not spose to run loose like he does, but turn your back a second an' he skedaddles. Today the little wart didn't even come home to lunch."

She smiled. "Maybe because he ate with us."

"Well, darn his socks!" Jeff said exasperatedly. "We told him a million times not to impose on people."

"Oh, he wasn't imposing." She shrugged. "We like him, an' it's nice Dennis has a playmate his own age. Besides, we only had hamburger sandwidges."

"That lucky little dickens," Jeff said enviously.

She nodded distractedly, gazing at him absently. "Take this afternoon—after baseball practice you'll prob'ly go swimming, or fishing, or wherever you please . . ."

"No baseball today," he told her. "We only practice two days a week now, some guys can't make it ever' day, an' that suits me fine. They got me on second when I'm a natural born right fielder." Suddenly he wanted to tell her how baseball had lost its joy for him, Mutt forever yelling at him, certain guys hinting he couldn't make the team if his dad wasn't manager, and how sometimes he wished he'd bust a finger or something so he could quit. She might feel

92

better, knowing that being a boy wasn't such great shakes, either, sometimes.

But her ma called: "*Al*-muhhh! Come put Papa's *a*prons on to boy-ull!"

"See!" Alma said, dark eyes indignant, and he gave her a grin of sympathy and felt a pang of regret when she disappeared around the shed—but also a curious sense of relief. Talking to her was a nervous strain—not the talking, her *looking* at him, maybe comparing him to other guys. He wasn't any jelly bean with his patched overalls, sleeveless shirt, stained baseball cap and dirty bare feet, not to mention his chubby freckled homeliness. He didn't cut much of a figure alongside neat guys like Mutt or Lige. The only guys he considered homelier were Hud, Jug Hazlitt, Spotty, Lefty Gronstetter and Jake Ballew.

Circling up past the drugstore, he paused, briefly tempted, then went on resolutely. Now that he could afford ice cream and stuff he just didn't crave it like when he was broke, and the more he denied his sweet tooth, the sooner he could buy a rifle and skates and so forth.

His dad wasn't at the shack this time of day, and Jeff winced across the hot oily cinders and creosoted crossties, then sighed with pleasure when his barefeet encountered the cool floor. He got a *Western Magazine* and climbed into the big padded reclining chair, and about three pages into an exciting story he began to dream his own crazy adventures.

It seemed he'd just dozed off for a few minutes, but the sun was coming through the west door at an alarming slant that gave him an immediate feeling of urgency. He drank some ice water and took off for Main Street, fearing that by the time he reached the swimming hole a lot of guys might already be getting out, doggone it. With patient Ranger at his heels he trotted across the tracks and down the slope past the shady elm-ridden park where horseshoe

93

pitchers were still at it. The business district drowsed in the afternoon heat. Turning north at the bank corner, he followed the shady west side of the street into what he thought of as poisoned dog country, Ranger being safely muzzled against tidbits, then west a block to old man Ketcham's long lane, where he found a problem worse than hot dust, concrete, etc. Since his last swim the alfalfa had been cut, raked and hauled off the field, leaving an unfamiliar desert of yellow stubble that obliterated the path and made barefoot walking a painful experience. The only way to keep from puncturing your feet was to sort of drag them like skating, to push the spikes down flat, and it was slow going.

The alfalfa field was about two hundred yards across and sloped down steeply by the creek so you couldn't see people on the bank until you were practically there, but usually you could hear them laughing and hollering long before you got there. At first, snailing across the stubble, Jeff imagined he heard distant voices, but as he got nearer there was a worrisome silence, and when he finally could see the pool it was placidly empty, not a ripple marring the surface, and the creek bank was deserted. They'd been there all right; the plank diving platform was still dripping from recent use. Scowling upstream, where the willow-lined creek curved south around the steep bank, and downstream where it swung north, concealed by trees and brush, he blew out a windy sigh. Dammit, he'd missed out on the fun. No swimming for him today unless he hung around and somebody else showed up late. Swimming alone wasn't safe, you might get cramps. Also, his imagination summoned up visions of seven-foot man-eating gars, giant snapping turtles, belligerent cottonmouths, etc. Killer frogs.

Then he noticed the little mound of clothes under a willow and his spirits revived. *Someone* was still here. "Hey, somebody!" he hollered. "Who's here?" No answer. "C'mon, I know you're here!" he yelled, skating down the stubbly incline toward the clothes. "Less hit it, whoever . . ." The shock of recognition and sudden fear squeezed the air out of him: the runt-sized striped shirt and gray knee pants belonged to *Jody!* Who couldn't swim a lick . . .

"JODY!" he shouted. "WHERE ARE YOU?" Knowing even as he asked the sinister silence, knowing with chilling horror, running back up the incline unmindful of the gouging stubble to stare without hope at the empty field and the deaf and drowsing distant town. "HELP!" he yelled, his voice amplified by terror, knowing even if someone heard they couldn't possibly arrive in time, knowing but not admitting that it was already too late, screaming one final hopeless plea for help: "DAD!"

Lunging down the slope, frantic, he was thinking he had no time to undress, and reasoning: Feel all around the diving platform first, he probably slipped on the slick wet planks and fell in, oh gee, he *knew* better, we told him a *million* times, don't ever ever *ever* come to the creek without one of us along, aw please, God. . . .

He went splashing all around the makeshift pier feeling with hands and feet, reversing and widening the semicircle, moaning and whimpering, scared sick and grieving, blubbering, aw *please,* God, don't *let* him be dead and the creek kept getting deeper so he had to swim under water groping desperately in all directions, eyes wide-staring and smarting as he tried to penetrate the murky, stirred-up, soupy gloom. At first when he came up for air he yelled for help, thinking someone might be fishing nearby, but then he couldn't spare the breath to yell and his lungs began to ache in protest as he stayed under longer and longer, knowing time was swiftly running out for Jody, if it hadn't already run out, thinking hopelessly: Maybe he didn't fall in *here*, but somewhere up or down the creek. And all the time he was groping and staring in the muddied opaque depths it was like the times he'd tried noodling for fish—he desperately yearned to find Jody but was sickened at the thought of touching a drowned slippery body, and he yanked his hand back a couple of times when he imagined he had. And he kept having one awful growing compelling longing desire: to just get out of there and run, and keep on running until he was forever gone from Cottonwood, never to know for sure that Jody had drowned. But he clung to that faint, expiring, futile hope that he could get Jody out on the bank and *do* something, shake the water out of him, make him start breathing again—if he could only *find* the little wart.

The creek was nine feet deep in the middle and it got harder and harder for him to swim down to the mucky bottom in his confining shirt and overalls, with the slingshot around his neck and rock-laden hip pocket, and despair was numbing his body as well as his mind and heart, and he began to fear his own drowning as he struggled, weary and waterlogged and sore-lunged, to search the blind depths. Each time he surfaced bleary-eyed for air he had to rest awhile, and it was one of those times, treading water and gasping for breath, wiping the blur of muddy water and tears from his stinging eyes, hiccupping with hopelessness and numb sorrow, that he heard Mutt say harshly: "Aw, cut it out, you dumb nut!"

He was facing north, and he wallowed around slowly to face the south bank, gasping: "Help me, Mutt . . . we got . . . to find 'im . . . before it's too . . . late!" And there, seen through the shimmering blur of his muddied and scalded vision, about half the town stood on the south bank, a gang of naked guys all ages and sizes gawking at him and holding their wadded-up clothes—except Jody, whose clothes were under the willow, who stood there beside Mutt gaping at Jeff like he didn't understand what was going on, skinny arms folded high across his puny chest, jug-handle ears looking bigger than ever because his hair was plastered to his skill. "Why are you swimmin' with your clothes on?" the ghost of Jody inquired wonderingly, and Jeff gave a retching sigh of relief as he understood the situation, and began swimming backward away from those sly grinning faces, outraged and embarrassed, to drag himself up onto the muddy north bank, crying partly from awful relief, partly from this public humiliation.

"Dirty rotten stinkin' guys," he sobbed.

"Can the crybaby act, dammit!" Mutt growled, like it shamed *him*, like he thought Jeff was doing it on purpose.

"I can't git over the look on his kisser when he seen us," Jake chortled. "His eyeballs bulged out a foot."

"He was really seinin' the crick," Lex Yancy remarked.

"Go to hell!" Jeff hollered across at them, getting to his feet and starting down the north bank, wiping his wet face. "Stinkin' lousy skunks!" he said by way of farewell. But nothing he said would alter the fact that he'd been the butt of a mean practical joke that no intelligent guy would have fallen for. They'd seen him coming late across the field, slow and careful because of the sharp stubble, giving the whole stinking bunch time to take their clothes and go hide up around the bend, then while he was making a big fool of himself they sneaked back to laugh at him like a pack of baboons. When he saw the dripping diving platform, after not meeting anybody leaving, he should of been suspicious, and if it had been anybody's clothes but Jody's he probably would have . . .

Behind him Lige bawled out: "Hey-ullp, heyy-ulllp!"

"C'mon, Jiffer, can't you take a joke?" Jake called out, and Mutt said, "Come back here, boy!" But he was speaking to his dog, not his crybaby brother. "Here, Ranger, *here,* Ranger!—you sonofagun, c'mere!"

The sopping wet dog caught up, waiting until then to shake himself and spray Jeff with water he didn't need. As they went on down the creek together, Jeff started brooding and burning. The story of his sappy humiliation would probably spread like wildfire and everybody would razz and jeer and tease him—for the rest of his life, probably. They'd tell it over and over, those baboons.

97

He'd lost his baseball cap, but that was the least of his worries. Who else had seen his disgrace? It didn't matter. There'd been enough guys to see that the humorous story circulated all over Cottonwood.

Some people were fishing at the dam, so he circled north and climbed the embankment, and went down the other side through rank weeds and into the timber, headed nowhere in particular, merely seeking solitude and quiet away from the human race. He was enduring a confusion of feelings now, mainly hot prickles of embarrassment but also great relief because it had only been a joke, resentment at being the goat but so glad to remember the little devil standing there with the others, alive and breathing. The laughingstock of Cottonwood . . . but oh, Jesus, what if it hadn't been a big joke? Right now he might be running back across the stubble field carrying . . . his mind boggled at the thought.

Feeling a need for the company of·a friend who didn't know and might never hear what a goofy sucker his partner turned out to be, he kept going downstream. Crossing at the ford above the rendezvous, he started whistling, in case anyone was in the vicinity, and he sat on the noodler's rock in the drying sunshine, waiting.

"Didn't expect you today, buddy," his partner remarked, having approached like an Injun. Jeff grinned sheepishly and said he just happened to be in the neighborhood. Dallas Strode returned the grin. "Looks like you fell in."

"Aw"—Jeff shrugged—"some guys pulled a joke on me."

Noodler rolled a cigarette, then took time to rub Ranger behind the ears. Lighting the cigarette, he said, "Tell me about that joke, pard."

Jeff told him, pretending to see the humor of it now himself, but his partner just frowned and shook his head.

"That was a mean, low-down trick," he said. "But you did right, an' if I was you I'd walk tall about it an' tell those jaspers to kiss my foot." Easy to say, but pretty hard to do, Jeff thought. Everybody razzing you, or at least grinning behind your back. "After they give it some thought I expect they'll feel ashamed of themselves," Noodler said, blowing a smoke ring. "If that same situation ever comes up again, you jump right in there, just in case it ain't a fool's prank. Might save a life."

Jeff nodded, feeling a lot better.

"Say," his partner remarked. "I'm well fixed for grub an' all now, so why don't you take them four cats to your maw?"

"Gee, thanks," Jeff said. His mother would be glad to have a mess of catfish, and he could let on he got all wet and muddy running his trotlines. Unless Mutt or Jody told her about her dumb son disgracing the whole family. . . .

"The days git kinda long down here all by my lonesome," the fugitive said. "Could you bring me some old magazines an' newspapers? Readin' helps kill time."

"That's easy," Jeff said, thinking of all the magazines stacked under his dad's table in the shack.

"What's the latest on that jailbird? They find 'im yet?"

"Nope," Jeff said, straight-faced. "Guess he's long gone by now. Nobody hardly ever mentions him anymore."

What people talked about mostly was the well-known evangelist who was coming to hold a big revival meeting soon, but the subject didn't seem appropriate here. So Jeff told his outlaw friend about how the railroad was going to drain the watertank to get the fish out of it.

"I dunno," Noodler said dubiously. "A metal tank that hasn't been dreened in years, my guess is they'll find maybe a few big bass an' perch an' possibly a few catfish, but the rest will be runty stunted little boogers. Probably no carp or other bottom feeders at all. That's a dog-eat-dog proposition where fish are cooped up in a tank like that an' no place to hide. The big 'uns eat the little 'uns an' the in-betweeners starve out."

Kinda sorry he'd told him, Jeff said tomorrow he'd bring eggs, hamburger meat, store bread and magazines, and he headed for home with the catfish.

He detoured around the elevator, so Mr. Calvert couldn't talk him into selling one of the fish. Thinking how easy it was to make money selling fish got his mind off other stuff, until he saw Mutt up the street—waiting by the gate with a scowl.

"Here's your damn cap, bawler," he growled. "You left it in the crick, when you made such a hysterical specktickle of yourself." But somehow he didn't sound as sarcastic as he was trying to. "Lissen, if you tell Mama I'll bust you one in the snoot, weepy."

"Oh, yeah!" Jeff said, puzzled. He'd figured Mutt would tell her himself.

"Lissen," Mutt said. "What happened wasn't my idea, an' I never knew Jody left his clothes there—that wasn't part of the joke, he just forgot 'em, that's all."

Come to think of it, his mother probably wouldn't see anything funny about people pretending Jody had drowned; she might even get sore at Mutt for a change. And clamp down on all three of them where swimming was concerned. He shrugged. "The trick sure worked an' you baboons had your fun. Put Jake back on second, I won't have time for baseball anymore." He took his gift fish in the house expectantly, wondering what his mother would say.

"What's the matter?" she asked, sorta sarcastically. "Wouldn't anybody buy them this time?"

"They're for us," he sighed. "If you want 'em."

"I'm overwhelmed by your generosity," she said, spoiling it for him. But he had plenty to be thankful for—there'd be all *five* of them eating those babies, instead of just four.

10

As summer wore on there was a growing interest in boxing because of the second Dempsey-Tunney fight coming up in Chicago in September. Hack Kelso, owner of the Teapot Dome filling station, got some sixteen-ounce gloves and promoted exhibitions in the street between various kids and boys and men who gathered there after supper.

Although Jake and Lige still razzed him occasionally, Jeff was surprised how nobody else ever mentioned the swimming-hole episode, but he was still wary, and liked to see who was present before deciding whether to join a group or steer clear of it. He'd skipped one baseball practice, and his dad asked how come, apparently not knowing about the humiliating hoax. Jeff said he forgot it was a practice day, and his dad said don't forget again, it looked bad if the manager's own kid skipped practice. So Jeff went to the next practice and Jake hollered: "Here comes the hero." And Lige said: "Hellup, hellup!" But during batting practice Vern threw him a ripe one he knocked into the cornfield for a homerun, and his dad said: "Even Babe Ruth wouldn't sneeze at that one, by golly." Some sportswriters predicted the Babe would hit fifty homers this season, but then he played a lot oftener than Jeff . . .

He was standing in front of the drugstore, looking toward the Teapot Dome to see if Lex or Von Yancy was there, wanting to ask a favor of them. Not seeing either of them, he glanced down the street and suddenly got that old self-conscious feeling—the sidewalk had been empty, but now Alma was down there, gazing over toward the park. He'd been staying away from her bailiwick, figuring she knew all about his sappy comical performance unless her brother got lockjaw on his way home that day, and now he pretended he hadn't seen her, concentrating on his problem.

This afternoon Granny Hanks had called him over to her alley gate and said, "Here's some corn for your mama an' I want you to go tell Turkey Dobbs I want to see him in the morning about a job." Then she walked away, as was her blunt custom, and he headed for the house scowling. He'd have to go past the Britton yard to reach Turkey's ramshackle home, or else go clear around the block. After supper Chink wouldn't be home, but his damn dog would, and it was scary to have him snarl and slobber and chew the fence. So while letting Jody help him shuck the roasting ears, he'd thought of the Yancy brothers.

Back in June they'd chopped cotton south of town, buck twenty-five a day, and they'd got sick and tired of Killer's crazy wild carrying-on every morning and evening when they walked past in the street, so they did something about it. One night they ran wire from Britton's fence to the McGraw hayloft and attached it to a hand-cranked electrical generator. Then mornings one of them would go on ahead and the other would crank the apparatus and give old Killer a good jolt when he started chewing the fence. Around five-thirty, when they'd be coming back to town, Von would give a shrill whistle just before they got to Brittons and *Jeff* would crank the generator. The third day, when Killer saw the Yancys coming he slunk around behind the house—he didn't know what they'd been doing to him, but he durn sure knew they did it. They took their dynamo home, but the wire was still there, and now Jeff wanted them to return the favor and electrocute that ornery sonofagun when he went past. . . .

"Mad or just stuck up?" Alma asked, and he nearly

102

swallowed his gum. She had snuck up on him quietly, surprising him tongue-tied. She looked nifty in a starchy blouse and skirt, with sandals on her small feet. She looked spiffy in just about anything she wore, and he was thankful he'd put on clean overalls and a shirt and his new tennis shoes, and had oiled and combed his hair for a change. "I just wanted to say sumpthing," she said earnestly. "Roy told me what a dirty trick those boys played on you, an' I just wanted to say it's the meanest thing I ever heard of, Jess—and I think you were very brave to jump in with your clothes on to rescue Jody the way you did. Even though he hadn't really drownded."

Brave, he thought, amazed. Not dumb or sappy, but brave, by gosh. He hadn't thought of it that way before. He recovered his powers of speech. "Say, this'd be a good time to have that ice-cream soda, Alamo."

She glanced down the street and nodded. "Okeydokey."

No one was in the drugstore except plump, jolly Mrs. Schuman, who handled all the non-medical business. Alma asked for strawberry, so he ordered the same, and they sat on the stools in a kind of companionable self-consciousness, with Doc's wife beaming at them from behind the tobacco counter like she figured it was rather romantic. Which it wasn't, naturally.

"Goin' to the revival?" Alma asked, and he said, yeah, that's why he was all dressed up and wearing shoes.

"We went last night, and that'll do me for quite a while." She gave a delicate shudder. "That hoarse rantin' and ravin', an' all that scary stuff about sinners spending eternity burning in hell, ugh!"

"I was layin' in the grass across the street an' fell asleep," Jeff confessed. "But ol' McCratty can sure raise the roof, an' make your hair stand on end the way he describes damnation and all."

"I bet he coulda been an actor if he'd wanted to—and wasn't so fat." Presently she added: "Who are your favorite movie stars? Mine's Charlie Chaplin, Mary Pickford and Douglas Fairbanks."

"Mine are Richard Dix, Tom Mix an' Hoot Gibson," he said, since those were about the only ones he'd seen.

"I miss going to the movies," Alma said, "but otherwise I like Cottonwood better than where we use to live. People here seem a lot friendlier." She made a cute face. "Some of 'em are too friendly." She slid him a meaningful sidelong glance. "An' some not enough." Well, what did she mean by that? They finished their sodas in silence, and she gave a contented sigh. "That was swell, Jess, but I better go or they'll have Roy out lookin' for me." She gave a different kind of sigh. "Only darn time I have any freedom is just after dark, when I come out on the sidewalk for some fresh air—like I do every evening." She gave him a quizzical smile as they went out, and watching her go down the sidewalk in her peppy, almost-strutting way, he wondered if she had possibly been hinting. Aw, nerts, he said to himself, don't be a sap.

He located Von at the barbershop and Von said he could use the generator if Hud went along. So he bought some licorice whips and went down to Yancys'. Hud was just starting for town to watch boxing on his way to hear preaching, and at first he was disinterested, but the candy loosened him up.

Jody was sitting on the front steps all washed and combed for church, and Ranger was tied up. Jeff gave both of them a few inches of licorice, and Hud muttered something about wasting candy on a dog. In the hayloft, when the apparatus was hooked up, Hud said, "I'll guard the candy until you git back—prezoomin' you git back." Jeff didn't feel much like laughing at the moment.

He went up the alley, eager to see how old Killer would react to a charge of juice, but apprehensive that something would go wrong. And it did. Killer came in a snarling rush and began to chew the fence, squalled and went rolling backward, and took off around the house yelping. Jeff was grinning when Chink came charging out of the house, hollering: "Whud you do to my dawg?"

"Never done a durn thing to 'im," Jeff said, thinking with dismay: He's suppose to be downtown!

"You done something!" Chink yelled, starting to open the gate and come out after Jeff—then howling like his dog had and yanking his hands back. Jeff took off running.

Tall, weathered old Turkey was in his small cluttered yard watering tomato vines, and Jeff stopped running long enough to deliver Granny's summons. Turkey nodded curtly, maintaining his reputation for never speaking unless he had to. As he sped on around the corner, heading east and expecting both Chink and Killer to come baying after him, Jeff recalled someone had once estimated that Turkey spoke an average of ten words a week, counting grunts.

Reaching the railroad tracks with no sign of pursuit, he followed them north, worrying that Chink would be waiting in ambush somewhere on ahead. But the street beyond Major Conklin's urban pig and fruit farm was empty, so he headed warily on west, and was flagged down by the major himself. Who in his own busy, puttering, ramroddish way was about as non-socializing as old Turkey.

"Ask your maw if she wants some Elbertas," he ordered Jeff. "Forty cents a bushel."

"Yessir," Jeff said, feeling like he should salute or something, resuming half speed. When he cut through Granny's yard she was driving stakes in the ground, so he stopped to report. "I told Turkey what you said to tell 'im, Granny," he panted, and she squatted on her heels, hatchet poised in mid-air, and asked: "What did he say?" Didn't say anything, Jeff told her. Just nodded. "All you could expect," she said. "Thank you, Matty boy." When people got real old their minds slipped. Sometimes she even called him Jody.

Hud blinked down at him from the hayloft with his mouth full of licorice, and when Jeff explained how things had gone awry he was suddenly in a big hurry to take the generator home. "I never knew the deal included *Chink*," he complained. "I thought it was just the dog. Man, don't you ever tell 'im I was in on it, durn you."

Well, Chink knew someone was in on it, but no matter who else he might think was in on it, Jefferson McGraw would bear the full brunt of his retaliation.

When they went around the house his mother was in the porch swing fanning herself, dressed for the revival, so he told her about the thirty-cents-a-bushel peaches. She nodded absently, looking up the street where early church-goers had churned up a haze of dust already, and said: "How is your mother, Hudson?" Just being polite. "Mean as ever," Hud replied solemnly, and she laughed and said well, this hot weather would make any woman hard to get along with, and Jeff suddenly caught his mistake. "Did I say thirty cents? It's forty cents a bushel."

"Or something like that, no doubt," she said, shaking her head as if you couldn't ever depend on him to get anything straight, and he went on down the street with Hud, thinking: How does she expect me to remember the price of peaches when the war with old Chink just flared up again hotter than ever?

By the time they reached the outdoor arena between the Teapot Dome and the bank, the coppery-red sun had slid down behind the Osage Inn and there were about twenty spectators present, including Dolittle, Hack Kelso, the promoter-referee, three men from the layover train crews, and a motley group of young guys and kids. Including baleful Chink Britton, who got there in time to watch Jeff and Hud arrive and sort of nod like okay, he knew who Jeff's accomplice was.

He knew durn well it couldn't have been Mutt, who was just finishing the third round of another match with Lige, McGraw representing the *Oklahoma City Times* and Bowzer the *Tulsa Tribune*. They had been tangling with sixteen-

106

ounce gloves almost daily for a week, trying to settle their personal and business feud, but they were so evenly matched and able to block punches that their fights were pretty dull to watch—no knockdowns, no blood, not even any black eyes. This one ended in a draw, too.

"Who's next here?" Hack Kelso inquired. "How's about you two, Kid Yancy an' Babe McGraw? Wanta spar a little?"

"I jist got up from the supper table," Hud said, so Mr. Kelso asked Jeff what his feeble excuse was, and he replied that he was on his way to church, and besides he couldn't fight worth a hoot. One of the railroaders laughed and said that sure didn't sound like one of the Slim McGraw's boys, so Jeff explained: "I mean I can't box worth a hoot."

"Boxin' is a science you gotta learn," Chink remarked in his know-it-all way. "An' I'd be glad to teach Jeffery a few of the tricks if he'll promise not to hit me too hard. Wotta ya say, kid, just spar a few rounds, hey?"

"Like heck," Jeff retorted. "You're too old for me." But he was sorta tempted. Maybe if he let Chink pop him a couple times with the relatively painless sixteen-ouncers the ornery sonofagun would consider the score settled, temporarily.

"Shoot," Mutt jeered, "the lummox won't even spar me, an' he outweighs me a good fifteen pounds."

"They say Jiffy's more of a runner," Lige put in.

His ears burning, Jeff said, "Heck, I just wouldn't wanta hurt my own durn brother, is all." Which was true enough, but a pretty dumb thing to say under the circumstances, causing Mutt to give a derisive hoot.

"Tell yuh what, Catfish," Mutt said. "I'll risk it, seein' there's enough people present to keep you from killin' me. Git 'em on an' put up your dukes, boy."

Jeff peered around at the crowd to see if anybody had sense enough to stop two hostile brothers from beating each other to a pulp, but even Dolittle looked neutral, although sympathetic. Maybe he even figured it was about time Jeff took some of the brag out of Mutt. All the others looked eager to see a good old family grudge fight, a real knockdown-and-drag-out brotherly slugging match.

Jeff tried a last reasonable demur. "If I won, you'd say you was tired from goin' three rounds with Lige."

"That just warmed me up," Mutt said. "Boxin' Lige is how I rest an' relax. I'm fresh as a daisy, boy."

Jeff felt trapped. He had to box somebody or his name was mud, and he sure didn't want Mutt humiliating him with half the town watching. Better to be klonked by an older bigger guy than an older smaller brother. "Well, besides," he said glumly, "Chink's got first call on me here."

Helping him don the sweaty gloves, Dolittle said wryly: "Sorta jawboned yourself into a tight fit, pard." Jeff tried to grin and asked if it had to go three rounds, and Dolittle said, "I wouldn't bet on it."

He was right. It didn't even go one round.

During the touching of gloves Jeff muttered: "I didn't do nuthin' to your dog, honest." And smirking, Chink said softly: "Follered the wire to your barn, kiddo."

In that case Jeff figured he might as well give it his sorry best; at least act like he wasn't yellow. So he went piling into his taller, older, longer-armed opponent with a windmill attack, and it was his aggressiveness that undid him. Chink just stuck out his left and Jeff's nose collided with it, like running into a tree. Stunned surprise and hot pain made his eyes water, blinding him and discouraging him, but he didn't quit. He kept swinging clumsily and had the dubious satisfaction of landing solid punches on Chink's elbow, shoulder and hip, but by then his nose was streaming claret and Mr. Kelso stopped the boxing lesson. Jeff leaned over so as not to bleed on his church clothes while Dolittle removed the gloves, hearing Mutt say with scornful humor, "I told that saphead fifty times you ain't supposed to lead with your nostrils."

108

The crowd laughed, but Jeff didn't give a darn. He was glad it was over, worried about getting blood on his clothes, and hoping Chink was willing to let bygones be bygones. For a while, at least, he thought as he walked bent over out to the horse trough. Hud pumped cold water and he sloshed it on his burning, smarting nose that felt as big as a dill pickle. When the blood quit dripping, Hud said gravely, "I hate to say it, but you're right, you can't box worth a hoot, Jiffer. Which makes two of us, I must admit."

Jeff said eddyway he drether have Chig bloody his doze thad his od brudther eddy tibe. His clogged nose gave him a strange accent that got a rare chuckle out of Hud, which almost made up for the pain, but not quite. They went back to the scene of carnage, and Chink was strutting around with the gloves still on, cutting up, wanting to be the main attraction awhile longer.

"I'll spar with anyone here under seventeen years old," he said. "Anyone wanta give me some action here?"

Suddenly, to Jeff's amazement, Vern Strode spoke up from where he'd been leaning unnoticed on a gasoline pump. "How's about me, you liar?" he demanded, and a hush fell over the spectators. Everybody *knew* Chink was a liar, but nobody ever called him one in front of witnesses before. In the shocked silence Jeff heard a bullbat swooping after bugs, and Slick Melton laughing over in the barbershop.

Chink gave a sort of strained laugh. "Well, looky here, now, if it ain't ol' Flew-the-Coop's whelp barkin' at me."

"Can that stuff, pronto!" Dolittle said sharply.

Chink shrugged, grinning. "Put the gloves on 'im quick, before he changes his mind, boys."

"No gloves," Vern said, stepping into the circle. "I aim to fight you bareknuckled unless you take back your dirty lie about me sellin' you a bass after stealin' it from Jeff McGraw. You told it back in May sometime, but I only got word of it just lately."

Chink scowled. "Who says I said you done all that?"

"I'll say you said it," Jeff blurted impulsively, then wished he'd bit his durn tongue off.

"You got a poor memory, sonny," Chink growled. "All I said was it *coulda* been one of the jailbird's kids for all I knew, seein' I wasn't acquainted with his brats. But I later found out it wasn't. I won't name who it was—I got my money back an' promised to forgit an' forgive. So the case is closed as far as I'm concerned."

"Not hardly," Vern said grimly. "Now you owe me *an'* my family an apology, as far as I'm concerned."

"I'm sorry," Chink said, "that I ever mentioned your jailbird tribe—in polite society." Then he sneered.

Vern lunged at him, but Dolittle and Mr. Kelso held him back, and after struggling for a while he gave up and went stalking away. Dolittle looked at Chink with disgust and said, "Britton, you're a rare breed of skunk."

Chink grinned uncertainly. "Well, maybe I was a little rough on the kid," he said, mealymouthed. "Fact is, I feel sorry for his family, all that shame an' disgrace . . ."

Various people said stuff like: Aw, baloney! Banana oil! And: Horse feathers! Chink had ripped his britches as far as most of the onlookers were concerned, and realizing it just seemed to make him more cocky and cynical.

"Oh, yeah?" he said. "I bet there ain't one of you birds wouldn't turn that kid's old man in for the reward money if you knew where he was at. Try smokin' that in your pipe!"

Jeff suddenly felt a moral obligation to go sympathize with his partner's son. Easing out of the crowd, he went loping after Vern and caught up as he was turning the corner west. "Hey, lissen," he said, "don't mind that brayin' jackass."

"Just leave me alone," Vern muttered ungraciously. "I ain't in much of a mood for talkin' right now."

Jeff shrugged, but kept walking along beside him, looking at the fat red sun about to disappear behind the blue timbered hills, solicitously feeling his nose. And suddenly he said what he'd been wanting to say for a long time.

"Vern, I know where your dad is."

That yanked Vern to a sudden stop. "Oh, yeah?" he said with sullen disbelief. "How could you know that?"

Since the cat was out of the bag, Jeff told him the whole story, and it sure took Vern's mind off Chink. He even grinned a couple times while Jeff was blabbing it all out. "Oh man!" he said, tickled to death. "Mama sure has been worryin' her head off. She'll be relieved . . ."

"You can't tell 'er," Jeff protested. "For some reason he don't want 'er to know. I wasn't even spose to tell you, but I was bustin' to, and it looks like I did."

Vern grinned happily. "Boy, I'm sure glad you did."

They stood there in the evening street discussing the various angles. Vern promised not to peep a word to his maw until he got clearance from his paw. He said he didn't think the law would have the time to keep watch on the Strode home, but somebody might, in hopes of collecting that reward money. In fact he'd sorta had a feeling someone was snooping around spying on them—old Milton had raised a fuss at night a couple times. And Vern had seen that dang Chink sort of following him down on the creek a few times.

Also, Jeff threw in, old Chink had taken to carrying his uncle's binoculars a lot lately, and had been seen up on the coal chute several times—from up there a guy could spy on the whole durn town, if he wanted to.

"Man, I can't git over it!" Vern enthused. "We never figured Paw was still around here. We thought he'da headed for Uncle Milt's place in east Texas. Hey, now that you went an' spilled the beans, maybe he'd let me come down there— I sure would love to see him."

Jeff shrugged dubiously. "Well, I'll ask 'im."

"We could go at night, when nobody could follow us."

That wasn't a great idea, in Jeff's opinion. Too durn spooky down there at night for his taste. He gave a non-committal shrug, and Vern said he was sure glad Jeff had been the one who located his paw instead of—well, hell, instead of anybody else he could think of. He shook Jeff's hand warmly and started on home, whistling cheerfully.

And Jeff went back to Main Street, his mind working around to other things by brisk degrees. Dolittle and Mutt were drinking from the town pump, and they eyed him expectantly, as if he was supposed to make a report, but he just shrugged. Dolittle said: How's your beezer? Stobbed up, Jeff said; cat smell a thig.

Mutt popped off, as usual. "In your business, Catfish, I'd call that a lucky break," he said. He meant fish smelled fishy. He probably meant Jeff smelled fishy, too.

"Well, gents, the show's about to commence," Dolittle said. "Shall we go repent our wicked sinfulness?"

"I need sub chewin' gub," Jeff alibied, starting on in the general direction of the drugstore. After buying the gum he stalled in front of the drugstore awhile, tempted to just go on to the revival, but his curiosity was stronger than his piety.

Alma met him by the Bull Durham sign. "Wasn't sure you'd show up," she murmured. "The way you acted lately I thought maybe you didn't care for my dull personality."

"Well, that shows how dumb you are, then," he said.

Softly, as befitted a clandestine rendezvous, she said yep, she was so dumb that if somebody shunned her society for a week it made her feel cross-eyed and warty. He said maybe he'd had the notion he wasn't her type of guy. She chuckled and said that showed how dumb he was.

He felt amazed in a numb sort of way—was this really happening? Holy smoke! "I thought you'd perfer more of a jelly bean like, well, Mutt, for instance."

Leaning on the signboard, she sort of absently hooked her little finger around his. "Nope," she said. "He's too stuck on himself, too braggish." She did a mocking imitation of Mutt, saying: "I'm a big cheese around here, captain of the baseball team, smart as heck an' rich to boot." She had old Mutt pegged to a T, and Jeff laughed. "He's also catty," Alma added. "Likes to run people down—mostly you, Jess."

Jeff sighed. "Yeah, that ain't news. How 'bout Lige?"

"He's full of hot air," she said, "an' so's his horse." She clapped a hand to her mouth. "Oops, that wasn't nice."

Maybe not nice, but very true. Lige's fat mare produced gas noisily when he galloped it up and down Main Street, a daily occurrence.

"He laughs like a hyena, he's so durn loud. And vulgar, always singing that awful song, you know the one?"

Jeff nodded. Horsie keep your tail up.

"As for other boys," she volunteered, "Clarence is just a friend—I couldn't go with a boy that wears specs. Also he sort of puts on airs. Boys are so dumb, they think talking themselves up impresses a girl." She looked up at him in the gray dark. "You don't brag, Jess."

Nothing to brag about, he thought. Until now. But then she hadn't actually said she was struck on him yet. "Any of those guys ever tried to . . . well . . . kiss you?"

"Never gave 'em any reason to," she said quietly.

Gosh durn it, how did you go at this business, anyway? Had she given him a reason to try? He felt paralyzed. "Is a guy spose to ask a girl if he can?" he wondered aloud.

"Well," she murmured, "I sure won't ask you."

Wondering why he felt so doggone scared, he turned to her uncertainly and said, "Well, is it okay with you?"

"Why not try it an' see?" she whispered teasingly.

Trembling with the first-time jitters, he clumsily took her into his arms like clinching with a boxing opponent so he couldn't hit you, drew a shaky breath, and went hunting for her mouth. His nose bumped her forehead and smarted, and he had trouble getting her lined up right, but suddenly and incredibly their mouths more or less fitted together in the first dizzying, astonishing kiss of his career. He was actually hugging and kissing Alma Dexter and she was returning the favor willingly! But presently he couldn't hold his breath any longer and had to quit kissing and exhale, due to his plugged nose. Then before he could resume with more confidence she hissed: "Somebody's coming—darn it!"

Not her dad from the butcher shop as he feared. His dad

from the café, on his way to the engines—and Jeff felt like he was about to get caught in a guilty and compromising situation. He edged away from Alma, leaning on the signboard feeling all hot and embarrassed.

"Evening, Mr. McGraw," Alma said cheerfully.

He returned her greeting, then said, "That you, Jeff? I hear you got bopped on the snoot. You okay?"

"Well, I didn't feel like goin' to church yet," Jeff said. "It's still purty sore."

"Don't tangle with longer-armed jaybirds henceforth," his dad advised. "Well, I've got to go see about the iron horse— that reminds me, Miss Dexter, did your paw butcher today?" He had that familiar kidding tone in his voice.

Alma giggled. "Yep, two horses an' a mule."

"Ask him to save me some mule cutlets," Jeff's humorous father joshed, and went his way, apparently finding nothing amiss in his being there in the dark with Alma, who said, "I like your paw, he's so good-natured, always joking—how did you happen to get hit on the nose?"

He told her; boxing Chink and walked into a left jab, and she said, my lord, he's quite a bit older, not to mention taller and heavier. "But we were just sparrin'," Jeff explained.

She giggled. "You remind me of a boy I knew, Delbert Jones. He couldn't breathe through his nose either—held his breath when he kissed, like you were doing." His silent hesitation must have worried her, because she said: "See, it was only once, at a party playin' spin the bottle—I *had* to let him kiss me is how I happened to know about him holdin' his breath. Asthma or something."

"None of my durn business," he said, and her mother got him out of the situation by calling: "*Al*-muh, better cuh-*min* now." Alma sighed and asked softly, "You mad?"

"Heck, you didn't bust my nose," he quibbled gruffly.

"You are mad," she said, sounding oddly pleased about it, and she suddenly kissed him kind of fiercely. "I never kissed anybody like that before," she informed him, and left him

114

standing there dazedly, leaning on the Bull Durham sign looking up at the stars.

Pretty soon he blew out his breath and started slowly up the street, feeling sort of amazed but also jealous, and strangely dissatisfied, let down somehow. Now that it was over he realized she'd tasted a trifle green-oniony, but that wasn't it, and it wasn't even that she might have kissed plenty of other guys in the past. It simply hadn't been the way he'd daydreamed of romance, and he felt a little trapped, obligated, sort of rushed into something before he'd had time to consider the consequences—like, for example, she'd probably expect him to show up every evening from now on. But heck, that's what he wanted, wasn't it?

Locating Hud across the street from the outdoor tabernacle, he felt an urge to brag about winning Alma's hand, but controlled it. Hud said: "The preacher didn't mention you by name, but he described you pretty close." Jeff grinned and lay back on the fragrant grass, hoping nobody had spit tobacco juice there lately, and wondered what she was doing about now. Getting undressed for bed, probably . . .

"Oh friends," the preacher charged sonorously, "we transgress God's holy laws not only in our wicked DEEDS but in our carnal and venal THOUGHTS, and HE can see into our hearts and minds every *minute*, every *second* . . ."

That didn't seem fair, doggonit, God eavesdropping on your private meditations. Heck fire, if just thinking and wondering about various stuff was sinful, then you might as well go ahead and *do* it. Boy, if temptation was a sin, then heaven would be a pretty durn lonesome place . . .

He awoke during the climactic singing, with the Reverend McCratty hoarsely urging the strayed and lost to come into the fold. Wondering what happened to his wad of gum, Jeff got up and went stumbling sleepily homeward, remembering blurrily that as of about eight P.M. Alma was his girl.

115

11

Some people said it was about the hottest, driest July they could remember, but some people said that every summer. Short memories.

The morning indoors "children's revival" forced Jeff to work out a new timetable. Get up around eight-thirty, eat fast, put on clean overalls and shirt ("Don't doll up, kids," Brother McCratty had hollered jovially. "Jesus doesn't care about fine feathers"), comb his hair and be at the church by nine. Sit through an uncomfortable, uneasy, fidgety hour, go home and change clothes, do whatever chores his mother had lined up, eat lunch, go purchase whatever he was taking to Flew-the-Coop, and leave town by a roundabout route so nobody could follow him down to the rendezvous. He made the sweaty trip every day now and gave most of Noodler's share of the profits to Vern, so all the Strode kids could buy new school clothes and shoes.

Except for batting, he had come to sort of hate baseball and would gladly quit it if his dad would let him. So far they'd played five games, winning four, and although he'd hit well he'd averaged about three blunders per game playing second base. He was solely responsible for the loss to Skedee and nearly lost the close one at Walston, but old Vern pitched a two-hitter and saved their bacon.

He didn't go near the Teapot Dome after supper anymore because of Mutt's challenge hanging over him, but also because he needed to get cleaned up and rest up for his regular evening visit to the butcher shop. When the sun slipped down behind the lumberyard he'd head for the depot and sit on a baggage wagon watching the autos, buggies and wagons arriving and parking up by the church. Then as twilight began to fill the town with blue shadows he would go on north past the watertank and wait until dusk settled on Main Street, feeling eager and excited but also, somehow, reluctant, troubled by a vague sense of guilt—and also a growing frustration. He knew darn well there was more to love than just hugging and kissing—and she knew it, too, and was very touchy about it. No-trespassing signs all over her, but she sure liked to kiss—and so did he, sinful or not, and in spite of her fondness for green onions. . . .

But his durn conscience bothered him sometimes. . . .

The first morning of the "young folks crusade" he sat with Hud, who was merely a curious spectator, whereas Jeff's attendance was compulsory. Hud's parents weren't Methodists or anything else, but he couldn't pass up any kind of free entertainment. The only part of it Jeff enjoyed was the singing, then Rev. McCratty's pretty big wife, Sister Ada McCratty, preached kind of a sermon about no matter how little or young you were you couldn't be too careful and it was never too soon to give your soul to Jesus because you could be snuffed out like a flickering candle at any moment. And she cited many examples of dumb unsaved kids who waited too long to come to Christ and were suddenly taken from this life by auto wrecks, lightning, cyclones, fatal falls, etc.

Several Methodist women helped recruit converts, one of them being dumpy Widow Hollis, who concentrated on Hud and Jeff, nagging at them to go kneel and ask Jesus to forgive all their past sins, stuff like fibbing and foul language, wicked thoughts and so forth. Jeff just sat there, hot with embarrassment, trying to ignore her wheedling until the ordeal finally ended. Hud did the same. No converts here, slow business the first day.

117

Escaping down the sunny street, Jeff said, "Darn it, how come ol' jabberjaw picked on us?"

And Hud said possibly because Widow Hollis was his mother's half sister, therefore his aunt once removed, and he wished someone would remove her again. Amazed, Jeff said he'd lived here all his life and never knew that, and Hud said, "Well, you know it now. She don't hobnob with us because Earl don't hold with church an' religion stuff. But it's me she's mainly after."

Jeff had heard that about Hud's dad being an atheist. His own dad wasn't what you'd call a red-hot Methodist; he cussed, chewed, smoked, took a snort frequently and even kidded about religion and preachers—like saying he'd always noticed that evangelists usually hit town at the peak of the roasting-ear and fried-chicken season and put on the feedbag with various members of the congregation—not including the McGraws. He said no railroader could get through a meal with a preacher without letting slip a cuss word or two, and besides, if the journeyman soul-saver ever found out what a great cook Jewel McGraw was, he'd probably stretch the revival to three weeks, and if everybody in town got religion it would be a hell of a place to live, especially if he got religion.

The people that got saved that first week were mostly backsliders from last summer's crop. Jeff's dad said it was probably easier to get salvation after you'd done it a few times.

Alamo's folks were Nazarenes so she didn't come to the morning services, and Jeff was darn glad of it on the third day when he finally agreed with Hud that the only way to end Widow Hollis's pestering was to go kneel at the altar and pretend to get altered, let on they had it. As they knelt there Sister Ada said happily: "Two more touchdowns for Jesus, haleeLOOyuh! Come on, you other boys, you're on third base and it's not far to the goalpost, come score one more for God!" With his hot face hidden in his crossed arms, Jeff couldn't suppress a grin. She didn't say who was doing the pitching for Satan, or playing right field, halfback or jump center, etc.

Nobody razzed him afterward—getting religion wasn't a kidding matter—but they gave him some odd looks, and Mutt said: "You finally got you an alibi for not fightin'." Jeff hadn't thought of that angle before. Hud asked him privately if he'd felt anything, and Jeff said heck, he was too durn embarrassed to notice at the time. Hud said ditto, but at least now his half aunt would leave them alone.

He didn't know that woman very well. The next morning she was right back after them, saying: "Now you must serve as apostles and try to persuade your unsaved friends to join you in the fold." Feeling irritated, Jeff went over where Spotty Higgins was sitting alone looking understandably nervous, and slid in beside him. Hudson picked Lefty Gronstetter, back near the door. Depend on old Hud to use his head at a time like that.

"I'm spose to talk you into makin' a specktickle out of yourself like I done yesterday," Jeff muttered, "so act like you're on third base." That got a snigger out of Spotty. "I hear you got a new dog," Jeff whispered. "What kind?"

Spotty giggled. "Duke's mixture, mostly rat terrier." Jeff tried to maintain an earnest gravity befitting a disciple, but Spotty kept snuffling, and his stomach hurt from the strain of not joining in. He was grateful when the session ended, although he hadn't made a dent in Spotty's resistance. Outside he asked Hud how he'd done with Lefty, a notorious cusser, and Hud said, "He's takin' a big lead off first base, hopin' he gits picked off, or caught in a double play. How 'bout Spots?"

"He ain't even playin'," Jeff said, and they laughed. Doggonnit, was it their fault if Sister Ada made the whole thing so durn funny? But Jeff's conscience bothered him about faking salvation every once in a while, like at night lying in bed, and when sparking Alma, and other odd times of

119

the day. For instance, while visiting with outlaw Dallas Strode down the creek in the sultry July stillness accentuated by the rasping of locusts in all the trees.

That was the day he told Vern's dad about the contest in connection with the watertank draining, which had been put off until August. Mayor Riley had suggested it in order to raise money for the baseball team, probably because he'd got stuck for most of the baseballs and bats so far. The idea was to have like a punchboard made up for each kind of fish, a big card divided into squares and each square representing a weight according to the reasonable weight limits of the particular species. You'd pay a dime and pick a weight trying to guess how much the heaviest fish in any category would weigh. The prize would be half the money bet on that kind of fish. For example, the bass card would be forty squares, going from a pound up to six pounds, jumping two ounces a square so it would be easier to get an exact weight without arguments. So, if all the chances were sold, the bass prize would be half of four dollars. But in the case of perch it would be in ounces, starting at zero and going up to three pounds (who ever heard of a three-pound perch, for Pete sakes?), or forty-eight squares. Catfish started at zero and went up to six pounds, two ounces a jump, so that was another four-eighty, etc.

Noodler squinted at him. "What about carp, drum, them kinda fish?"

Jeff nodded. "My dad says they're includin' nearly every fish known to be in the crick. One kinda bass, three of perch, three of cat, carp, drum, buffalo, redhorse and hog-sucker, an' even gars. Carp goes from a pound to six pounds like bass. If they sell even half the chances it'll be twelve or fifteen bucks for the team, Dad says." He added that, naturally, with a revival in town some people had spoken out about what they called gambling, but his dad said it wasn't any wickeder than raffling off pies at a pie supper, and not near as much danger because nobody had to eat the fish.

The fugitive jailbird chuckled, and picked his teeth with a stem of grass, scratching his chest, and said: "I'd still be willing to bet if they find any rough fish at all, like carp, buffalo, an' hog-suckers, they'll not be much bigger than minners. Likely be about two foot of slimey mud on the bottom of that tank, an' your bottom-feedin' rough fish, he can't live long on just mud, nor can the things he'd normally eat. My opinion is there could be five- or six-pound bass in there an' some big perch and a few channelcats, livin' off the supply of minners that git pumped in, or hatch out in there. But there won't be any bugle-mouthed suckerfish in there, unless someone puts 'em in . . ." He stopped and gave Jeff an owlish stare. "Say, now!"

Jeff was quick, some ways. He grinned, but the grin faded as he thought about things. "The tank's about twenty feet high with a dinky iron ladder that starts about nine feet from the ground, an' you'd hafta do it at night . . ."

The outlaw shrugged. "Any twelve-year-old boy can toss a *small* fish that high, an' small suckers would do the trick. The trouble would be gettin' 'em there alive."

Jeff got a sudden twinge of conscience and had to wrestle with it. He hadn't been baptized yet, so his religiousness wasn't what you'd call official yet, probably. Anyway, if Noodler was right and the tank contained no carp, etc., *nobody* would win on those kinds, which didn't seem right.

"Bottom-feeders might live three, four days in there," Noodler said, "if they were healthy when they got there."

"One of my troubles is overthrowin'," Jeff said. "But I'll bet Vern could toss fish up in there easy."

Vern's dad grinned. "Need him in on it, all right. Be suspicious if you won too many times." He suddenly sobered. "Whoa, now, we'd hafta know exactly how much our entries weighed. I can't guess in ounces too good."

"Heck, I been needin' some hand scales anyway," Jeff

told him. "Some customers always argue the catfish don't weigh what I claim they do. Mr. Riley's got some for around a dollar."

"Seein' as how it's a business expense, I'll foot half," his honest outlaw-partner said, getting up off the rock with his groceries. He looked up at the cloudless sky through the canopy of trees. "See you tomorrow, pard."

Jeff followed the creek to the street above the dam, pausing now and then to baptize the catfish so they'd stay alive, entertaining an occasional twinge of guilt about the scheme he'd helped cook up, but somehow it didn't seem very crooked, illegal, wrong, dishonest or unethical. Anyway, they hadn't actually done it yet, and the time to feel guilty about something was after you did it.

Soaking the fish thoroughly at the foot of the street, he loped all the way to the horse trough on Main Street and soaked them again, pleased to note they were still vigorously alive. At the hardware store, while buying the hand scales, he asked in a casual, offhand way if the rules of the contest said anything about the prizewinning fish having to be *alive* at the time of the draining.

Mayor Riley's mouth turned up in that perpetual cherubic smile, but under the bushy brows his eyes peered at Jeff in a bright alert way. "Good point," he said. "We never thought about that possibility, Jefferson. How did you happen to wonder about that point of order?"

"Some guys were discussin' it," Jeff said, wishing he hadn't asked, especially after buying the scales. It would look funny to Mr. Riley if he won on dead carp. . . .

That night at supper his dad said they'd decided dead fish counted if they weren't *too* dead. Not stiff or bloated. And his mother said, "That's a lovely thought while eating, for heaven sakes."

She was very moody and touchy, sorta gloomy all the time, never laughed, seldom smiled, had to lie down oftener with headaches and looked red-eyed sometimes.

Jody changed the subject. "I'm priddy durned tired of okry," he sighed.

"Don't cuss in front of Jeff," Mutt said, grinning.

"All I said was *durn*," Jody explained, missing the little joke there. "I'll tell yuh wot else I'm priddy durn tired of, is budderd beets. N'carrots, cucumbers. Ol' garden stuff. Except roasty nears an' tomadoes. Well, taters. I still like *some* garden stuff."

It seemed to Jeff his mother was looking at Jody in a kind of hurt way, so he said, "Boy, ever'thing tastes delicious to me." But it didn't seem to cheer her up much. Then Mutt said, "A hog'll eat anything, they tell me," and she looked more hurt and said well, thank you very much, and went into the kitchen to mope.

"I never meant it that way, dadgummit," Mutt called after her. "Gittin' so a guy can't say anything without bein' misconstrued." He grinned a little like he figured using a two-dollar word would amuse her, then he changed the subject back to fish, asking his dad what all kinds he thought there'd be in the watertank.

And durned if he didn't say practically the same thing Noodler had said. A few big bass and perch, maybe some cats, a lot of runty *little* bass and perch, minnows and tadpoles, but no frogs, and he'd be mighty surprised if there were any carp, drum, buffalo, or rough suckerfish like that. "I don't think they can earn a livin' in a tank," he said.

"How come you figure it that way?" Jeff asked him, and his dad said, "I was there *last* time we drained it."

"If there's tadpoles, how come no frogs?" Mutt wondered, and his dad said, "Search me. My guess is, soon as they grow legs they crawl out on the bank, which is quite a drop. I've occasionally noticed small frogs dead around the tank, but maybe most of 'em survive the fall, or something eats them. Beats *me*."

He was a whole minute late, and Alamo said: "Took your

123

own sweet time." Nag, nag, nag, he thought, following her past the Bull Durham sign and into the deserted barbershop. She had that radishy-oniony taste again that took a little while to get used to, not strong but persistent.

"Want a stick of Juicy Fruit?" he mumbled into her girl-smelling hair, and she said, "I can't kiss and chew gum at the same time, silly." He *knew* that. She stiffened suddenly. "Say, are you insinuating I've got halitosis or something?"

"Heck, no," he said, and her mother called from the meat market: "AL-muh!"

"Hell *eena!*" Alamo muttered. "Lissen, you could come around afternoons, just walk past and slip in here, an' maybe I could duck out."

The idea sort of appealed to him—kissing her before she ate supper, instead of too soon afterwards. . . .

Since the night Chink threw clods at him he'd taken to roosting in a private, secret pew on the roof of the lumber-yard paint shed, under the overhanging maple tree. Not even Hud knew about it yet. You couldn't see much but you could hear everything, lying back in ease and comfort on the warm shingled slope, gazing up at the patterns cast on the leaves by the streetlamp. You could really relax, listening to the hypnotic, sonorous voice of the preacher without paying too much attention to what he was saying. It was a much better place to doze and dream than the dew-damp grass, but it had its drawbacks. Like nobody waking him up after the meeting ended, and having his dad come looking for him.

"Jeff! Where the hell are you?"

The lights were out over by the church and the street was full of moonlight and shadows, deserted except for a worried, aggravated Slim McGraw.

Jeff started scooting his half-awake body down to the limb he used to reach the sidewalk. "Up here, Dad," he mumbled, jaws locking in a great yawn. "Here I am."

"Well, dammit to hell!" his dad said.

On the sidewalk, Jeff yawned. "Went to sleep."

"You always do, dammit, but you always made it home to bed before," his dad growled, steering Jeff's weary hulk under the streetlamp. "Hell, maybe I oughta thank you. I came within a whisker of getting religion about an hour ago, but this little affair has restored my equilibrium. It wouldn't take, wouldn't last a week. I wasn't cut out for that desist and abstain and give-it-up brand of living." He snorted. "I'm just a railroader, an average run-of-the-mill taxpayer, not as good as some, but no damn worse than most." He was silent awhile, guiding Jeff's stumbling feet down the moonlit street. "Those salvation orators sure create a mess of confusion, trying to sell a man a bill of goods he can't possibly pay for, dammit. I'm a guy who cusses, smokes and chews, takes a nip occasionally—always have and always will." When they were nearly home he said, "Trouble with religion, it's whole hog or none. If a man could keep one or two of his sinful habits—hellfire, there oughta be degrees of salvation. Oughta grade it like a school does, maybe lower the passing mark to sixty. Or like the damn railroad, give a man brownies for going on a toot, cussin' excessively—but, dammit, show me in the Bible where it even mentions tobacco."

Helping sleep-drunk Jeff up the front steps, he said: "If you're barefooted you'll hafta wash your feet."

"Tennis shoes," Jeff mumbled. The mere thought of washing his feet in cold water hurt. Oh, man, just let him flop on that old bed . . .

He'd been too groggy to comprehend all his dad had said on that ten-mile walk from the corner, and the next morning he wasn't sure he hadn't just dreamed it. So at breakfast, with Mutt gone to peddle his papers and his mother starting to do the dishes, he sidled up to it. "I dreamed Dad nearly got religion." Speaking to Jody, but aiming it at his mother. Jody grinned. "Then only me an' Mutt won't have it yet."

"What about Mama?" Jeff said kiddingly.

125

"She don't *need* it," Jody said. "She's *already* good."

"Well, bless your little heart," Jewel McGraw said, half-laughing, but then she sorta hunched her shoulders and stared out the kitchen window awhile. "Your dad is a decent man, whether he's saved or not," she said. "It's easy enough for people without any bad habits to give up worldly pleasures and sit in judgment on others, but I've seen too many backsliders, and known too many hypocrites who *pretended* to be good Christians . . . I just hope the Lord has been too busy to read *my* mind and heart lately," she sighed, and went on washing dishes.

Anyway, even if he'd been a true convert, something happened that sort of shook Jeff's faith in God's mercy and fairness. Actually it was two things. Friday morning Mr. George Rose, who owned half the town and most of the bank, came driving his big Chandler down Main Street while Lige Bowzer was cutting up on his mare (still trying to impress Alamo; didn't know when to call it quits), and ran over Lige's dog, Bozo. But the wheels straddled his terrified, crouching body, and the high underside cleared him. Scared him silly, but didn't touch a hair. Mr. Rose went whizzing on east like he didn't know anything had happened —or nearly happened. Jeff was glad Bozo wasn't hurt, but kinda disappointed he hadn't been hurt a little, slightly crippled up permanently.

Then that afternoon, after selling Claude Calvert some catfish, Jeff had the horrifying, unforgettable experience of seeing one of the nicest dogs in town get killed. He saw it, his dad saw it, a highschool girl named Dorothy Crow saw it (and in a way caused it), but worst of all, poor ten-year-old Bubby Coonrod saw it.

The northbound local was switching on a sidetrack, the engine's bell ringing a cheerful warning, backing cars across Main Street. Leaving the elevator fondling his money, Jeff saw his dad coming from the shack, and saw Bubby and

126

Prince on the brick sidewalk headed downtown, waiting for the slow-moving train to pass, and between cars saw Dorothy approaching on the other side with her little bitch Fluffy. He'd exchanged grins with his dad and they were converging on Bubby when Prince began wagging his tail in a friendly, curious fashion, seeing Fluffy (smelling her, more likely), and casually started across the tracks between two boxcars, and the nightmare slowly unfolded before Jeff's horrified eyes. The near wheel of the trailing boxcar urged Prince gently down across the rail and cut him in two, and he lifted his head to look at himself with a kind of astonished dismay before he died. Jeff was petrified; Bubby collapsed on the sidewalk screaming and sobbing, covering his eyes; Slim McGraw said: "Aw, Jesus Christ!"

It seemed to Jeff they were all frozen there for an infinity as the slow cars kept passing over half of Prince, then the engine came backing across Main, and Blackie Arthur, the engineer, grinning down at stunned Jeff from the cab window, called out: "Howdy, Jeff, how's the fishing?" And the engine kept backing up, its bell tolling a knell for Prince although the fireman pulling the rope didn't know it, and Blackie didn't know it. And Prince didn't know it.

White-faced Dorothy Crow had picked up her small dog, and as soon as the way was clear she came across the tracks with her eyes averted, and Jeff envied her because she could beat it, but he couldn't somehow. All he could do for Bubby was not leave him there with his dead dog. Nothing much anybody could do for Prince, but what needed doing, Jeff's father did.

"Back in a minute. Stay with him, son," he said, and went long-legging it back to the shack and returned carrying a wooden box that had held sticks of journal grease. He fitted Prince gently into the box and put the lid back on. "Come on, boys, we'll give him a decent burial," he said. And when they reached the back of the shack he said, "Get the spade, Jeff."

127

He cleared a space in the lush weeds by the stockpens, and dug a grave, and they buried Prince, who had been alive just a minute ago. Death could happen so shockingly, unexpectedly sudden, Jeff thought, still not quite believing it.

"I shouldn't stood . . . so clo-close to the—the tracks," Bubby moaned. "If-fiff . . . if I'da just *held* 'im . . ."

"Wasn't your fault," Jeff's dad told him.

"We wuh-waited a hun . . . a hunderd ti-ti-times for tray . . . trains to pa-pa-pass like that," Bubby moaned, wiping his eyes.

Jeff's dad shook his head. "Just one of those unforeseen calamities, Bubby. A lousy coincidence, unlucky timing—a he and a she dog on opposite sides of the damn tracks."

They walked with Bubby to the street and watched him head east at a shuffling trot, wiping his face, a grieving kid victim of the blind chance that ran things. Jeff wondered if God was in charge of killing dogs or had a mean angel do stuff like that. God was in charge of misery and sorrow, punishing people for their sins, but what could Bubby or Conrad Coonrod have done that was so bad He would do *this* to them, or let it be done?

"Goddammit!" his dad said. "This must be the saddest day of Bub's life, so far. Awful thing for a kid to see."

"For *anybody*," Jeff said gloomily. He'd probably have some real lulu nightmares about it. But he'd learned a lesson, paid for by the Coonrods, about dogs' dumbness when it came to the flanged wheels of slow-moving railroad cars. Get a grip on your dog and hold on tight . . .

He couldn't shake off his feeling of shock and morbid anxiety, and that night he skipped Alma, waiting at home until Hud came up the street and telling him what a great pew the paint shed made. He didn't much want to be up there alone with his haunted thoughts. But he discovered that even with Hud beside him he was *still* alone with his thoughts, and the awful tragedy kept happening over and over again in his mind's eye. Bubby sobbing, Blackie grinning down from the cab, asking how was fishing, not knowing he'd been chosen by God to kill an innocent, good-natured dog. White-faced Dorothy Crow pretending not to see. His dad saying: Aw, Jesus Christ! But most horrible of all, the way Prince lifted his head and looked back at his severed hindquarters like he didn't know what had happened but sure wished it hadn't . . .

On Immersion Sunday morning Hud came up the street and asked if Jeff was going to participate in the ritual and Jeff said heck, no, he wasn't no hypocrite, and besides, it would be miserable hot out at Russell's pond with no shade. Hud agreed wholeheartedly and with obvious relief and said: "We could sorta have our own babsousin' down at the crick—or at least go swimmin' where there's shade." So that's what they did, and if Jeff felt no more religious for it, at least he felt no guilt, as he would have if he'd pretended to have his sins washed away in Russell's pond, which was probably full of cow pee and frog slobber anyway.

12

After the excitement of the revival it was hard for people to settle down again, but most of them finally did. The last few days of July registered 100° weather and August started off by pushing it up a couple of notches, and an epidemic of inertia hit the boys and a lot of the men. Nobody swam as often because the swimming hole was stagnant. Jeff hadn't been there for weeks, but Hud told him the water was scum green and full of frog slobber. The creek still ran clean, if sluggishly, down where Jeff took dips in his own private waist-deep gravel-bottom pool, on trips to the rendezvous.

Nobody took long walks during the heat wave except Jeff and old Turkey Dobbs, it seemed like. Normally this time of year there'd be guys going down to Clem Parker's watermelon patch, but the drought had stunted the melons so bad they weren't worth hauling to market, and Clem announced publicly they were free to anyone who'd come get them. With the fun of stealing them removed, they weren't worth the bother to anyone except Flew-the-Coop, who kept a supply in the spring branch to share with his partner during business conferences.

He'd noodled about all the good catfish out of that stretch of creek and thought he'd set some real trotlines and limb-lines. He could get minnows, crawdads, grasshoppers and so forth for bait, and he'd like to try liver, too. "Come to think of it," he said, "I'd relish some liver an' onions myself." So Jeff made a note: cord and hooks for trotlines, liver and onions for his partner. Rolling a cigarette, Noodler said casually, "You might bring Vernon down someday around sunset, and we'll figure out how to win that fish-guessing contest." Jeff figured he'd tell Vern at baseball practice, if there was any. Last time only eight guys showed up, including Dolittle. Funny how all winter you yearned for summer, then when it came it got old in a hurry, too dang hot to enjoy. Going barefoot was more often a tribulation than a pleasure, especially having to wash your feet at bedtime.

Only seven guys showed up for practice, including Jody tagging along with Mutt, who said, "Go play on the slidin' board."

Jody shook his head. "It'd burn my bottom."

"Then go play with Woody Higgins, why don't you?"

"Too fur to walk," Jody said, and headed for the shade.

Mutt scowled around at the skimpy turnout and said, "Aw, hell, less call it off, we don't have a game Sunday anyway. Lissen, you guys. Pass the word, next practice day if *ten* guys show up send someone to notify me an' I'll show up." So Vern said make it nine guys and send someone to notify him, too. Which sorta put Mutt in his place.

Mutt took his catcher's gear and Jody and headed for home, and all the others except Vern went looking for a cool place. When they were alone Jeff split the day's take with Vern and told him about his dad finally agreeing to a visit. Vern got pretty excited and said well, what's wrong with today? Jeff agreed, figuring the sooner he took line and hooks to his partner the better for business. Anyway, all sundowns were alike for him; he had previous engagements with Alamo in the gloaming, and better try to tell her in advance he couldn't make it. . . .

He strolled past the meat market, then back west to lean on the Bull Durham sign, hearing the tireless clank and thump of horseshoes in the park. Never got too hot for those guys. Feeling conspicuous there on the empty street in the hot sun, he went into the ex-barbershop, acting like he might rent it if the owner fixed it up.

She was waiting for him in the small, oven-hot back room with a conspiratorial smile, sweating a little. "Slipped out the back way," she said. "Can't stay long, I hafta fix supper. What makes your pockets bulge like that?"

"Fishin' line an' stuff," he said, feeling shy. It was easy to kiss her at night, but in daylight he could see her—even worse, she could see him, smiling quizzically, acting a bit uneasy herself, and abruptly tucked a folded piece of paper in his pocket. She'd done that before, at night. Little notes and poems. One reason she liked him was being fellow poets, probably. Clumsily embracing her, he kissed her, and it was different. She'd never tasted like strawberry ice-cream soda at night, and he was instantly suspicious and jealous.

"Had you a strawberry soda recently, huh?" he inquired, and she said *yup.* "Buy it yourself?" he asked, and she said: *Nope, what's that in your back pockets?* "Pound of liver an' two big onions," he growled, seeing how she was trying to change the subject, "plus my slingshot an' a bunch of rocks— who did buy it?" *Sure wasn't you,* she said with a teasy smile—*we're wasting time talking. I can't stay long.*

"Well, it's none uh *my* beeswax," he said gruffly.

She sighed. "What's it matter if someone treats me to a cold drink? You're the only one I'm *kissin'* nowadays."

He still felt sulky. "Okay, just skip it."

She blew out her telltale breath exasperatedly. "It was Matt. So there! You feel better now?"

He felt worse, but hid it. "All in the family." He shrugged and kissed her mainly to end the conversation, thinking: That's why Matt didn't want to practice, he had a date to buy a soda for his possible future sister-in-law.

She sighed. "Guess I better be gettin' on back."

"Well, lissen, I might not make it tonight," he said.

She squinted up at him. "I get it, you're mad."

"Heck, no," he said. "I hafta go down the crick after supper an' may not git back in time it all." She looked dubious. "Honest, I'm *not* sore," he said. She went to the door, turned back, and said: "Well, if you're not mad now you probably will be when you read my poem."

He unfolded the bit of paper and read it.

> I sure do wish
> you didn't smell like fish,
> don't get me wrong,
> it isn't very strong,
> but I sorta hope
> you'll use more soap.
>
> Alma Dexter

He sort of resented her criticism and began thinking up a poetic retort about her after-supper kisses always tasting a little oniony but the only rhyme he could think of was bunions. Besides, he felt self-conscious and kept coming up with stuff like: It makes me feel punk that you think I stink like a skunk, I guess I'm sunk, etc. All in her favor. But just the same, in the kissing game, a girl was dumb not to chew gum—and if she had to accept treats from another, he wished it wasn't his own brother . . .

For supper Jewel McGraw tried a new recipe she got from Mrs. Riley who had got it from Alma's mother—meatballs stewed in a mixture of okra, corn, tomatoes, peppers and onions. "I like this," her husband said. "I hope we have it once a year from now on."

Vernon was waiting at the stock pens and in a hurry, and they didn't talk much until after they met Turkey Dobbs just inside the pasture gate, carrying a couple nice cats and a dozen large perch. "You got some nice fish there, Mr.

133

Dobbs," Jeff said. Turkey nodded curtly, passing on, so Jeff threw a direct question after him. "How come you always catch bigger perch than anybody else?"

Turkey stopped and turned around, sour-faced as usual. "I go where nobody else goes, an' use the right bait." Then he went on, looking sort of scarecrowish, and kinda lonesome, Jeff imagined.

"Ol' Turkey used up a whole day's worth of talkin' there," he said, grinning, and Vern said, "I hear he's sorta touched in the head."

Jeff told him how crazy old Turkey was, as they walked across the dusty, grazed-down pasture. Granny Hanks wanted Turkey to dig a new cellar, as her old one was caving in and mildewed, etc. He offered to work by the hour or day, but as she told Jewel McGraw, if you pay a dad-durned man by the hour he'll piddle and loaf, and maybe even quit before the job was done. So she told Dobbs she'd pay fifteen dollars for the whole job. Dig it eight feet deep, seven wide, ten long, with dug steps at one end, lay supporting timbers across it, nail boards on top of the beams trickle-tight, then mound the dirt and clay back on top. She would carpenter the shelves and slanting door herself. She would pay him a third when it was four feet deep, another third when the excavation was done, and the rest of the money when it was roofed over to her satisfaction.

So the first day Turkey only dug about a foot in the dry hard ground under the hot sun. Then he located some boards and made a trough so he could pump water from the well into the excavation. Since then he came early mornings, scooped out the soaked top layer, pumped in more water, and left for the day. Late afternoons he came back, scooped out another thin layer, pumped in more water, and departed. Granny complained that at the rate he was going it would take him all summer. But all she could do was fume and fret, since she hadn't stipulated any deadline in the verbal contract. She'd outsmarted herself. If she'd hired him by the hour or the day she could boss him around, but a contractor was his own boss. So Turkey worked about an hour mornings and an hour evenings, and went fishing in between.

"Only drawback," Jeff said, "is he pumps a heckuva lotta water." And Vern groaned: "Man, don't tell me about pumpin' water."

The father-son reunion didn't come up to Jeff's expectations. It wasn't very sentimental. They were pretty self-conscious.

Hey there, Paw. *Howdy, son.* How you doin', Paw? *Right well, Vern, how's Mama and the kids?* Don't you worry, Paw, we're gittin' along fine. *Well, you look purty well fed.* So do you, Paw. You put on some weight, seems like. *My pard here keeps me well supplied with grub, but I miss your mama's cookin'.* Well, she misses your eatin' it, too. *Buddy here tells me you have a nice flock of chickens now, son.* Lord, yes! Mama let all them ol' Rhode Islands set an' damn near ever' egg hatched. We're eatin' fried chicken two, three times a week, an' she's cannin' some of the biggest roosters— but we're eatin' a lotta fish, too. *Gawd-almighty, so am I, Vern . . . How'd the garden do in this long dry spell?* Real good, Paw, we pour all the wash water on it an' stuff has really growed. That garden hadn't been worked in years, an' the soil's rich as heck. *You got any fall crops started?* You betcha. We got late corn an' beans . . . etc.

They hadn't even shook hands, after not seeing each other since back before Christmas, over seven months.

We dug ten bushel of nice taters, an' three of onions. Mama canned thirty-some jars of green beans, more'n that of wild greens, twenty-some of scraped corn, about sixteen quarts of tomatoes so far an' a dozen half-gallons of soup mix. *How about pickles?* Aw, you know Mama, she's really puttin' up the pickles an' chowchow. As for berries an' fruit an' jelly, well, it'll do us over the winter. *Vern, I'm mighty glad to hear that, mighty relieved.* I even left out some,

135

Paw . . . black-eye peas, pickled beets, carrots. I tell you that cave under the house is so stored with eatin' stuff you can't hardly git in it anymore.

Well, hell, Jeff thought. They could of at least shook *hands.*

Tell me about the house, son. Well, it ain't bad atall, Paw, it's got a good roof an' fairly easy to heat in winter—there's a fireplace, one of the few in town, they say. *I always hankered for a fireplace—but whatta you do for wood, son?* Well, last winter I drug dead limbs up from the crick to saw up, but then I found out cobs are free at the elevator, so I made me a two-wheel cart to haul 'em in, so we mainly use cobs to heat wash water—I'm tryin' to git a big pile ahead for cold weather. But I aim to haul deadwood from the crick for the cookstove an' fireplace both. *Wish I had my team an' wagon for a couple days. I could lay you in a few ricks of oak for the winter.* Now don't go frettin' about us, Paw, we'll make out fine—me an' ol' Milton made some money on hides last winter, an' put a right smart of meat on the table.

I'd leave, Jeff thought sarcastically, if they didn't need me so bad.

If I had me a target an' a lantern, me an' Milt could hunt possum an' coon at night come autumn. *Speakin' of which, son, this money Buddy is passin' on to you, first I want you to see all you kids has shoes an' clothes for school. I know them little fellers especially are outgrowin' ever'thing.* Well, Paw, Denver can wear Buck's hand-me-downs, but Buck can't yet wear mine, he's the main one needin' new clothes, an' Goldie's sewin' herself some dresses—she made straight A's all year. *Buddy told me that, an' it sure made me proud, son. Ashamed, too. But never mind that. Soon as the shoes an' clothes is taken care of, you buy you a twenty-two target an' a Coleman lantern to possum-hunt with. There's good money in hides, an' also meat, an' ever' damn dollar you can bring in—son, it hurts a man to think of his little woman*

136

washin' clothes for a livin', especially in cold weather. It scares him, too, she could ruin her health. Yeah, I know, Paw. Scares me, too—especially since she aims for me to go to school, meanin' I won't be home to help her with the dang work. *I sure wish there was some other way she could make you kids a livin'—an' I just wish to hell I hadn't got so smart with the goddurned sheriff, turnin' a three-month sentence into a long lonesome year in jail . . . I coulda been out last spring an' takin' care of you all . . .*

Jeff was embarrassed and restless.

Shoot, Paw, you're helpin' as it is. I already got over eight bucks Jeff give me—you keep callin' him Buddy, but he's Jeff McGraw. An' a durn good friend of mine. *Mine, too, son. We agreed not to worry about right names, but it don't matter now. Howdy, Jeff McGraw.*

"Howdy, Mr. Strode," Jeff said, relieved to be noticed. "Here's the hooks an' cord, an' the liver an' onions you wanted. So why don't I head back to town?—you could show Vern your hideout an' fry the liver before it turns blinky. An' you can talk all night if you want to."

"That's right thoughtful, pard—an' I sure appreciate *havin'* you for a pardner. You brung me luck."

"Lucky for me, too," Jeff said. "Well, I guess Vern can make it back to town okay." And Vern said with a big grin: "All I need is some of Paw's liver an' onions to give me the strangth."

By hurrying, Jeff beat the dusk back to town, hoping she'd be out there—but then suspicious because she was.

"Expectin' someone?" he inquired, and she said, "Nope. Said you couldn't make it, I seem to recall."

"I made it," he said. "You rather I keep on goin'?"

"Suit yourself," she said. "I'm sure not expectin' anybody else, if that's what you're hinting. But I thought you'd be pretty mad at me."

"Nope," he said. "I guess anybody would rather *know* it if they smell fishy. Or taste oniony."

"Oh-oh," she said. "Just what does that remark mean?"

"Well, for example, you ever eat onions for supper?"

"Oh, lord," she said, and was silent, not looking at him, and he feared he'd offended her. But finally the pale blur of her face turned up to him and she said, "Got any gum on you? I seem to recall we had onions for supper."

They didn't get much done before her mother called her in, but Spearmint sure improved the situation.

He awoke the next morning to the sound of Granny's squeaky pump and wondered if Turkey ever got tired of fish, but since there was no aroma of coffee and bacon he went back to sleep. Get all you can before school starts, he told himself, and dreamed he caught a twenty-pound perch.

His mother must have heard Granny's pump screeching, too, because after breakfast she put the family slave to pumping water for the garden. But he didn't really mind, considering all the present and future good eating involved. The way he looked at it, he was saving the McGraw tribe from starving to death next winter.

Jody came out and asked, "Wotcha doin', Jeff?" This was the same kid that made all those A's on his report card.

"Washin' the garden," Jeff said. "This time of year you hafta keep garden stuff clean or it ain't safe to eat." Jody went wandering around the house, free to do as he pleased, and Jeff thought: We can keep on trotlining through the fall. I can run down there after school and hurry back in time for chores. I could do most of it after dark. But what about winter? A guy couldn't camp out in freezing weather. . . .

His dad paused on his way to the spider closet and squinted at him. "I can't get over the change in you this summer, Jeff. All of a sudden you're a money-making, ambitious sonofagun like Mutt. And sticking with it during this hot spell. How come? Do you know?"

"Well," Jeff said, "I wanted a twenty-two rifle, to hunt squirrels an' so forth. I'm twelve, an' you always said . . ."

His dad nodded, scratching his whiskers. "I always said a boy of twelve was old enough for a rifle or shotgun. Well, it's your money. You've got my okay." He left Jeff grinning at the pump, feeling pretty good.

While he was watering the corn next to Rileys' chicken pen, Caroline stopped on her way back from the hottest toilet in town to try getting his goat again. "I'm going to go visit Alma after a while," she said. "Want me to deliver any love letters?"

"Thanks, but I do my own deliverin'," he said.

"I certainly don't see what she sees in you."

"That makes two of us, Coaloil," he replied, and she stared at him through the chicken wire, not grasping all the subtle meaning of what he said. Funny how having Alamo think he was nice-looking gave him a sort of confident nonchalance with other females.

Next time he went in for a shot of leftover coffee his mother was standing by the dining-room window dabbing at her eyes and sniffling, so he tried to pretend she just had a summer cold or something. He didn't know *why* she was crying, and it worried him.

When he came out again he saw Granny over in her yard by the new cellar hole, and his curiosity led him across the alley to check on the progress. She swung her wrinkled brown face around at him accusingly and said: "Men! Laziest animals on God's earth! Shiftless piddlers! Skeert of a little hard work!"

"Not me, Granny," he said. "I'm a hardworking dude."

"Well, you're young, you'll grow out of it," she snapped. "He only pumps enough water each time to soften up a little thin layer."

The excavation looked impressive to Jeff. It was down about three feet. "Gonna be a nice big cellar, Granny."

"If it's ever finished," she said. "Aw, well, that pore thing,

139

he's gettin' old. We're all gettin' old." She glared at Jeff. "You're gettin' old, too, Matty boy, and don't you forget it. That's what people do, the minute we're borned we start gettin' old, an' ain't a blessed thing you can do about it because it's God's will."

Jeff hadn't ever thought about it that way before, and going back across the alley, he thought about it that way and was startled when a rock whacked the barn. He sprinted for cover, cussing himself out for being absentminded. Chink was usually home this time of day, ready to take potshots at saps who wandered into the alley. One thing about him, he never shot you in your own yard or garden. Maybe even Chink had a code of honor.

It was mid-afternoon when he got to the rendezvous and found his partner pretty upset, with good reason.

"I was prowlin' down the crick lookin' for places to set trotlines," he said, "an' nearly stumbled over a man."

Jeff felt immediate alarm. "Did he get a look at you?"

"He would of," Mr. Strode said, "if he was alive."

Jeff gaped at him. "You mean . . . he *wasn't?*"

"He's either dead or paralyzed," the fugitive said. "I keep hopin' he was just asleep, but I don't believe it." He got up off his personal rock, finger-combing his long mane of yellowish hair. "If he's still down there when we git there, I'll be convinced he's stone cold dead."

Nossirree! Jeff's mind protested. "When *we* get there?"

"Well, I don't know him, an' someone's got to notify somebody he's dead—an' I sure can't do it, pard."

Jeff swallowed. "Never saw a dead man. Or *wanted* to."

"I'm sorry about that, pard," Dallas Strode said. "Wish I could spare you, but if you went to town an' said there's a dead man down here but you didn't know who, then it turns out you *do* know him, it'd look mighty odd. Folks would wonder how you got clost enough to know he was dead but didn't recognize 'im. Wouldn't make sense."

140

Jeff saw the logic there, and along with shivery dread he felt sort of curious and excited—maybe seeing a dead man, he'd get over his fear of death. But he sure hoped it wasn't anyone he knew. . . .

He would have recognized the dead man from two blocks away, but was within twenty feet before he saw him, slumped back in a sitting position at the foot of the high slanting creek bank.

He cleared his throat nervously. "It's Turkey Dobbs!"

"Well, seein' as how he hasn't moved for over three hours, you'd best git to town an' tell somebody Turkey Dobbs is dead, an' *you* found 'im. Meanwhiles, I'll roll my gear an' go camp somewhere else for a few days, Jeff. You better cut up over the bluff so you can show how to git the ambulance the closest to here."

Jeff sneaked another look at his first corpse. "I thought he always fished away down below," he said shakily.

"Maybe today he didn't feel up to goin' no further."

"Well, who do I tell, in a case like this?"

"First grown man you see. Let him take it from there."

The first man Jeff saw was his dad. He made a beeline for the shack, running, trotting, loping and galloping, never slowing to a walk, hoping his dad would be there, terribly glad he was. Winded, he panted: "Turkey dead is Dobbs, Dad!" A month later they'd be able to laugh about that, but not now. "Down yonder . . . on the crick!" His father didn't question his reliability, taking his word for it and accepting the responsibility.

They went over to the grain elevator and told Claude Calvert, and his dad phoned Mr. Riley, and the mayor phoned the county courthouse, and the sheriff arrived within an hour in his Chevrolet sedan with a deputy, followed closely by a gruesomely ornate hearse from the funeral parlor in Blackthorn . . . followed by Hack Kelso's gasoline truck, Lige Bowzer on his flatulent mare, a growing straggle of running boys and men, a few women and girls, Mayor

141

Riley's Model T, etc., until it seemed that half the town was there to watch Jeff and his dad climb into the back seat of the sheriff's auto. Including a worried-looking Alamo, who seemed to fear Jeff had committed a crime or something.

The sheriff was a beefy, dour-faced man with a belly that hung over his belt. His deputy was younger, lean and solemn, not as intimidating as his boss. They both wore wide-brimmed straw hats. The sheriff kept asking questions over his shoulder and sweaty Jeff did his best to answer them. Look like Turkey was shot? *Nossir*. Kilt in a fight or some sort? *Nossir, he just looked like he sorta keeled over while fishing.* Jeff's dad answered some of them. *Nope, Turkey didn't have any enemies—or real friends, either, for that matter.* Could he have fell? *Well, it didn't look that way.* Did he have a bad heart?

"Doc Schuman would likely know," Jeff's dad said. "He's coming along."

Jeff directed the sheriff across Buffalo Wallows to the old dead tree where he'd come up over the bluff, and when they were getting out of the car the sheriff said, "Does Dallas Strode's wife still live here in Cottonwood?" Jeff's dad said she did. The sheriff scratched his florid jowl and hitched up his belly and said, "I figgered by now she'da took off to join him wherever he skinned out to." He watched the gas truck bumping over the pasture and the horsemen (Hud and Lige) and straggling people on foot (half the boys in town, including Mutt, and quite a few men) coming across the pasture, and snorted. "Like a goldanged circus! Holler dead man an' ever'body from miles around comes arunnin' to gawk!"

"Don't get much excitement around here," Jeff's dad said. "I only came because Jeff's involved, and probably wishes he wasn't—right, son?" Jeff nodded, but tentatively. He'd caused all this commotion and wasn't at all sure now he'd rather someone else had done it.

The gruesome bone-colored hearse arrived, and the sheriff asked him how far was it, and he said a couple hundred yards. The hearse driver said he'd need some help with the stretcher, and twenty people volunteered, including kids nine or ten years old. Everybody wanted to get in on the big event.

The mayor's Ford arrived without the mayor, Dolittle driving, and old Doc scowling and muttering—no reason why he had to come down here; they could of brought the corpse into town to be certified as officially dead.

"Awright, boy, lead the way," the sheriff said, and Jeff did so, feeling like the Pied Piper. Feeling important. Seeing Turkey again wouldn't be so bad with a crowd along, including his dad. . . .

"There he is!" he said, and backed against a tree as the morbid mob surged forward to gape at poor old Turkey, who'd never liked people and probably would hate being gawked at if he knew it was happening.

Doc Schuman pronounced him deceased and said it looked like a common everyday heart attack—there didn't seem to be any wounds, injuries or signs of a struggle.

A syrup bucket beside the body contained some fried perch, biscuits, two ripe tomatoes, an onion and a salt shaker. The sheriff made a shrewd professional deduction: Turkey died before he ate his lunch.

Jeff's dad, Dolittle and Hack Kelso helped the hearse driver carry Turkey back through the timber. Jeff lagged behind, and Hud said, "You found 'im, huh?" Jeff nodded. "How'd you know he was dead?" Hud inquired. Jeff shrugged. "He wasn't doin' no breathin', mainly."

During similar conversations with about fifty people the next few days he'd get better at telling his side of it, not lying exactly, just making it more interesting. "Saw old Turkey while hunting places to set lines and I says: *Howdy, Turkey, catchin' any fish?* No answer, an' I noticed he wasn't movin' so I says: *You sick or something?* Still no answer, and suddenly I realized! *My lord!* I says to myself. *He's dead!* And I lit out for town."

His mother had already heard about it from Mrs. Riley

when he got home, spoiling that telling, but then he thought somebody ought to notify Granny, so he went on across the alley and did his duty. She clapped a hand over her mouth and stared into space for a while. Then she croaked: "Merciful God, that pore old thing! Likely he's been feelin' sickly is why he skimped so on the work. I knew that wasn't like him atall. Had I known he was in such pore health I never woulda hired him. My lands! Just keeled over, you say. Fishin'! Well, I hope he went fast and never suffered."

I wish he'd got to eat his lunch first, Jeff thought. But I guess it didn't much matter.

Granny heaved a sigh. "Well, the livin' has to go on livin', and I still need my cellar dug. Just have to find somebody else, but I'm blessed if I know who. Mr. Dobbs was always the man to git for odd jobs." She eyed Jeff. "You're big and stout, Matty boy."

"I better be gittin' on home to supper," he said.

"Pay you ten dollars. You and your brother."

He stopped backing away. Old greedy Mutt would jump at the chance and sure wouldn't hire his brother to help. He'd get some guys to do most of the work for a couple bucks apiece and stick the rest of it in his pocket. "Gee, I dunno," he said. "I'm pretty busy."

"Call it twelve," she said shrewdly, and he thought: Hud would like to earn some extra dough. And Vern sure could use a couple bucks—there won't be any fish money for a few days, with Noodler laying low. "Okay, then, it's a deal," he said.

He remembered to sprint, crossing the alley.

After supper he found Hud talking to Windy Mills, the bat-breaking shortstop, and Windy volunteered his brawn, too. Jeff could count on Vern, so he ended up with a three-man crew willing to work for two dollars each.

By mid-morning of the next day old Granny was so pleased by the way Jeff's crew went at the cellar-digging that she whomped them up what she called a harvest-hand dinner. Fried chicken, roasting ears, mashed spuds and gravy, cole slaw, sliced tomatoes, homemade bread, canned peaches and iced tea. Afterward Hud rubbed his belly and said, "If she's ten years younger I'd marry 'er." Granny's fried chicken couldn't touch Jeff's mother's fried chicken, but it sure was some meal for a Friday noon.

The next day Granny was too busy helping set the ceiling beams and nailing on the boards to cook, but she fed them headcheese sandwiches and apple pie with thick cream. They finished around four o'clock and she gave Jeff a five and seven ones, he paid off his crew, they gathered up their tools and headed for the drugstore.

Vern bought a dime's worth of mixed candy for his whole family to enjoy and said he'd better go pump water or something. Tight Hud blew a whole nickel on an ice-cream cone and went to get ready to go after the cows. Windmill, who had done most of the pick and mattock work, bought some jawbreakers and went limping homeward to rest his aching muscles and recuperate.

Less weary and better paid than his employees, Jeff drank a leisurely ice-cream soda and shook his head in amazement. He'd earned six bucks without straining himself, due to his shrewd, crafty brain, et cetera. If you know anybody that needs any cellars dug, he thought expansively, notify Contractor McGraw.

Turkey's funeral was scheduled for Monday, and there was a soaking, drought-breaking rain Sunday night with a lot of thunder and lightning that seemed like kind of an omen, or something. Maybe when he got to the Pearly Gates old Turkey said, Lord, them folks sure need rain bad down there where I come from . . . they got to dig my grave and the ground is dry and hard. But Turkey probably wouldn't say that much even to God.

Jeff's mother thought he ought to go because he was the

145

one who found poor Mr. Dobbs, but when Jeff opposed the idea she surprised him by letting it go at that.

Jeff had other things to worry about, like checking to see if his partner had come out of hiding yet. But he wasn't crazy about going down to that death-haunted place alone, so he asked if he could take Ranger along, and Mutt said, "I don't lend my dog, but I'll rent 'im, for a dime." That buzzard could think up more ways to make money.

When he reached the rendezvous he knew Flew-the-Coop was back in business because the chughole contained six big catfish. So he gave a loud yodel and waited, and presently Mr. Strode came out of the sweltering underbrush.

"Howdy," he said amiably. "Tell me all about it."

After Jeff told him how things had gone last Thursday, the fugitive said he'd noodled those catfish down where he'd been laying low, had come back yesterday, and had set trotlines and limblines up and down the creek.

After they gabbed awhile about digging cellars, baseball, etc., Vern's dad said he was low on tobacco, lard and matches, out of eggs, and craving a mess of beefsteak.

At supper he asked about the funeral, and it turned out his mother had gone. And Granny Hanks. In fact, about forty people had showed up, either out of morbid curiosity or compassion for a fellow human with no family or friends to mourn him. Jeff's mother said she was glad so many people turned out—it would be terrible if nobody came to your funeral.

It seemed to Jeff it would be terrible enough just to die, never mind what happened afterwards.

The undertaker had put a legal claim on Turkey's estate, since no evidence of heirs or living kin had been found, and the weather-beaten, two-room house and double lot was auctioned off by the sheriff on Tuesday morning. Nobody particularly wanted the place and money was tight, and after the banker bid it up to forty dollars, Dolittle surprised everybody, including himself, he said later, by bidding forty-two fifty and winning the raffle.

The undertaker complained he was getting shorted, so the spectators contributed, including two bits from Jeff who felt he owed Mr. Dobbs something for digging part of the cellar. So the undertaker got forty-five thirty to defray the expense of burying Turkey Dobbs in a plain wooden coffin Hud said couldn'ta been worth more'n seven-fifty, handles and all.

After the others departed, Jeff helped Dolittle appraise his impulsive purchase. The first thing they noticed inside was the calendars on the walls, dating back to 1907. The furniture wasn't worth keeping—a saggy iron bed, battered armchair, homemade table and bench, a small heating stove, an old kitchen range, propped up by bricks, a coal-oil lamp, a few pots and pans and a dog-eared Bible. There were three orange crates full of new potatoes, bunches of onions hanging all over the kitchen, and a small wooden keg half full of salted-down catfish. Otherwise there was only salt, pepper, lard, flour, cornmeal, coffee, baking powder and molasses. Dolittle said he guessed Turkey had been living off his garden and fish—and doing all right by golly. The big well-tended garden had tomatoes, black-eyed peas, corn, okra, lima beans, peppers and sweet potatoes. Dolittle said hell, the garden alone was worth ten dollars—and don't forget that keg of salted catfish. A priceless rarity.

They picked a couple of big ripe tomatoes and went inside where the salt was and examined the calendars some more.

Except for the current one, each of them had all but four months torn off, and certain dates were marked with penciled X's. February third, April twelfth, July ninth and December fifth. The mystery was solved when they found one with names by the X's and deduced they were birthdays. "Mother" was February, "Me" was April, "Ellen" was July and "Paw" was December.

"Feature that!" Dolittle said. "That poor ol' loner remem-

147

berin' his parents' birthdays when they've probably been dead for ages. I wonder who Ellen was?"

"Maybe his sis," Jeff said. "Lissen, what I don't git is how come *you* want this place."

Dolittle started to shrug, then gave Jeff a broad conspiratorial wink. "All old hermits hide their money—Turkey only had chicken feed on him when he died, so there may be a fortune hid around here. Unless he just happened to be broke, which occurs even in the best of families." He grinned at Jeff. "The real truth is, I only bid because I hated to let Bradman get it too cheap, an' thought he'd go higher. But I'm not blue. Since Paw is a carpenter, we can spruce her up an' maybe I'll have the last laugh yet. Sell it for a nice profit someday."

Jeff liked the buried-fortune idea better—it seemed reasonable to a guy who kept his money in a fruit jar under his mattress and used to hide it in the cob pile.

Dolittle picked up the old leather-bound Bible from the bedside apple box. "Turkey never struck me as bein' religious," he said, holding out the Bible. "Here, Jeff, this will make a good keepsake, a remembrance of the time you found a dead man fishin' in your favorite hole."

Jeff didn't much want any Bible that belonged to a ghost, but he didn't want to offend Dolittle by refusing, and it occurred to him that Flew-the-Coop liked to read and the Bible might be a sort of comfort to him. . . .

So he smuggled it down the creek to his partner, who didn't act awful thrilled but accepted it, saying: "I have read some of the New Testament, but I never got past the begats in this ol' feller—who knows, it might cure my wickedness." Grinning like that was highly improbable, he thanked Jeff for the beefsteak, tobacco, etc., and said he sure would like some ripe tomatoes.

On his way to town with a large carp and two medium cats, Jeff fretted about that request. His mother knew all the McGraw tomatoes by their first names and was canning the ones they didn't eat sliced. So he turned the tomato problem over to Vern, whose mother still didn't know her husband was camped out down there. For some reason Mr. Strode didn't want her to know. Vern said it worried him to carry all the fish money around all the time, but he didn't know of a safe place to hide it. That reminded Jeff of what Dolittle said about possible buried treasure, and he told Vern.

That night somebody ransacked Turkey's house, pulling all the calendars off the wall, ripping up the old mattress, even dumping out the taters. Dolittle didn't say who he suspected, but most people figured well, hell, who lived right next door and had a shady reputation?

Jeff wasn't so ready to find Chink guilty, nor did he suspect Vern. The only other person he'd mentioned possible hidden money to was Hud, who might have told Von or Lex, and Jeff had them pegged as the sort to pull a stunt like that. He figured it had to be more than one guy, since few guys would mess around a haunted house *alone*. The more he thought of it the less he blamed the culprits and the more he envied them—that must have been a pretty exciting adventure, hunting money which, in a way, didn't really belong to anybody.

What confused the issue was the way Chink didn't bother to claim he was innocent. When asked about it he just grinned slyly, like he'd found a fortune next door but wasn't fool enough to admit it. Jeff asked Hud if he thought Chink did it, and Hud just shrugged. So he said casually, "If it 'ud been me I'da looked under the linoleum." Hud gave him a surprised look and started to say something, like maybe, "What linoleum?" but then he clammed up. So Jeff could only suspect he knew there wasn't any linoleum in Turkey's house.

The ransacking of Dolittle's property became another local mystery, like who poisoned the dogs. And who would win the fish-guessing contest when the watertank was drained.

13

It was Vern's idea to use his cob cart, the only idea they had at the time. He wheeled it over to the elevator in broad daylight, as usual, only he left it there. Which might have aroused someone's curiosity—if they were the suspicious type like Alamo's mother. She had started bringing a chair out on the sidewalk at sundown like a chaperone, causing Jeff to go kissless two dusks in a row. But it gave him an alibi for not showing up this night.

After sundown he eased over to the elevator with his toy railroad lantern and pushed the cart down to the northeast corner of town, where Vern waited with a washtub, and some garden stuff for his dad in a gunnysack. When they got to the pasture Jeff waited while Vern backtracked in the deepening dusk to make sure nobody was tailing them. He was barefooted, but Jeff had on tennis shoes and was durn glad of it, because of stickers and sharp rocks—and the possibility of snakes. Boy, don't overlook snakes!

It gave him a start when Vern materialized silently out of the charcoal gloom like an apparition, to report nobody was tailing them. They headed for the creek, and because it was on his mind, Jeff told Vern about the scare he'd had that afternoon. Walking along the muddy edge of the creek hunting frogs, he'd come to where the bank overhung the water and turned back, following his footprints, and discovered that while coming downstream he'd stepped within a foot of a water moccasin in the process of shedding its skin

—a time when snakes were blind and ornerier than usual. He still shivered at the memory. "It's a wonder he didn't slam them ol' fangs into my leg," he said. "Pure D luck, boy."

"Glad you told me now 'steada waitin' 'til tomorrow," Vern said sarcastically. "Light that dang lantern, man."

"Gladly to do so," Jeff said. In the past he'd found snake-skins, and plenty of live snakes in the pasture.

Vern said, "Lead the way. I'm new around here."

The closer they got to the creek the better their chances of encountering a cranky pit viper hunting its supper, and the little lantern didn't furnish much light. Vern's dad had killed three copperheads along the bluff so far. Deadly as rattlers, they came out after dark, to hunt, mainly frogs. This nocturnal mission was about as scary as Jeff had feared it would be, so far.

Vern told him a story. About a soldier in the cavalry in the old days, who was picking up sticks at twilight for a fire when a diamondback rattler bit him three times in the face. The Army doc said it was hopeless, but gave him a quart of whiskey to ease the pain. The soldier gulped down the whole quart in no time at all—and danged if he didn't recover from the bites.

Jeff found that hard to believe but didn't say so.

"The moral is," Vern said, "next time we come down here at night we bring along two quarts of likker."

"One will do," Jeff said. "I ain't comin' next time."

Jeff hoped Flew-the-Coop would be there, but he'd said he wouldn't and he wasn't. Couldn't blame him. He wasn't needed, no use taking chances. The fish had already been weighed on Jeff's scales and only needed transportation.

The return trip was worse, slower because they had to concentrate more on the cart than where they stepped, trying to keep all the water from sloshing out of the tub. Cheating was too durn much work, and he worried about it taking so long. His mother might be awake and wondering about him, getting upset.

Before they reached the edge of town he had to douse the lantern, and he still had snakes in his britches, believing that copperheads liked to lie in the dusty streets at night because the dirt retained warmth. He stepped on something squashy and jumped about three feet in the air, but then he smelled what it was and almost wished it *had* been a nice clean snake, instead of a damn cow pie. "Cut my foot on a German cactus," he muttered. "Lissen, if we meet somebody, whatta we tell 'em?"

"Dunno," Vern said. "How 'bout good night?"

Jeff chuckled nervously, wishing he had owl eyes, and they didn't meet anybody, naturally. Only crooks and snakes and tomcats and spooks prowled at night, unless you wanted to throw in tarantulas, skunks, mad dogs and bloodthirsty bats. He didn't step on anything else, but it was a big relief when they finally reached Main Street, which was silent and empty. Vern stopped by the elevator.

"Wisht I knew where your dad an' his big flashlight are at right now," he said. The northbound local had left its string of cars so they blocked the view of the watertank and depot, and Vern suggested that somebody oughta ease ahead and whistle if the coast was clear. Jeff volunteered, and had almost reached the nearest boxcar when they both heard a muffled laugh over by the watertank. Vern joined him and they climbed on top of the boxcar in time to see indistinguishable dark figures going down the embankment beyond the main-line tracks, and to hear someone say: "Watch out with that ladder, dammit!" A little later they heard laughter on up by the Yancy barn.

"Von an' Lex," Jeff said, yawning, "an' possibly their cousin that lives out on the river—I saw his truck in their yard today. Wonder what they been up to?"

"Search me," Vern said. "Man, look how close we are to the top of the tank up here. That was polite of the train fellers to put this boxcar here 'stead of a flatcar. Anyone could lob fish in there from here."

152

"I'd probably overthrow it," Jeff said, yawning, and Vern said, "Hey, it must be after ten. You best scat for home. I can hannel it from here on easy as pie."

Jeff didn't need any urging, being tired and sleepy and worried that his dad might be out looking for him, his mother waiting up. He envied Vern, who could stay out late as he pleased and not have to explain how come.

All the way up the street he invented alibis and discarded them, and quit trying when he saw the house all dark. But she might be awake—she hadn't been sleeping well lately—so he sneaked around the house, hoping Ranger wouldn't bark at him, hoping Mutt was asleep. Ranger didn't and Mutt was, but the screen door was hooked. Mutt's bright idea, most likely. Jeff slid his knife blade through the crack, pried the hook loose and eased inside like a thief in the night.

Undressed, he pulled back the sheet, and was about to crawl in when he suddenly realized he could see what he was doing. His mother was in the kitchen with a lamp, peering through the screen door at him.

"What are you doing?" she asked, and he said, "Gittin' back in bed. I hadda go to the toilet." Which wasn't a lie since he didn't say when he'd had to go to the toilet. His statement covered a lot of territory.

He could see her in there setting the lamp down, getting aspirin tablets, a dipper of water, swallowing, picking up the lamp and going into the dining room, where Jody said sleepily, "Mama, I need to nummer one." She said: "I warned you about drinking so much iced tea—go do it off the front porch." He said: "It's dark out there, an' I had a bad dream." She said: "Bad dreams are the only kind I have anymore. Come on, I'll protect you from the boogers, fraidy cat." Jody said: "Well, I bet you wasn't so brave at my age neither. I dreamed a whole bunch of cows was chasin' me, with horns six feet long—can I git in bed with you, Mama?" And she said in a peculiar tone of voice: "No,

153

Jody, you have to start being a big boy, and I have to learn . . . try to . . ." She took time to blow her nose. "Never mind," she said, sounding cranky. "Come *on,* I'd like to get *some* sleep tonight."

I know that cow dream well, Jeff thought, drowsily.

When he went to the hardware store the next morning to risk some hard-earned cash on the fish lottery he saw all three Yancy brothers coming out. Lex and Von went on toward Main Street, but Hud stayed and said, "Wotta you fixin' to do this hot mornin', Juh-ferson?" Jeff grinned and shrugged. "Dunno, I never plan that far ahead, Huddleson. Wot'r *your* plans?"

"Avoid work, stay outa trouble, maybe sweat a little," Hud said. "You enter the guessin' contest yet?"

"Naw," Jeff said. "Too chancy. Heck, I never won anything in my life. Did you sign up?"

Hud nodded. "Don't expect to win, just doin' my patriotic duty to the baseball team. You still on it?"

Jeff sighed. "Dad won't let me quit. Say, you make me feel ashamed. Guess I oughta go in there an' contribute my fair share, you reckon?"

"Good for your soul," Hud told him. "I feel so proud I wouldn't mind goin' fishin' down at the dam awhile."

"You're talkin' my lingo," Jeff said. "Hold the fort."

He went in the store and told Mayor Riley he felt lucky and would like to see the contest cards for, oh . . . well, lessee, carp, maybe. And what comes after C . . . the *drum* card. Blow in twenty cents in a good cause.

Mr. Riley gave him that little curly grin. "Jefferson, we never got around to making up cards. In fact, we changed the rules a bit." He explained why. If only *one* person could guess a particular weight, that limited the take considerably. But if all guesses were secret, maybe a dozen people would pick the same weight for a particular fish, adding a dollar-ten to that category, you see. That was an exaggeration, of course, but there were bound to be a few duplications—already had been, matter of fact. So if Jeff would state his guesses he'd write them in the secret ledger and give him a receipt.

"Well," Jeff said, "what if three or four people do guess a winner? They hafta divide it up among 'em?"

Mr. Riley's smile didn't falter, but managed to express a certain ruefulness. "Each would be paid whatever a single winner would get—that's the chance *we* take. It's an honest game and the house pays off. But we think the odds are on our side."

Much relieved, Jeff picked his sure winners in the carp and drum divisions, then to ease his conscience he invested a dime on the bass, guessing five pounds even. On his way out he marveled at how casual he was about money anymore. Sure nice to have a regular supply, but the funny thing was, now that he could afford a rifle he just wasn't in any hurry about it. Besides, he might decide to buy that secondhand Winchester pump instead of the bolt-action single, for seven bucks more.

"If we had some hossgrappers," Hud said, "we might hafta eat bass for supper. You got fishin' line with you?"

Jeff had to laugh—grasshoppers. That durn Hud. "Sure do," he said. "I'd be lonesome without it. Hey, I hear they been catchin' good perch on doughballs made outa bakery bread." "They" was Vern. "Good day to try it."

So he led the way to Ballew's grocery. Mr. Ballew was a big jowly partly baldheaded man and quite a kidder. "What'll it be, gentlemen?" he asked affably, and Jeff said, oh, he just needed some bakery bread for perch bait. "How many slices you figure you'll need?" Mr. Ballew inquired. Banter from grown-ups always confused Jeff, and he said he didn't know. "Well," Mr. Ballew said, "how many fish you planning to feed?" And Hud said, "We'll take a whole loaf, an' bring back what we don't use." Jeff sighed inwardly and thought: Now why the heck didn't *I* say that?

As long as he was charging a loaf of bread, he decided

155

to get some baloney to go with it. By the end of the month his mother probably wouldn't remember whether she ordered it or not. "Oh, yeah," he said. "Dad needs a plug of Day's Work." Maybe that would cause her to think his dad bought the bread and baloney. If not—well, it was a long time until the end of the month. Worry about it later.

Outside, Hud said, "I realize the bread an' tobacco's for fish bait, but what's the bull-only for, I hope?" Jeff grinned and said it was to help use up the extra bread, and Hud nodded. "Well, then, that means I hafta swipe a couple onions between here an' the crick. A sanwidge without onion would insult my intrills." And he zigzagged back and forth across the street until he found a garden where the onions hadn't all been pulled yet. Since they belonged to one of his cow customers, he hollered: "Miz Keefer, it's me, Hud! I like to borry a couple onions from your garden." And she hollered back: "Help yourself, Hud."

So he got three big ones, and was surprised to discover two big ripe tomatoes inside his shirt as they ambled on down the street. "Now how'd they git there?" he asked Jeff, who didn't know, but was glad they had.

The fishing was good, tightlining with whippy willow poles, once they learned how small to make the breadballs, and the bread was a rare treat for Hud, whose father thought it a sin to buy bread. All in all, it was one of the best mornings of the summer.

They managed to finish the baloney, tomatoes, onions and bread in time to go home for lunch, each with a string of summer-fat perch. The difference was, Hud would have to clean his and Jeff wouldn't.

His mother was making pickles when he got home, and she wiped her moist face with her apron, nodded resignedly at the fish, and asked, "You see Jody anywhere?"

"Nope," he replied. She always asked that and he usually said nope. "What's for lunch?" he inquired, and she said,

"Whatever you can find." He always asked that, and she usually gave him that same answer.

"Listen, Izaak Walton, I'm in no mood to clean perch," the overheated canning woman said. "You either clean them yourself, or give them to some fish-hungry family."

"You know me," he said. "I'll take Granny Hanks a few, an' the rest to Mrs. Riley. You reckon?"

"I reckon," she said. "And *give*, don't *sell*."

Did she think he was money crazy, like Mutton? Come to think of it, was he getting to be that way? Could he ever stand to be broke again? Wealth spoiled a guy. . . .

He took six perch off the stringer and put them in a pan of water for Granny, then carried the rest of them next door and asked Mrs. Riley if she wanted them. Oh, my, yes, she said. They hadn't had perch in ages. However, would he be willing to clean them? For a reasonable recompense, naturally? Say a dime, perhaps?

Hiring out wasn't *selling*, so he agreed.

"Caroline will help," Mrs. Riley said, and he almost backed out of the deal, only he couldn't. He said he didn't need any help, just a pan to put 'em in, but when Caroline brought the pan out to the pump she had a paring knife.

"Show me how to do it," she said, but not bossily. Practically a request. And she looked different, somehow. He hadn't really noticed her up close for months, just across the fence. "I like to learn to do things," she said almost shyly. "I'd even like to learn to fish."

Well, if she could be polite, he could be civil. "It's easy," he said. "Say, you look sorta different."

She smiled and sorta blushed. "I'm letting my hair grow longer. I got tired of bobbed hair. Then another thing, I've gained six pounds this summer, since I had my tonsils out."

He said: "I didn't know you had your tonsils out!"

"Right after school ended," she said. "The doctor in Blackthorn said that's all was wrong with my health."

157

"Oh," Jeff said. "Well, here's how you scale perch. Start back at the tail. They scale easier after they stiffen up. Watch out for the fins."

He finished his and started to gut it, and suddenly felt embarrassed—he couldn't explain *that* to her, where you inserted the knife. Even if he called it the belly button. "Tell you what," he said. "You scale an' I'll gut, an' it won't take any time at all." She nodded agreeably, and he looked at her, puzzled. Having her tonsils out changed her personality this much? Or was it just that he'd never really noticed her before? "Since you're doin' half the work, you git half the pay," he said.

"I couldn't do that," she said. "Maybe . . . sometime . . . if we happen to be at the drugstore at the same time, if you wanted to . . ."

No matter what anybody said, Jeff had a quick mind. He looked at her down-turned blushing face and remembered his own wallflower days. Shoot, a little thing like that, just buying her a Coke or something, it wouldn't hurt him and it might do wonders for her. . . .

"It's a deal," he said.

She smiled, and he realized her eyes were blue. He'd never noticed that before. "But maybe Alma wouldn't like it," she said.

"Why not? It ain't her money," he said.

Caroline sighed. "She will be thirteen before I'm even eleven . . . in October." She glanced at him shyly. "Did you happen to notice I don't breathe with my mouth open like before I had my tonsils out?"

That was one of the differences about her. Boy, at the rate she was improving, Kerosene might surprise a person in a couple more years. . . .

When he took the fish to Granny Hanks she was frying chicken and invited him to eat with her. "Trouble with cooking for just myself," she said, "though I can't eat but part of a fryer, I still have to kill the whole chicken. I don't even like the drumsticks, or the gizzard." She peered at him over her grease-spattered spectacles.

It happened that drumsticks and gizzards were the parts Jeff, Jody and the real Matty boy fought over, so he accepted her invitation. She was a gabby person and nearly talked his leg off, but he didn't pay too much attention.

"When do your folks expect little Jeffy's daddy to come for him?" she asked, but he was thinking about how changed Kerosene was, and didn't get the full gist of the question. "Jeffy" confused it.

"I dunno for sure," he said. "Soon now, I guess."

"Too bad," she said. "Grab that other drumstick." He got the full gist of that, all right.

Later, loping along Bradman's hedge on his way downtown, he saw his dad going into the hardware store, and noticed the Ballews by the back door of the grocery, looking across the street, and people at the front corner looking back across the street. Jake hollered: "Go back, Jeff! Mad dog! Go back—or else come over here!"

"Where?" Jeff asked, cutting across the street.

"Under that car yonder," Jake said. "Your dad went in the hardware to git a gun to kill it with."

He saw the dog under the old Chevy, and his dad coming out of the hardware store loading a double-barreled shotgun. "I don't reckanize that dog," Jeff said.

"A stray from the country, I reckon," Dock said, and they watched Jeff's dad walk down the middle of the street until he was even with the Chevy, then kneel down and aim the shotgun at the dog cringing under there. "Sure was slobberin'," Dock said, and Jake said, "More like droolin'. It really cleared people offa the street in a hurry."

Jeff's dad was holding the shotgun pointed at the sky, looking at the dog. Presently he said, "Come on out, old boy. Let's have a look at you." He said it twice, and durned if that mad dog didn't come crawling out from under the auto, whimpering and cringing. Jeff had never seen a mad dog this close before except in dreams. "Come on, ol' feller," his dad said. "Keep acomin', boy."

Dock gave a snort. "He gonna beat it to death?"

Jeff's dad just knelt there with the shotgun aimed at the sky as the dog kept inching closer on his belly, mouth open and slobber dripping out, and Jeff had cold chills, feeling scared for his dad.

"Whatta yuh waitin' on, Slim?" Chink Britton hollered from the corner, but Jeff's crazy dad just leaned down closer to the mad dog! It didn't hafta bite you; if you just got slobber on your skin, that's all it took sometimes.

"Good gravy!" Dock said, and Jake said, "Cheese'n rice!" Jeff couldn't say anything—his dad was patting it on the head! Unloading the shotgun! Turning his back to that mad dog! "Got all muddy!" Jake murmured.

"Take the gun back, Jeff," his dad said. "False alarm."

"You mean it ain't mad?" he asked, and his dad said, "Well, he's plenty *sore*. Got a rusty fishhook in his mouth. Looks like he durn near swallowed it, poor guy."

"There's the line wrapped around his neck," Jeff said.

"It's string, not fishline," his dad said, bending over the whimpering dog as people approached cautiously. What's up? someone asked, and Jeff's dad said, "This old feller ate something he wishes he hadn't. He's got a fishhook just north of his tonsils." He had cut the string from around the distressed dog's neck. "Well, looky here. There's a note rolled around this string. Let's see what she says."

It said, "To whoever reads this: moving to California and can't take him with us. His name is Bill, a good watchdog, gentle with kids. Hope someone here in Tahlequah will give him a home. The Ed Johnson Family."

Jeff's dad stared around at the spectators. "Tahlequah! Hell, that's around two hundred miles." He bent over to pat the dog's head. "Sonofagun! I've heard of dogs finding their way back home from a long ways off, but never one trying to follow somebody to California before."

"Whatta you gonna do with 'im, Slim?" Chink inquired.

"Same thing I'd do if it was you," Jeff's dad said. "Take him to Doc Schuman and get that hook removed."

That got a laugh, and Jeff's dad started toward the alley leading down behind the drugstore, saying: "C'mon, Bill, let's go fix you up so you can resume your journey." And the ex-mad dog got up off his belly and followed obediently, as if he understood. Mr. Riley, who was standing in front of the hardware store, said, "That's what I admire about Gabe McGraw—anyone else woulda shot first and asked questions later."

Jeff nodded with family pride, thinking how sad it would have been if Mr. Marheddon or Mr. Ballew or somebody had shot poor Bill and discovered the mistake later.

Jake was hanging around. "Say, lissen," he said. "Now the excitement's over. Sumpin' I wanta say."

"Spit 'er out," Jeff told him, and Jake said, "Well, a deal's a deal. You skinned me on that glove swap, but I ain't a guy to crawfish. So the deal stands, see."

"Dadburn," Jeff sighed. "I sure miss my old mitten."

"It's old, all right, but it's my mitten," Jake said.

Jeff shrugged and went on his way, smiling to himself. As he rounded the corner he almost collided with Alamo, roller-skating, and she had to grab him to keep from doing a preacher seat on the sidewalk. She grinned at him. "Why don't you watch where I'm goin'?" she said, and kept hold of his arm. "I heard there was a mad dog."

"He had reason to be mad," Jeff said. "When last seen it was goin' down the alley towards your place." She looked so alarmed that he went ahead and told her about it, and she seemed rather disappointed. He'd felt that way himself; being present at the execution of a mad dog would have been a major event in his young life, but he was glad his dad had taken time to make sure.

"Start walkin'," Alamo said, hanging onto his arm, and let him pull her along, although the sidewalk sloped enough

161

so part of the time she used him for a brake. There was something possessive about the way she clung to his arm that he sorta liked but didn't like.

"Where'd you git the skates?" he asked. She said Clarence Olive loaned them to her.

"He wants to sell 'em an' I'm tryin' them out. He wants two dollars for them."

"Dollar apiece," Jeff remarked. "Lissen, I'm spose to find Jody an' send 'im home to lunch."

"He ate with us," she said. "You got any gum?"

He gave her a stick of gum and asked, "Hamburgers?"

"Yeah," she sighed. "Look, go you know where an' I'll skate on past, then come back."

Well, he had his orders. He wondered if she realized how bossy she was sometimes. She did all the planning. Also all the skating and bicycle riding.

She came back, walking on the skates between the buildings, and klomped into the back room, grinning. "More than one way to skin a cat," she said. Hugging her was different, on account of her being taller. Not necessarily better, but different. Somehow he just couldn't relax and enjoy kissing in broad daylight. Too easy for someone to catch them at it.

"I had a keen idea," she said. "From now on when Mama comes out of an evening, I'll say I hafta go to the watchamacallit, an' I'll meet you out there by the . . . by the shed. Hunh?"

When he went out the side door, his dad was coming from behind the building next door carrying the dog. He asked what Jeff had been doing in the old barbershop. "Cuttin' through to come see if Doc got the hook out okay," Jeff said, thinking: He almost caught us! "Is he dead?" he asked, because the dog looked dead.

"Doc gave him ether," his dad said. "He'll come around soon." He was carrying the limp dog under his right arm, bloody saliva dripping from its mouth.

Jeff followed him to the street. "What you gonna do with

'im?" he asked, and his dad said, "Take him over to the shack and look after him while he recuperates. You go buy a half pound of hamburger meat and a can of Carnation. Old Bill won't feel up to doing much chewing for a while."

Jeff hated to go in there and face Mr. Dexter with the taste of Alma's kisses still on his lips. It always seemed to him that grown-ups could sorta read your mind, or see guilt in your eyes, or something. But all Mr. Dexter said was: "A whole half pound of ground beef? You must be havin' company for supper." He was quite a kidder, like most men, but if he knew Jeff had been kissing his daughter he wouldn't feel so durn comical.

At the tracks they met Vern coming from the elevator with his cart full of corncobs, and he looked kind of surprised to see the baseball manager carrying what appeared to be a dead dog. "Strychnine?" he asked.

"Ether," the manager replied. "How's the arm, Vern?"

"Fine," Vern said, giving Jeff a wink. "I was tossin' a few yesterday evenin' an' they went right in there." He eyed Bill curiously. "Takin' it somewheres to bury it?"

"Well, no, I'll just keep him in the storeroom a few days," Jeff's dad said, starting on. So Jeff stayed behind to explain about Bill, and confirm something. Yep, Vern said, tossing the fish in the watertank had been a breeze. Simple as falling off a log. Yep, he'd signed up in the contest. "Say, if you're headed down yonder, tell ol' what's-his-name I said howdy."

"I'll do that," Jeff said. And he did, a while later, and old what's-his-name nodded absently, squinting, and asked: "Did you know my hide's worth thirty-five dollars?"

"Sure," Jeff said. "Why?"

Dallas Strode grinned and scratched his bristly cheek. "Pardner, you sorta restore a man's faith in the human race."

When Jeff told him about the mad-dog scare, Flew-the-Coop told him enough mad-dog stories to give him nightmares for two weeks, if he strung them out a little. His business associate threw in the case of a house cat that went

163

mad and bit a whole family eating supper. He said cats were worse than dogs because they moved faster. He said any animal could get hydrophobia, possibly including turkeys and chickens, since bats were well known to get rabies.

"I wonder if snakes can?" Jeff asked.

The fugitive ruled out rabid snakes, but that reminded him of snakebite stories, including one about a woman in Kansas who got bit by a rattler on washday morning, away out on the lonesome prairie, with her husband gone, the nearest neighbor miles away, and three or four little kids to worry about. So she cooked up a big bunch of food and went ahead with the washing and chopped wood to last a few days, then took a bath and put on her best dress and says to the oldest kid: "I am very tired and I am going to bed and I don't want you to disturb me until Daddy comes home." So she went to bed and slept a few hours and woke up, instead of dying like she'd expected to, because all that hard work and cooking and fretting about her family had caused her system to throw off the poison some way. Dallas said she probably just sweat it out of her.

Jeff said he'd always heard if you put a cud of chewing tobacco on a snakebite it would draw out the venom, and Vern's dad said he once heard of a man that got bit by a rattler, what he did was boil some tobacco and drink the juice like tea, and he got quick relief at both ends, you might say, and survived.

"That reminds me," he said. "Smoke your pipe yet?"

"Nope," Jeff said. "Haven't hardly had the time."

"Well," his partner said with a grin, "I expect you'll find the time eventually, but there's no hurry."

He went back by way of the shack to see about the dog, and Dolittle was there in his Sunday clothes talking to Jeff's dad. He'd been in Blackthorn looking at automobiles, but hadn't found one he wanted to buy.

"Know something?" he said. "It ain't easy to make up your mind when you get right down to a thing like that."

Jeff's dad grinned. "That's why I never bought a car. Never could decide which brand I wanted. What worries me is whether Bradman's got any money left in the bank. That musta been the biggest withdrawal he's had in a long time."

Jeff went in the storeroom, and old Bill wagged his tail in a weak, friendly fashion. You could see he didn't feel so hot. Jeff wondered how long it took him to come from Tahlequah. No use asking Bill, though. He probably hadn't kept track of the days. . . .

Dusk found him lurking in the ex-barbershop, and Mrs. Dexter keeping her daughter company. Presently Alamo said, "I need to go to the watchamacallit, but I'm scared of the ghosts, Mama—you want to go along an' protect me?"

"Oh, don't be silly," her mother said. "Ghosts don't come out until ten o'clock, central standard time."

Admiring his sweetheart's guile, Jeff headed for her backhouse, to wait by the adjacent shed. She came hurrying out of the butcher shop and said, "Are you out here?"

Before he could answer, her dad said from inside the toilet: "That's nobody's dang business but mine!"

Jeff didn't wait to see what else they said. He lit out. Her keen idea had a flaw in it.

That night he dreamed about mad turkeys and chickens, even worse than mad dogs except that in the dream he could jump twenty feet in the air and hover up there indefinitely, so it wasn't too scary.

14

There were four passenger trains a day through Cottonwood and the newlyweds came in on the mid-morning southbound. Because of wanting to make a good impression on the new aunt, they had to dress up and wear shoes, then sit and wait in the sweltering August morning. It was a dreaded relief when Jeff's dad came up the street with the company. Jeff was on the front porch with Mutt and Jody, and his first impression of the bride was sort of unnerving—she was taller than Uncle Tobe, and almost as tall as his dad. But then she was wearing high heels.

"Hello there, Mutt and Jeff," Uncle Tobe said as they turned in at the gate. "Meet your new aunt Gus—Augusta for short. Named after the hottest month of the year." He grinned at her and she made a playful slap at him.

Mutt said, "Please to meetcha, ma'am," and Jeff said, *huhm num*, being sort of tongue-tied. She kind of took his brains away, being pretty much of a flapper in appearance, wearing a real short dress, a little straw hat tilted over to one side, rouge, lipstick, earrings, and beads around her neck. Her hair was bobbed short, and she was easily the most glamorous-looking female Jeff had ever met. It was generally agreed later that she put on airs and was a hoity-toity type.

"Howdy, old Jody boy," Uncle Tobe said. "This is your new mama, how do you like her?"

Jody had been grinning shyly, but he quit and looked uneasy. "I still like the old one," he muttered.

Uncle Tobe looked up at his bride. "That's the feller I been tellin' you about, Gus. Whatta you think of him?"

"I think he doesn't look much like you," she replied.

Jody said, "I look like Albert Gronstetter. For a long time Miss Burns couldn't tell us apart at first."

"Miss Burns teaches first and second grades," Jeff's dad explained, and Uncle Tobe said, "What does Albert Gronstetter do?" It wasn't really funny, but they all laughed like it was.

After the sisters-in-law had been introduced they all sat around in the parlor suffering from heat and social strain, trying to carry on a polite, wary conversation. Jeff's dad passed out fans to the women and flyswatters to Jeff and Jody, saying, "Jody is the fly-killing champ around here." Uncle Tobe said, "He gets that from me." That was about the general level of the conversation. How was the train ride? Well, about what you'd expect in hot weather, stifling with the window down, gritty with it up. Yes, it was extremely hot weather.

Jeff's dad said, "Maybe a little music could cool us off." He put a record on the Edison and cranked it up, Paul Whiteman's orchestra playing "Who Stole My Heart Away?" "I'll dedicate this to the bride and groom," he said, and they all sat there grinning, smiling, listening, and Uncle Tobe asked, "When you gonna get electricity, Gabe?" His brother shrugged. "When it gets this hot in January."

Jody swatted flies everywhere except within five feet of his stepmother, giving her uneasy looks now and then. Jeff was uncomfortable in all departments, yearning to be out of his Sunday duds and in his overalls. And shoeless. Why'd they pick the hottest dang day of the year?

After an eternity, Jeff's mother said well, she'd better start dinner. Aunt Gus asked in a tired, polite way if she could help, and the hostess said, oh no, thank you, it's unbearably hot in the kitchen and you're tired from your trip; besides all I have to do is fry the chicken and make the gravy. Uncle Tobe said: "Now doggonit, Sis, you didn't need to go to all this bother. A cold lunch woulda been fine." Jeff wished he'd shut up. Fried chicken was going to be the only good thing about all this social misery. His dad said it for him: "Can it, kid brother, I've got my mouth all set for fried chicken." Then after the cook went out to the kitchen he said how about some more music, and played one of his favorite records, "Oh, Dem Golden Slippers." He also liked "Golden Stairs to Glory," "Leather Britches" and "Over the Waves."

Jeff got so fidgety he eased out onto the porch where there was a slight breeze and took off his bow tie. Presently Jody came out and said, "How long they gonna stay?"

"Overnight, I guess," Jeff said. "How you like her?"

"Well, hosh durnit"—Jody sighed—"I don't even know 'er —but I'll admit one thing, she sure is tall."

Jeff was dreading dinner, but that worked out great. His mother caught him when he went to drink from the dipper. "Son, there's only room for six at the table without crowding. Would you mind eating in the kitchen?"

He managed to conceal his joy and relief. "Naw, I don't mind," he said. "Whatta you think of our new relative?"

She looked through the door to make sure nobody was coming. "I think she's the cat's pajamas," she said.

He really enjoyed eating by himself, and they were still sitting around the table talking when he skinned out the back way. He was glad to escape the social formalities. He felt so good he let Ranger off his chain and took him along, making him happy, too.

Dreading the evening festivities, he stretched the afternoon, and came home around five-thirty, hoping supper would be another feast. But Mutt was the only one in evidence, and there was something wrong with him because he didn't say a word about Jeff taking an unmuzzled Ranger

168

with him—although he remembered later to collect the dime rent. "Where is ever'body?" Jeff inquired.

"Halfway to Kansas by now," Mutt said.

"That's what I call a fast visit," Jeff said, surprised and relieved. "Why isn't Mama fixin' supper?"

"Too busy cryin' her head off," Mutt said.

Jeff gaped at him. "Why?" he asked. "What happened?"

"Well, wot the hell you *think* happened?" Mutt said in an angry, disgusted tone. "They took Jody with 'em."

Jeff blinked at him. "Oh, for a visit, huh?"

Mutt glared at him kind of glassy-eyed. "For good, you chunkhead! Forever, dammit to hell! Are you so dumb you didn't know they only come jist to git him?"

That's how dumb Jeff was. Too dumb to expect anything so awful to happen, so wrong and unjust.

"No tellin' when we'll ever see the little dickens again," Mutt said, sniffling. "Git outta here, dammit!" And he turned so Jeff couldn't see his face, but Jeff couldn't see it anyway. He beat it out to the barn loft, where he did all his private grieving, and did some more. It was almost as if Jody *had* drowned. He'd always taken the little wart for granted, considered him a pest and a nuisance a lot of the time. Now if he could live life over, he would appreciate Jody, take him fishing and stuff like that. But it was too late. Jody was gone forever, to a faraway world named Kansas. . . .

His mother didn't even fix supper that day, but stayed in her bedroom crying for the child she'd mothered from infancy. But his dad didn't come home for supper anyway. He got drunk, and the mayor had Mutt go get Dolittle to take care of the locomotives. It was the beginning of a long sad time for the McGraws. Jeff's mother always fixed supper after that but seldom ate any. She couldn't bear that empty chair at the table, or the silence. The whole town was haunted by the ghost of a jug-eared, unpredictable, grinning little dickens who wasn't dead but somehow seemed to be. There was a void in the world, an absence of laughter, too many tears. Jeff got his all done that hour in the hayloft, but his mother never quite finished, and she didn't have any special time or place for weeping. She could do it any hour of the day, in any room. . . .

All you could do was go on doing the things you usually did, and if you were twelve the sorrow was like a festered splinter that didn't hurt most of the time but could suddenly flare up when you least expected it, and ache like heck.

The day after Jody vanished from the face of the earth, Dewey Little bought a six-cylinder two-door Oldsmobile coach, for eight hundred bucks because the dealer had used it awhile to haul prospective customers around in, but it was still good as new.

The next day he took Jeff and Hud for what started out to be a little spin. Main Street was deserted, and they were loafing by the lumberyard corner when Dolittle came from the south in his almost-new Olds, going home to lunch after doing some work on the Turkey Dobbs mansion. He stopped and grinned at them like a kid with a new coaster wagon.

"You gents care for a little spin?" he asked, and naturally they said heck, yes. Jeff got in the front seat and Hud climbed in the back and said: "How come you ain't snoozin' this time of day, Do-sumpthing?" That was his nickname for the assistant engine watchman.

"Try it sometime with noisy kids next door," Do-sumpthing said. "I've given up sleep 'til school starts."

Then he shifted gears and drove slowly north, and they had the rare privilege of witnessing a bank robbery, although they didn't realize it. They just saw a guy come out of the bank, get in a car and drive east on Main.

"Feller in a hurry," Dolittle remarked, yawning.

They were almost to Main when banker Bradman came out into the street waving his arms. Dolittle stopped, and the banker was too agitated to speak for a minute. Then he said, "The bank's been robbed, call the sheriff!"

"You call him," Dolittle said. "I'll give pursuit."

170

"I think he went west," Mr. Bradman said, and Dolittle said, "Nope, he went east—you guys pile out."

"Heck, no!" Hud said. "We're goin' along, boy!"

"No time to argue," Dolittle said. He swung the auto in a turn around the town pump and headed south, saying, "That sonofagun might try doubling back. Besides, this way we only have one corner to take."

He opened the throttle all the way south and slid his Olds around the corner to go whizzing east, and Jeff wasn't so sure he wanted to go along. Chasing a bank robber struck him as being dangerous. That darn Hud.

Halfway to the railroad tracks they saw the auto turn the corner yonder in a cloud of dust, and Hud bellowed: "Hot diggity! There he goes!"

"No use crowdin' him," Dolittle said. "He leaves tall tracks. I sorta wish we had some bullets." Hud said eagerly: "You got a gun?" Dolittle shook his head. "That's the next thing I was gonna wish for."

Two miles east of town the bank robber turned north on a section-line road, his streamer of dust betraying him, and Dolittle continued to drive just fast enough to stay about two hundred yards behind the getaway car.

"You could run 'im into the ditch," Hud suggested, and Dolittle said, "There's a ditch on my side, too."

They followed the guy north, then west, then north again, and Dolittle seemed puzzled. "He's headed for the river if he doesn't turn at the next crossroads—an' the nearest bridge is four miles upstream."

The bandit didn't turn at the next crossroads, and Dolittle sighed. "Either that dude's fixin' to swim the Arkansaw, or he's got a boat. This road don't go nowhere except down to the river-bottom timber."

"One thing to remember," Jeff said nervously, "your average bank robber, he's usually got a gun."

"That possibility had crossed my mind," Dolittle said, and presently he stopped and said: "Pile out an' make it snappy!"

Even Hud didn't argue this time. They got out and Dolittle started on down the road pretty fast.

"C'mon, let's foller 'im!" Hud said, running down the dusty road into the tall timber, and Jeff took off after him, either not wanting to miss the fun or not wanting to be left alone, he couldn't figure out which.

It seemed like a mile, but was more like a quarter, when they went barreling around a bend and saw the bandit's car reared up on a small tree it had tried to climb, and fifty yards beyond that the parked Oldsmobile, and Dolittle chasing a guy carrying a canvas pouch. The bandit hit slick mud on the river bank and went skating all out of control, flailing his arms, and dropped the pouch, and went sliding into the water beside a rowboat, which was pulled up on the sloping bank. He didn't try to get in the boat but yanked it into the slack water, and swam backwards towing it, hidden by it. Dolittle didn't go in after him, but just picked up the pouch, watching the guy get into the current still swimming backwards, using the rowboat for a shield. He didn't need a shield, and it was a little late for a disguise because Jeff had got one clear look at him, and supposed Dolittle had, too. When the bandit had swum and drifted about fifty yards he climbed over the end of the boat and started rowing frantically across the strong current, and soon disappeared behind a narrow brushy island.

"He never even fired a shot," Hud panted.

"Don't sound so damn sad about that," Dolittle said. "Personally, I appreciate it. Nice of him to leave the loot behind, too." He untied the neck of the pouch and looked inside, and got a funny expression on his face; walked over to lean on a tree and scratch his jaw, shook his head and finally said: "Jeff, step over here a minute."

Jeff went, curious, still puffing and panting.

"Can you keep a secret for the rest of your life?"

"Sure," Jeff said. "Well, I dunno," he qualified.

Dolittle sighed. "I'll risk it. I might need a witness bad

172

when we get to town." He opened the canvas sack and let Jeff look inside, and all it seemed to have in it was bundles of newspaper cut like bills, and a couple pounds of washers. No money. He gaped at Dolittle.

Dolittle said quietly, so Hud couldn't hear: "You're my witness, if I ever need one, pal."

"How much you figger it is?" Hud asked, and Dolittle said, "I dunno—hey! I shouldn't of untied this sack! If it checks out ten bucks short, they'll think *I* took it."

"Well, shoot," Hud said, "we just tell 'em we never even untied it, so what? She's just the way we found 'er."

"That's a smart idea, Hud," Dolittle said. "For all *we* know this pouch could be full of horse biscuits." This struck everyone's funnybone and they all laughed kind of hysterically, having a nervous reaction to the extraordinary adventure. Even after they were driving back up out of the river bottom they kept having the giggles and sniggers. Then when they had about regained their sanity, Dolittle started them off again by saying: "It might even be counterfeit horse biscuits."

They didn't meet any other posses on their way to town, probably because Dolittle took the shorter route west instead of retracing their irregular pursuit pattern back around to the east, and every once in a while they were overcome with glee.

When they entered town from the west they could see people milling around the bank corner, and Dolittle said, "Let me do the talkin', gents. I might add a few embellishments—like how we threw rocks at the bandit. Let's see now, how many shots did he fire?"

"Emptied his gun." Hud laughed. "It musta been empty or he'da used it, seems like."

"Well," Dolittle said, "we may never chase another bank robber so we might as well make the most of our golden opportunity."

"Hey, how about I was shootin' at 'im with my slingshot?"

Jeff suggested, and Hud said, "Yeah bo, me too! Maybe we hit 'im was why he dropped the money."

"Or the horse biscuits," Jeff said, and the giddy two of them were giggling some more as Dolittle honked his way through the perturbed populace to park by the bank. The crowd opened a path for them and asked a hundred excited questions, but Dolittle said, "Later, folks." The mayor was in the doorway, keeping out worried depositors and the merely curious, and he looked at his watch and remarked: "Fast trip—I make it twenty-four minutes. What happened to the perpetrator of the crime?"

"Took himself a boat ride," Dolittle said, and they went inside, where Mr. Bradman was talking to Mr. George Rose, who owned most of the bank. Dolittle approached the high marble-topped counter with the pouch hanging by his thigh and said, "He got away, I'm sorry to report."

"Damn!" Mr. Bradman said. "You lost 'im, eh?"

"Headed for the river an' escaped in a boat," Dolittle said. "But he slipped on the muddy bank and dropped something." He plunked the canvas bag on the counter so the washers jingled, and the banker sort of shivered and gaped and mopped his face with a handkerchief.

"Great guns!" mysterious, gray, glint-eyed Mr. Rose exclaimed with a grin. "Bully for you, sir!"

"Yes," Mr. Bradman said in a shaky voice. "My goodness! My goodness! Yes, that's a . . . terrible relief."

"Would you check it an' see if it's all there?" Dolittle said, and the banker nodded and took the bag to his desk before he opened it and stared inside. "Y-yes, it . . . appears to be all here," he said.

"We didn't check the contents," Dolittle said.

Mr. George Rose shook Dolittle's hand. "We're very much obliged to you, Little. I commend your courage and quick unhesitating action. Bradman estimates about two thousand missing, which would be a substantial loss."

"Wasn't only me," Dolittle pointed out. "I had a couple spunky sidekicks along, don't overlook that factor."

Mr. Rose beamed at the boys. Jeff had never seen him up close before—but Old George had never seen *him* up close before, either. Mr. Rose reached over the counter and shook hands with him and Hud, then produced a dollar bill. "A small token of appreciation for your bravery, boys," he said. "Treat yourselves to some ice cream."

They grinned self-consciously, awed by his attention if not his generosity. Mr. Rose turned back and said, "I feel we ought to reward you, too, Little."

Dolittle shook his head. "I only did what any man with a new Oldsmobile woulda done."

Mr. Rose laughed. "Well put, sir, I like your sense of humor. Did you get a look at the man?"

"Not his face," Dolittle said. "I don't believe I'd recognize him if I ever saw him again."

"Bradman thinks it may have been that jailbreaker," Mr. Rose said. "What's his name? Stone? Stearn?"

Dolittle shrugged, and Jeff bit his tongue to keep from saying heck, no, it wasn't Dallas Strode. "*I* got a good look at 'im for a second," he said. "He wore a cap but had dark hair an' was dark-complected." Whereas Flew-the-Coop had yellow hair, anybody ought to remember.

"Funny," Dolittle said. "Ordinarily I'd be tryin' to get some sleep at noon, and I only bought my auto yesterday. But that feller sure picked the right time to do it, otherwise. Ever'body home eatin' dinner."

"I was, when Bradman called me." Mr. Rose nodded. "And he was just about to lock up and go home to eat."

"We better go tell our story to the people, then we can all go eat dinner," Dolittle said.

The eager audience outside was short on men, but long on boys and girls and women, including Alamo, Kerosene, Alamo's mother, Mrs. Riley and Eunice Tifferton. Mutt was present, looking sick with envy, as did Jake and Dock, Lige, Clarence, Lefty, Jelly, Spotty, Windy, Jug and Conrad Coonrod. Word of a bank robbery got around town fast.

Dolittle didn't lie but he let people use their own imaginations. Like saying: "The only artillery we had with us was a couple slingshots." And: "His gun must of been empty by then, or he surely woulda used it, you'd think."

"Why didden you dive in after 'im?" Jake asked, and Dolittle shrugged and said, "Didn't have my bathing suit along." That got a laugh, and then somebody asked if he'd had a good look at the bank robber, and Dolittle said no, but Jeff did. So everybody focused on Jeff, causing him to have a mild case of stagefright.

"Never seen 'im before," he managed to say, "but I'd know 'im if I ever saw 'im again, I expect."

"Me, too," Hud announced, wanting in on the importance.

There were a lot of other curious questions. How close did they actually get to the bandit? *Too damn close*, Dolittle said. Were the guys scared? *No scareder than you woulda been*, Dolittle said with a grin.

"Did you see his pistol?" Dock inquired, and Dolittle said: "If I didn't, I sure imagined I did." Embellishment, that's all. And it would be embellished even more as time went by —especially by Jeff and Hud, who would eventually argue over how many shots were fired, who shot the most rocks at the bandit, etc.

When the avid crowd began to run out of questions, Hud said, "Less go spend our *re*ward money. I need a root beer to calm my nerves after realizin' how clost I come to gittin' my fool self kilt." Alamo followed them to the drugstore and, being a female, made them go over the whole thing again. But this time it suddenly occurred to Hud that the bank robber looked kinda like Chink.

"Couldn't be him," Alamo said. "He went on the gasoline truck with your brothers and Mr. Kelso."

"Didn't look like Chink to *me*," Jeff said.

"Your dad an' Slick, the barber, took the mayor's Model Tin," Alamo said. "Papa an' the blacksmith an' Mr. Hallet went with the elevator man in his grain truck, an' another bunch went in Major Conklin's 1921 Case tourin' car. Gosh, I never saw so many guns in my whole life."

Summing it up in his mind afterwards, Jeff decided it was the second most exciting day of his life so far, but Turkey Dobbs was still first. For one thing, he had to split the importance of the bank-robber deal with two other guys, and Dolittle was the real star of the drama because it was his Oldsmobile and his decision to chase the bandit. No matter how you looked at it, Jeff and Hud were just passengers.

15

They finally got around to draining the watertank on the next to last Sunday before school started. On Sundays the locals were tied up and fewer freight trains stopped for water. It took all day because they drained by letting the northbound passenger and freight trains fill their tenders and lower the water level. So it began around seven A.M., with the last freight due in at five P.M., after which Jeff's dad would open the four-inch drain—the bung, he called it—and let the rest of the water run out. And the fish, of course.

After Sunday school Jeff decided to go on down the creek instead of waiting until after noon, because the noodler craved hamburgers for his Sunday dinner. He headed for Arlene's Café feeling worried. Maybe the transplanted fish had died. Maybe cheating on the Sabbath was more sinful than doing it weekdays, like storekeepers, etc.

Passing Bradman's place, he wondered how the banker was—he'd had a sort of nervous breakdown after the robbery, and Mr. Rose had brought in a man named Purdy to run the bank. The sheriff hadn't solved the robbery yet, and Dolittle confided he probably wasn't trying very hard, since the bank had got its washers back.

Arlene was alone in the café, and he ordered two hamburgers to take out, heavy on the fried onions. She grinned and said, "Yes, sir, hero." She was chubby but pretty, and rather flirty. He might still be sort of a hero to a few people, but it was dwindling pretty fast. When the hamburgers were sizzling on the grill Arlene said, "I don't suppose you know of a good cook I could hire?"

"Granny Hanks," he said, and they both laughed. "I thought you did all the cookin'," he added, and she held out her plump left hand. "That's an engagement ring, sonny—believe it or not, I finally caught me a man. But I'll keep the café if I can find someone to run it."

"Anybody I know?" Jeff inquired, and she gave him a dreamy smile and said, "Elmo Vance, the Golden Crust bread man, a widower with no kids and a lovely home in Blackthorn. I can come over every day and help out, let the cook have a few hours off." She grinned. "I don't expect anyone to put in the hours I do now."

Alma wasn't on the street and he was kind of relieved about that, being in a hurry. He went by the shack and took old Bill along, and the first thing Flew-the-Coop said was: "Well, got your own dog now, or is this another rented one?" Jeff explained that Bill was the mad dog he'd told him about that was headed for California. The fugitive urged him to help eat the hamburgers. Reluctantly, Jeff refused, saying he'd be having smothered chicken in a couple hours.

"Buddy, that's a first-rate hamburger. Who done it?"

"Arlene's Café," Jeff said, and just to make conversation he mentioned that Arlene was fixing to get married and looking for someone to run the café for her.

"I know a dandy cook," Mr. Strode said, "but I don't reckon she'd wanta hire the wife of a famous jailbird, if I still am one." He still was. In fact he was worth eighty dollars since the bank robbery. Somebody had sweetened the pot, possibly Mr. Rose, or banker Bradman, or somebody. But Jeff didn't tell him.

There were eight catfish, but it took a long time to sell them. People didn't like to skin catfish on Sunday. The smothered chicken dinner was delicious, but something happened that almost spoiled it for him. They were discussing the rumor that banker Bradman wouldn't go back to the bank because of his health, when suddenly Jeff's mother stopped picking at her food and said: "I want you to order me a pass—I intend to go see him before school starts, Gabe."

His dad said, "I don't think you should, this soon . . ."

"I don't care what you think," she said, and got up and ran into the kitchen, crying. The rest of them just sat there not eating, shocked and dismayed, and presently she got herself under control in there and said, "I have to see him, and I'm going, Gabe, with or without a pass."

"I can't get a pass that soon," he said.

"Then I'll go on a Saturday," she said, and he sighed. Okay, he'd order a pass, but still thought it was too soon, they'd think she was meddling. She sort of yelled: "I have a right to visit him!" He said okay, it was settled, come on back and try the grub, it wasn't half bad. So she came back, blowing her nose.

And Mutt remarked: "Make that pass for two. I'll go along an' look after Mom." So Jeff said make that pass for three, he had as much right to go as Mutt did, and their dad threw up his hands and groaned. But then he calmed down. "What about the papers?"

"I'll pay Jeff to deliver 'em," Mutt told him. Jeff said he wouldn't do it for fifty dollars. Mutt grinned and said, "I wasn't aimin' to offer you fifty dollars."

"I'd like one of the boys along, but I won't choose between them," their mother said, and Mutt said, "I'd pay you a buck, which is about what I make Saturday an' Sunday."

"Whoever stays home will have to eat his meals at the café," their dad said. "And miss Sunday school."

"Well, heck," Jeff said. "Seein' Mutt's the oldest, he probly oughta be the one that goes—darn it."

His mother gave him a shaky smile and his dad said, "Now that's white of you, son. I know how awful you feel when you miss out on Sunday school."

They all laughed, and it wasn't until later that he saw the catch to it. When they went to Kansas he'd be all alone

180

in the house until midnight, just him and all the spooks, including the ghost of Turkey Dobbs. . . .

After dinner his mother felt so good she took a dish of potato salad and went to visit Granny Hanks, and Jeff felt so restless and nervous about the fish contest that he decided to climb a tree, something he'd been too busy to do in quite a while. And because the top of a tree was a very private place, it seemed like a good time to try a pipe with tobacco, instead of cornsilks.

The big old elm in front of the house was one of his favorite climbing trees, and he went up in it with his pipe tamped full of Granger Rough Cut, his stomach in a happy smothered-chicken mood but his mind a bit troubled—not about smoking, about what if his fish had died, or what if nobody else bet on carp and drum and instead of winning he came out a dime loser. Also, his conscience bothered him about the cheating angle. But not too much.

At first the pipe tasted hot and much stronger than a cigarette, but after half a dozen cautious puffs he began to relish the taste and develop a pleasant tingly sensation, a feeling of well-being. This was the real stuff!

For a while the tingly numbness continued, then gradually something went wrong—the mild euphoria became a dizziness and vertigo and distress, the view got sort of blurry and wavery and his well-fed stomach began to act up, threatening nausea. Worst of all, the world was shifting and the tree seemed to be sliding and sinking and slowly revolving, causing him to hang on for dear life. Shutting his eyes only made it worse; he felt like he was falling and his arms and legs were too weak to hang onto the limb. It was the scariest sensation he'd ever experienced, and he figured he'd better get down on solid earth before he fell, or fainted or threw up or something. He needed to get off the merry-go-round quick.

He made it okay until he was about six feet from the ground, then his pants leg caught on a snag and he fell the rest of the way with a head-ringing, breathtaking thud, and a very painful impact. He lay there for a few seconds with his eyes shut, recuperating and taking inventory of his injuries. Skinned forehead, bruised shoulder and a throbbing left arm. Presently he sat up, feeling a bilious queasiness, and discovered Caroline standing there looking kind of anxious.

"Did you hurt yourself?" she asked, and he grinned sheepishly and said, "I'm the one that did it, all right."

Then Slapper Hallet came marching across the street. Oh lord, he thought, looking around for his pipe. If she knew he fell due to smoking, it would soon be all over town. He didn't see the dang thing anywhere, and Slapper said sort of accusingly, "Are you all right?"

"I dunno," he said, holding his left wrist. "I think I mighta busted my arm, the way it feels."

"Wiggle your fingers," she ordered, and he did. "Tisn't broken if you can wiggle your fingers, but you're lucky it isn't. Let this be a lesson, leave tree-climbing to monkeys and squirrels. Go wash your face."

Who the heck did she think she was? But he got unsteadily to his feet, glancing around surreptitiously for the damn pipe and not seeing it, and stepped over the sagging fence as Slapper said, "Well, Caroline, looking forward to school?" Caroline said yes, ma'am, but didn't sound too enthusiastic. No wonder—she'd be in Slapper's room for another two years, poor thing. . . .

By the time his mother came home the arm had swollen considerably, but she had him wiggle his fingers and said, "Just sprained." She wet a dish towel, sprinkled soda on it and wrapped it around his arm, saying that would help keep the swelling down. He shrugged—he had the word of a teacher and an ex-teacher that his arm wasn't broken; what more could he ask? He went back outdoors and found the damn pipe in the ditch; it must have bounced off a limb on its way down. He didn't need anyone to tell him what to do with it—put that sonofagun back where he got it. Smoking a pipe might not stunt your growth, but it could shake you out of a tree and make you sick as a dog.

It was one of the longest, achingest afternoons he'd ever endured, and before it was over a dozen different authorities had assured him if he could wiggle his fingers his arm wasn't broken. He couldn't stay put anywhere very long because of the feverish tight, throbbing pain, and he kept trying various things to ease his suffering. Some cold smothered chicken helped for a few minutes, and holding his arm submerged in the rain barrel eased it a little for a while, but nothing really helped for long. He rubbed it with a piece of ice, then tried hot water, but it just went on throbbing.

At five o'clock he headed for the watertank with his injured member tucked inside his overall bib. The northbound freight was there, taking on water, and about fifty men and boys, including his dad, Mutt, Dolittle, Hud, old Chink, etc. They all knew about his sprained wrist, and the novelty had worn off. They had other stuff on their minds, but so did he.

The big locomotive finally quenched its thirst and headed on north, whistle tooting and bell ringing, chuffing and clanking and hissing steam, and Jeff's dad began to open the tank's big pet cock with a huge Stillson wrench and sledgehammer. It was rusted tight, but finally the seal gave, the cap began to turn, and Jeff's dad said, "Back off, you birds, unless you want wet feet." He had on gum boots.

When the pet cock came free a thick mucky stream began to pour like sorghum, but the barefooted guys didn't back away from it, they just rolled up their pants legs and grinned as the slimy guck spread across the cindery ground. Jeff missed out on the fun; he couldn't roll up his pants legs. Besides, he just didn't feel like horsing around.

The muck pouring out of the tank changed to a gout of muddy water, and guys were slipping and sliding around, having a gay old time. Then somebody spotted the first fish, and as everybody crowded in closer old Chink accidentally on purpose bumped Jeff's sore arm. It hurt so bad he couldn't grit back the stinging tears, and public crying was a disgrace, so he took off around the tank, not wanting to be seen in his moment of sissy weakness.

Chink's meanness caused him to miss all the long-anticipated excitement of seeing fish draining out of the tank, but he was the only guy there who watched the section hands climb up the ladder with ropes and shovels to clean out the accumulated mud in the tank. All three of them had sons more interested in fish than in watching their fathers do something dangerous. Lefty Gronstetter's dad went up the ladder first and tied two ropes, leaving one hanging outside and dropping the other inside. Then he disappeared inside the tank and Conrad Coonrod's dad went up, fastened himself to the narrow ladder with a pole-climber's belt and began pulling up the tools on the outside rope, lifting them over the rim and lowering them inside. Then he dropped the belt down for Mr. Mills and went into the tank.

Excited yells around yonder tempted Jeff, but he wanted to watch Windy's dad go up the ladder, so he sat on the end of the brick platform nursing his aching arm.

Mr. Mills reached the top, fastened the belt around the ladder and began retrieving one of the ropes from inside. And suddenly the belt came loose and he fell backwards, holding the loose rope in both hands. Jeff opened his mouth to yell and nothing came out. Mr. Mills was falling horizontally when the rope snapped taut, whipping him in a violent arc, and he came sliding on down rapidly. When his feet hit the cinders he collapsed in a sitting position and began shaking his hands, blowing on them, and Jeff finally said, "Watch out!"

Holding his hands under his arms as if to warm them, Mr. Mills blinked at him and asked solemnly, "You know a quicker way to git down?" He glanced around to see if

184

anybody else had seen his near-disaster and grinned at Jeff. "You gonna tell anyone about this?"

Jeff shrugged. "I don't know—who'd believe me?"

Mr. Mills got up with a sigh. "I hafta go back up there, Jeff, so stick around. I may try that again—I think I've got the hang of it now." He went carefully up the ladder, wincing like his hands were raw, and Jeff said hey, you forgot the belt, and he said hell, he wouldn't trust that damn thing to even hold his pants up. Jeff hung around awhile, but Mr. Mills just leaned over looking inside, and he was about to go around the tank when his dad appeared. He gave Jeff a quizzical look, then hollered up to ask Mr. Mills how it looked in there. Mr. Mills said there was about a foot of mud left, and Jeff's dad said he'd go on down and start the pump, leaving the bung open so they could rinse out the tank. Mr. Mills nodded, then said, "Slim, ask your boy what I did a minute ago."

When Jeff told about Mr. Mills's fall, his dad looked owlish, then grinned and said, "Do it again, Curly. Show me how it happened." Mr. Mills said he needed to grow some new skin on his palms first. Then he asked how many fish they'd got, and Jeff's dad said about two tubfuls, was all.

"When'll we know who won?" Jeff asked, and his dad said not until tomorrow at noon. The mayor, Dolittle, and Professor Hallet were in charge of weighing the fish this evening and deciding the winners. Jeff had to grin about calling Slapper's henpecked husband Professor. But it was a gritted-teeth grin, and when his dad asked if he wanted to stroll down to the pumphouse he begged off. Walking jarred his sprained wrist.

"Those things can sure hurt," his dad said. "I'll stop at the drugstore later and get some pain-killer."

But he forgot to, and at supper, which Jeff didn't have much stomach for, he said he'd do it as soon as he finished eating. But then he got delayed downtown, and Jeff was already in bed, suffering unendurable pain, when the laudanum arrived. Even then his mother only gave him a little dab, saying he was putting on like a baby. It took him a long time to get to sleep, mainly because there was just no place to put a sprained wrist; it didn't fit in with any of his usual sleeping positions. He dozed fitfully and woke up several times, groaning and whimpering, and was awake, crying forlornly, when his dad came home around midnight.

One thing he admired in his dad was how he understood about pain and suffering. When he located the medicine he gave Jeff a generous dose, and either that or sheer exhaustion caused him to sleep until morning.

The swelling seemed to have gone down a little, but the pain was as bad, or worse, and he didn't want any breakfast —which finally convinced his mother that maybe he'd better go let Doc Schuman take a look at his arm. And old Doc was about the only person in town who didn't tell him to wiggle his fingers, although he still could. . . .

Usually it impressed people if a guy showed up with his arm in a cast, but Jeff didn't cut much ice with the crowd at the hardware store. All they were interested in was who won. He found Vern at the edge of the crowd looking worried. "Busted?" Vern asked, and he nodded. Doc said it was a green fracture, but "busted" sounded better. Vern said that was a dang shame. Then he said worriedly, "I'm hopin' my fish died. I don't feel right about riggin' it up." Jeff nodded, troubled by his own misgivings, and let down that nobody seemed to care much about his busted arm.

Presently Mr. Riley came out of the store with a sheet of paper and said, "The winners of the big event are as follows, beginnin' with A, for anchovies—no winner for anchovies." Nervous laughter. "B for bass—Curly Mills guessed closest at four pounds and wins a dollar forty." Curly Mills wasn't present; none of the section gang was present. "C for carp," the mayor continued. "Lex Yancy only missed by three ounces. It weighed a little over six pounds—and there were only two carp in the tank. Lex wins thirty-five cents." That got a hooting kind of laugh, but not from Jeff, who felt relieved, but indignant because, obviously, Lex had cheated. For thirty-five cents.

"D for drum," Mr. Riley said. "Another amazing coincidence—Von Yancy guessed five pounds and only missed by two ounces, and only two drum in the tank. Von wins fifteen cents for his lucky guess."

This time there were boos and catcalls mixed in with the laughter, and Jeff was truly relieved. If Lex and Von hadn't cheated, he'd be the one getting hooted at. Oh man!

"Hey, Mayor, you skipped buffalo," someone said, and Mr. Riley looked nonplused. "Doggoned if I didn't—in fact I'm all messed up here, skipped catfish too. Tell you what we better do—let's all go home and eat lunch, then return. Give me time to straighten this out—and will also give anyone wanting to withdraw from the contest a chance to do so, for whatever reasons. All in favor?" There was a loud chorus of "No's," but he said, "Motion carried, I'm hungry. Anyone wanting to retract, see Mr. Little." Then he headed for home.

Most of the others left, too, but a few lingered, and Vern was pretty upset. "I got to back out, but I sure hate to be seen doin' it," he groaned, and Jeff, spared embarrassment and shame by a lucky fluke, said, "Heck, I'll do it for you, pal." As he went in the store he met a sheepish Hud coming out and wondered what category he'd withdrawn from. Dolittle looked a little surprised until Jeff explained he was acting on behalf of Vern who wanted to cancel his redhorse and hog-sucker guesses.

"Just as well," Dolittle said. "There weren't any of those in the tank." But then he winked, which Jeff took to mean he'd just said that for Vern's benefit. Then he said, "Congratulations, pard—on not winnin' on carp an' drum." Jeff went on out, his face burning, knowing Dolittle knew he'd sort of cheated.

Vern was vastly relieved. "Man, I'll never do anything that dumb again," he said, and Jeff devoutly agreed. Crime didn't pay—look at Von and Lex. Even if they acted like it was all a prank, they'd been exposed as swindlers.

He went home to lunch and wasn't in any hurry to get back, and it was nearly over when he returned. Apparently the rest of the winners were just honest and lucky, and the baseball fund earned six twenty-five. Everyone seemed to think it was pretty funny about Von and Lex, just the sort of crazy stunt you'd expect them to pull, but Jeff figured if he'd won, especially if he'd won twice like he'd expected to, those same people would consider him a crook and scorn him forever. He'd had a close call and learned a lesson, and vowed to be strictly honest henceforth.

Except, maybe, in dealing with the fair sex. Like when he told Alamo his mother didn't want him messing around outdoors after dark until his arm was healed, so he'd have to skip the romantic stuff for a while. Heck, for all he knew his mother felt that way and just hadn't mentioned it yet. Alamo just sighed and said hurry up and get well, if that was the case. He said that was the case.

Mutt wanted him to hurry up and get well, too, only he said it differently. "I spose you figure on gittin' outa all the work around here for the next month," he growled, and Jeff said, "Darn right, why else do you think I done it in the first place?"

16

At first his fractured radius had seemed like a calamity, possibly the Lord's punishment for smoking a pipe on Sunday, although a broken arm seemed a high price for doing something that made you sick, too. But he soon began to realize the benefits of his mishap. If he couldn't use his slingshot, he also couldn't play second base, or swing a weed cutter, or hoe the garden, although he could still "run" his trotlines and peddle fish. But the main benefit was the immunity his injury gave him.

He could go to the Teapot Dome after supper without being challenged to "spar" somebody, and just enjoy watching Mutt and Lige perform what Hack Kelso called the mating dance of the one-eyed shidepokes. They would never settle their grudge wearing sixteen-ounce gloves, but neither seemed anxious to go at it with bare fists. Jeff was strictly neutral; he didn't want either to win, he wanted them both to get licked.

That last week of vacation he rediscovered the fun of riding on the back step of the ice truck eating slivers of ice, and standing behind Mr. Yancy on the road-grader watching the big blade sheer the rutted streets down to a smooth surface that felt good on bare feet and was great for shooting marbles, one thing a one-armed guy could do.

While the street was still slick smooth he played marbles with Kerosene, and it turned out about like he expected—she was pretty good, but no match for a veteran like J. McGraw.

He couldn't get over the change in her; not only being plumper, and breathing through her nose, but her personality, too. He couldn't remember the last time she'd stuck her tongue out at him.

"How is Alma these days?" she asked, and he said, "Sassy as ever, I guess. Why?" Just wondered, she said, and he wondered how it would be to kiss a girl that hadn't ever been kissed before. Ten was too young, of course, but eleven wouldn't be, at the rate she was developing.

Being disabled allowed him to do things he'd been too busy to do, or hadn't done because of the danger involved, like passing the Britton place. Even Chink wouldn't pick on a one-armed guy—not when Dolittle was within hollering distance, anyway. So Friday morning he went to inspect the remodeling of Turkey's house, and as usual Chink's dog had a crazy fence-chewing fit, and Dolittle came out to see what the racket was all about. Or who. He looked over next door and said, "Sometimes I wonder just how mean that sonofagun would be if that fence wasn't there."

"I dunno," Jeff said, "but I'm sure glad it's there."

The Littles were adding on a long shed-room and screened back porch to the house. Dolittle said as long as he had some cheap help he'd decided to turn the place into a family dwelling. "Paw's slow an' lazy," he said, "but if I prod him he does a halfway mediocre job."

Mr. Little grinned at Jeff. "I'd suspect he's fixing this place up for hisself, but I know he won't never leave home unless we cut off his corner of the table. He likes all that free grub an' laundry service too much."

"Free!" Dolittle said. "Costs me five bucks a week."

"That's just bother money," his dad told Jeff. "What we call a nuisance fee for puttin' up with the kid."

Jeff knew they were enjoying themselves for his benefit, but he also felt kind of in the way, so presently he said he guessed he'd better get going and started to leave.

"Wait a minute," Dolittle said. "How do you feel about findin' out just how mean Chink's dog really is?"

Jeff wasn't crazy about the idea, but he just shrugged, and Dolittle thought about it for a minute and figured out a plan, and Jeff didn't want anyone thinking he was a coward, so he agreed to do his part. Carrying a claw hammer as dubious life insurance, he walked past the Britton yard, causing Killer to go into his customary hysterical rage and follow along inside the fence, which enabled Dolittle to slip up on his blind side and open the gate. Then Jeff circled back in the street to where Dolittle was waiting, brandishing a length of two-by-four, and the raging dog came back along the fence carrying on so crazily that he shot right on past the open gate before he realized it was open. Then he started to rush out into the street, but suddenly stopped and crouched, looking rather surprised.

Jeff edged nervously behind Dolittle, who said, "Keep on comin', big boy. No fence stoppin' you now."

Killer's savage snarls changed to a kind of cranky muttering, and he looked around uneasily and began to edge back to the gate, mumbling to himself and looking almost embarrassed and sort of indignant.

"Come on, big mouth, you wanted out," Dolittle said, and Killer gave a whining bark, almost as if to say: This isn't fair. Dolittle handed the two-by-four to Jeff and squatted in the street. "Okay, then," he said, "if you don't want trouble, come and get acquainted, feller."

It was funny, remembering it afterwards. Old Killer bellied down and looked everywhere but at Dolittle, giving little yelps and grumbles, like he was arguing or griping. But as Dolittle kept talking to him in a friendly tone, the dog scooted forward on his belly and gave a few tentative wags of his tail, squirming and whining like he wanted to be friendly but wasn't supposed to. Then he inched forward some more, rolled over on his side with his tail thumping the ground, and sort of threw in the towel.

191

"What you are," Dolittle said, patting Killer's head, "is a big blowhard, like the company you been keepin'—or you were, anyway." He stood up. "Come on, boy, on your feet. All is forgiven, you're among friends."

The dog got up, still mumbling sheepish alibis and fawning on Dolittle, acting like he'd been starved for human friendship but was still a little nervous and uncertain.

"Henceforth," Dolittle said, "your name is Wilbur." He grinned at Jeff. "You give a dog a bad name an' he'll try to live up to it, I guess. Maybe that fence protected him from people more than the other way around. I always had a sneaking hunch he was overdoin' that man-eater stuff." He took the hammer and two-by-four from Jeff and winked. "Let's keep this just between the three of us awhile, okay?"

Jeff nodded, still watching the dog warily, finding the abrupt transformation hard to believe. If Killer was like his master, it might be some kind of cunning trick. But as Dolittle started away the rechristened, reformed Wilbur went trotting along beside him, looking up at him with respect and admiration, or something. Like he'd just been wishing for someone to call his bluff and free him from the need to go on putting up a big phony front, so he could just be himself for a change, or something.

Turning north, Jeff caught a glimpse of Chink's uncle in his wheelchair inside the screen door, and took off at a lope, his scalp prickling. Captain Britton had been living there about eight years and that was only the sixth or seventh time Jeff had even seen him. But that was probably oftener than most people had seen him. . . .

After dinner he was sprawled in the porch swing, feeling lonesome for Jody, when Caroline came out of her house all dolled up, with a ribbon in her hair, and as she came along the cracked sidewalk he remembered something the little wart said one time and grinned, and she took it personal.

"See sumpthing funny?" she inquired coldly.

"I wasn't grinning at you." He went out to the gate to explain. "I jus' remembered sumpin' Jody said once."

She blinked uncertainly, unconvinced. "What did he say?"

"Well," Jeff said, "back last spring Dad ask 'im if he knew who was the President, an' he said sure, an' Dad ask who, an' Jody said Hervin Cooblidge."

Caroline laughed, but then she looked sad. "Papa said just this mornin' that everyone in town misses little Jody."

Jeff nodded glumly, thinking: But especially *us.*

"Well," she said, "I better be goin'." She gave him a sort of puzzled look and departed, and he watched her go up the street wondering how come he ever had the notion she was pigeon-toed and knock-kneed. . . .

Ten minutes later in Marheddon's store, he saw Alma go past, all dolled up like Caroline, and figured there must be a hen party somewhere. Then, going down the street, he met Hud coming out of the drugstore in clean overalls, his hair slicked down, which was unusual as heck, and Hud stared at him and said, "You fixin' to go like that, ol' overhauls an' no sleeves on your shirt?"

"Goin' where?" Jeff inquired, and Hud said, "Clarence's birthday party." And Jeff understood the situation. Clarence was having a party and he wasn't invited. "Dadgummit," he said, "I forgot all about it. Heck-fire."

Hud grinned. "Or else too tight to buy 'im a present, I'd suspose. Way I lookit it, I blew in a dime for a gift but I'll eat enough ice cream an' cake to come out away ahead on it." He started moving. "I don't wanta be late."

"I perfer drugstore ice cream anyway," Jeff called after him, and headed on east, smarting, feeling left out. Today Clarence was fourteen and Monday he'd be a freshman, but an age difference was no reason to not invite someone. The whole idea of a birthday party was to invite *everyone,* so you'd get more presents. They didn't have to be friends.

If Mutt was invited, why hadn't he mentioned it? How come this dang party was such a big secret? Not that he

193

wanted to *go* to the dumb thing, but he'd much rather not go on purpose. A guy felt like a durn outcast if someone had a party and he wasn't even warned about it . . . something pretty darn snotty about that old sneaky stuff.

But after the initial humiliation began to wear off he guessed the reason for his exclusion. Alamo. Clarence wanted to try making time with her, a ridiculous notion that made Jeff laugh scornfully, but didn't make him feel any less insulted or humiliated. Outcast McGraw.

At the rendezvous he found his partner in a mood almost as melancholy as his own, and soon found out what caused it.

"I gotta decide what I aim to do when summer quits on me," Dallas Strode said. "Sure can't winter down here. I either hafta skin the country or go back an' finish out my sentence." He smoked and scratched awhile, then grinned. "Well, you could turn me in, an' we'd split the reward."

Jeff shook his head. "I wouldn't want any of it."

"Wouldn't work anyway," Mr. Strode said. "If you took me in, even holdin' a gun on me, it'd look mighty peculiar. But if you just told 'em where to find me that fat sheriff would probly cheat you outa the reward." He stretched and yawned. "Well, I'm not ready to end my vacation for a while yet. Autumn's my favorite season, an' it comforts me some to know I'm helpin' out my family, even if it ain't much."

"It comforts me, too," Jeff said. "Even blowin' in quite a bit on ice cream an' stuff, I've got about fifteen dollars saved up. I aim to buy me a rifle any day now."

"Wish I had one," his partner said. "Lots of fat squirrels an' swamp rabbits down here along the crick."

On the way to town Jeff thought about that from the business point of view. If he furnished a rifle, maybe they could start selling squirrels and rabbits. But if he bought a rifle, how could he explain not keeping it at home, not carrying it with him? It wouldn't work.

While splitting with Vern, another outcast who wasn't

194

invited to the party, he mentioned the rifle idea, and Vern solved two problems simultaneously. He said the only reason he hadn't bought him a four-dollar bolt-action target already was, how could he explain where he got the money to his mother. "I'll go ahead an' buy it an' you can take it to Paw," he said. For a guy that had quit school, old Vern was sharp as a tack. . . .

Jeff was rolling a hoop when Caroline came home from the big social event looking sunburned. She said she ate too much ice cream and cake and instead of worrying about being too thin like she used to she was beginning to worry about getting fat. Jeff eyed her critically and opined that for her height she was just about the right weight. She probably blushed—it was hard to tell with the sunburn. The Olives didn't have much shade in their yard.

She asked, hesitantly, why he hadn't gone, and he said, "Too busy. Plus I'm not too crazy about ol' Clarence."

"Me either," she said. "He played his dumb violin. Matt wasn't there either—there were a lot more girls than boys an' it wasn't much fun." She looked at the T-shaped hoop roller. "That looks like fun to do. I've watched you an' Hud an' wished I could learn to do it."

"Well, shoot, sometime when you're not all dolled up I could show you how," he told her, and she said eagerly, "I could change in no time if you'll still be out here."

He said he was just waiting for supper, and she went hurrying to change, and while he waited he thought, with a grin: I'll make her a hoop roller if she'll steal her own laths from her dad like everybody else does.

Mutt came home with Ranger and the first thing he said was: "Were you invited to Clarence's party?" Jeff just shook his head, and Mutt scowled. "Sumpin' funny goin' on. How come he invited everyone but us?"

Jeff shrugged. "Couldn't invite you an' not me, an' he didn't want me there on account of Alamo, I guess."

"Well, nobody snoots me an' gits away with it," Mutt

growled. "We'll have a party some night an' invite ever'one in town but ol' four-eyes. What I got in mind is a weenie roast out here in the street, say early October. Have a big bonfire an' play games, sing songs. Some Friday night when there's a big ol' moon. If we put up, say, a buck apiece, I bet Dad would let us charge that much stuff at the store, weenies, buns, mustard . . ."

"Heck, I'm not a dollar's worth of mad at Clarence," Jeff said. "I wouldn't of went if he'd begged me." Caroline was coming back, in everyday clothes, and he felt a little trapped and said, "Anyway, by October I may be flat broke."

Caroline spoke to Mutt, then smiled at Jeff. "I'm ready for a hoop-rolling lesson," she said. So he gave her a demonstration, with Mutt standing there sort of leering, then let her try it, and as she went sort of awkwardly down the street rolling the hoop, Mutt said, "Taken up robbin' the cradle lately, huh?" So Jeff said, "Take another look at 'er, boy. She'd need a fair-sized cradle. She's fixin' to be eleven in about six weeks, an' she's really growin' lately."

Mutt's sneer faded and he rubbed his chin, looking after Caroline, and said, "Hey, maybe we could make that weenie roast like a birthday party for her, then her dad would put up half the cost of it." When it came to slinky minds, old Mutt really took the cake. . . .

At supper their dad said Dolittle had paid a visit to Captain Britton and the maimed war veteran had some complaints about his nephew. Sloppy housekeeper, sorry cook, gone most of the time, insubordinate and sassy, cheating on the grocery money, etc. Mr. Britton had written to his brother in Ark. City and Chink's mother in Sapulpa about the kid's unsuitability as companion for an invalid, but apparently the dang boy hadn't mailed the letters. So Dolittle had agreed to see that the next complaining letters got mailed.

"But his brother and sister will probably ignore his

complaints," Slim McGraw opined, "since they figure he's shell-shocked and maybe getting more feebleminded all the time—and sure don't wanta have to take care of him themselves."

"I'm surprised that dog didn't scare Dolittle away," his wife said. "Nobody else will go near the place now."

Jeff was sorely tempted to tell them how he and Dolittle had tamed that savage beast, but he'd sort of promised not to.

"All I know about that boy is hearsay," his mother remarked, "but I certainly don't envy him. How many boys his age would be willing to take care of a crippled, disfigured, and probably irrational old man, uncle or no uncle?"

Mutt said it seemed to him Chink had a pretty good deal. Plenty of spendin' money, smoked tailor-made cigarettes and ate suppers at the cafés a lot, and Dock Ballew said about all the groceries he ever bought was stuff like bread, butter, baloney, bacon, sardines, cheese, weenies, eggs, Post Toasties and stuff like that. No steaks, roasts, pork chops, just easy quick stuff to fix.

Saturday morning Vern bought a bolt-action single-shot rifle and some shells and Jeff took it to his delighted partner, who said, "I'm gonna have fried young squirrel for supper, an' maybe rabbit stew for dessert, by golly." Which gave Jeff an opening to suggest maybe branching out and selling a few squirrels and rabbits to the fish customers, and Dallas Strode said, "Well, why not?" But then he looked rueful and added, "I'll tell you why not, Jeff. It would look mighty peculiar, you comin' down here without a gun an' goin' back with squirrels an' rabbits with bullet holes in 'em."

Jeff felt sheepish. "Shows how dumb I am," he said. "I guess I hafta buy me a rifle to carry back an' forth."

"You do that," old Flew-the-Coop said, "an' we'll give it a try, pard. If folks don't want to buy what I shoot, I reckon your mama might like a mess of squirrel now and then."

197

Jeff said she sure would, but he bet he could get two bits for a skinned squirrel, and his business associate said they'd not only be skinned, but gutted and wrapped in some of the newspapers Jeff had been bringing him. But rabbits, being so easy to skin, he'd just gut them. Anyway, the fugitive said with a smile, he wouldn't be needing much store-bought meat from now on. Take him until Christmas to get tired of game, and he didn't aim to be there that long. As an afterthought he asked if they'd ever caught that bank robber, and Jeff said nope. And furnished the information that the banker had moved to Walston to run a feed mill for Mr. Rose, who owned the bank.

There were a dozen catfish in the pothole that day and they were all about the same size, around a pound, and Mr. Strode said, "Why don't you try sellin' these to that woman at the café, or does she serve fish dinners?"

"Not that I know of," Jeff said, "but I'll try her."

When he got to town he dunked the fish in the horse trough to freshen them up, then went around to the café's back door, and Arlene said believe it or not, some of her customers had been asking why she never featured catfish on the blue-plate special. But when she asked how much he wanted for them and Jeff said oh, about two bits apiece, she threw up her hands and said, "I only charge thirty cents for the whole meal, including coffee. Sorry . . ."

Jeff was sorrier. He'd been hoping to unload all the fish on one customer and be done for the day. "Well," he said, "if you took 'em all I'd give you a special price, an' maybe take part of it in trade . . ."

Arlene gave him an amused look. "What did you have in mind, Mr. McGraw?"

Jeff shrugged. "Hamburgers an' chili, mainly."

"Okay," she said. "Twenty cents apiece, ten in cash and ten in trade, but no T-bones—just stuff I make a little profit on, agreed, hero?"

Durn tootin', he thought, handing her the fish. She gave

him a buck-twenty, and he had that much coming in chili and hamburgers, etc. Then as he was leaving Arlene asked kiddingly if he'd found her a cook yet, and he said, "I hear Mrs. Strode use to cook in a Fred Harvey place."

She raised her plucked eyebrows. "The escaped convict's wife? Kiddo, if I brought her in here, half of my customers would start eatin' across the street."

Jeff shrugged. "She didn't do anything," he said, but Arlene had already turned away.

He had already examined the Winchester pump several times as a potential buyer, but now he gave it a thorough inspection. Anything wrong with that baby, he wanted to know about it now. He frowned critically for Mr. Riley's benefit, having learned how to haggle from his fish customers. "I dunno," he said. "Twelve bucks for an ol' *used* gun with a couple scratches on the stock . . ."

"I've had that price on it for over a year now and nobody ever questioned it before, Jefferson," Mr. Riley said.

"Nobody bought it before, either," Jeff retorted.

"Well," the mayor said, "there's not much call for that octagonal barrel model lately. Most men seem to prefer the lighter round barrel kind." He shrugged. "I might get the twelve bucks if I hung onto it awhile, but then I might be glad to take less a couple years from now. Maybe the smart thing to do is get shut of it now. Tell you what, Jeff, for eleven dollars I'll throw in . . . a cleanin' kit an' a couple boxes of shorts? Plus an ironclad two-week guarantee?"

He was kidding, but Jeff knew he was also being pretty generous because he was a neighbor and a friend. The rifle had been worth about twice that much new and was still as good as new, a real bargain. So he took it home with him, jauntily cradled in the crook of his right arm, tempted to go around by Main Street just to show it off. He felt a great swelling pride about finally owning his first real gun.

When his dad came home to supper he admitted, uneasily, that it was about the best .22 rifle ever manufactured, but

199

dangerous as hell in the hands of an unskilled, thoughtless person, and he laid down some simple rules to follow until he could personally take Jeff hunting and teach him all the rifle safety rules. Never shoot toward town or toward any farmhouse, or where you weren't sure the bullet wouldn't hit a cow or something. In fact, always shoot *up* when hunting squirrels—*never* shoot at a running rabbit—and dammit, always hunt alone, except when with *him,* was that understood?

Jeff said he aimed to be careful and always hunt alone.

His mother wasn't too thrilled about the rifle but she just shrugged, like she figured her objections would be outvoted by the men in the family. Mutt tried to hide his envy by saying he planned to buy a twenty-gauge shotgun, so he could hunt ducks and quail, not just squirrels and rabbits.

That Saturday night his dad didn't come home until Sunday morning around three o'clock, due to letting poor Dolittle catch up on his sleep, even though there wasn't much for an engine watchman to do on Saturday night. It was a kind of relief to Jeff because he'd been worried that his dad might decide to go to the creek with him Sunday to teach him all the rules about being careful with a rifle, instead of sleeping past noon to make up for lost sleep.

By the time he reached the rendezvous Jeff understood why some people didn't much care for the octagonal-barrel model Winchester, especially one-armed people. It was heavy. But taking it along was amply repaid. His partner had made a gray daybreak visit to a cornfield on down the creek and had four tender young fox squirrels skinned and gutted and wrapped in newspaper for Jeff, plus about nine pounds of catfish. He admired the repeater rifle and asked if Jeff had tried it out.

"I shot at some walnuts on a tree," Jeff said, "but didn't hit any. Mainly due to my broken arm, I guess."

Flew-the-Coop examined the rifle and said the rear sight was set a notch too high, but otherwise, in his opinion, no

200

better rifle had as yet been invented; the octagonal barrel might be heavier but it carried straighter and farther than the lighter, shorter round-barrel model. Jeff was proud that everybody seemed to feel that way about his rifle, but sort of figured the lighter model might be better for a kid. At least a kid with a broken arm.

Getting back to town with the rifle and squirrels and fish presented a problem, which he solved by shoving the newspaper-wrapped bundle inside his overall bib and tying the stringer of fish to the rifle barrel. But the biggest problem didn't crop up until Claude Calvert, after buying some fish, asked how in hell Jeff had managed to skin and gut four squirrels with just one hand, when most people had difficulty doing it with two hands.

"Another guy was with me," Jeff said, and made a quick getaway, abruptly worrying. His own family, at least, knew he'd never skinned a squirrel in his life. And although he managed to sell all the fish, he couldn't persuade anybody to buy the squirrels for Sunday supper. While splitting a buck-sixty with Vern, they studied various possibilities but decided there was just no way to clean squirrels one-handed. "Even Paw couldn't do it," Vern declared.

So Jeff dawdled homeward, not wanting to throw the young squirrels away, but worried about being late to dinner, and he was thinking about hiding them somewhere until he'd eaten, then trying to find some new customers, when he got one of his shrewd ideas. He took the squirrels home and presented them to his mother and awaited the inevitable question.

She stared at him dubiously. "You mean to stand there and tell me you cleaned these animals yourself?"

"Not me, I never learned how yet," he said. "Run into Vern Strode, an' he knows the easy way to skin anything."

She nodded. "Well, I must say these are all nice young ones. They'll fry up nice and tender."

He told his conscience he hadn't said a word that wasn't

true. And from now on he could just say Strode cleaned them for a share of the profit, and if people thought he meant Vern it wouldn't be his fault. But it made him feel pretty dishonest when his dad said, "By golly, you must be quite a marksman to do so well with an unfamiliar rifle."

"Well, I missed a lot of shots," Jeff said.

Being smarter than some people, Mutt naturally figured out a way to take the misery out of washday mornings—by pumping and carrying water Sunday evening. While doing his share of the pumping, Jeff thought how dumb he was not to have thought of it himself long ago, and the word "dumb" led into thinking about another school term beginning tomorrow, with the usual mixed feelings of anticipation and dread, but with a little nagging extra anxiety he couldn't pin down for a while. He looked forward to seeing people he hadn't seen all summer, and to having his own private desk at which to read, write, draw and study, in a cozy classroom full of the good school smells of new tables and pencils, old books, ink, paste, chalk, oiled sawdust, etc. Including the fragrance of people, especially girls. And there was a sense of adventure about moving up to a different room with a new teacher, and with eighth-graders instead of fifth-graders. Even being in the same room with Mutt again would beat being cooped up with old sad-singing Alice Brubaker, and old mean-eyed, scowling . . .

Chester! Well, heck-fire, was that what he felt so durn uneasy about? For gosh sakes, he didn't need to fret about that ornery sonofagun for at least a month, and by then he'd probably have a bunch of new guys to chase. Sighing, Jeff grinned to himself, thinking how lucky he was to break his arm just before school started, instead of, for instance, back in June or July.

17

Alamo claimed she had a secret diary, so Jeff decided to try keeping one in the back of his Big Chief tablet, but he didn't seem to have any secret stuff to write. Monday he wrote: *First day of school, hot and sunny. Old Chester sure looked funny when he saw my arm in a cast. Let him go chase someone else this year.* Which turned out to be one of the longest entries in his erratic log.

He felt uneasy in the same room with his brother, and self-conscious in the same class with Alma, and no matter how you looked at it he was in for nine months of incarceration and mandatory studying and homework. It always took a few weeks to get used to school again, and the toughest thing was getting up earlier. All he tried to do was get there before the bell rang, but Alma was an early bird who liked to socialize before school, so they didn't walk together as he'd assumed they would. Instead he walked with Hud, as usual, and Caroline, which was unusual. But shoot, she just happened to go to school the same time he did. After school he walked with Alamo as far as the lumberyard corner, then took out for home to change clothes and head for the creek. There wasn't much time between four o'clock and suppertime.

Thursday when he went home at noon his mother was in seclusion, because of a letter for him, or rather just an envelope with a hard lump in it and a slip of paper. It was addressed in uncertain printing: *Jeffy,* and under that in a neat, adult, sort of civil-servant longhand: Cottonwood, Oklahoma. The lump was a coffee agate and the slip of paper said simply: "Burtday present"—and there was only one person who printed and spelled like that and had a spare agate. Which accounted for his mother's indisposition, and the sudden lump in his own throat. That little dickens. It wasn't as much a birthday gift after all this time as it was a homesick cry for help, and Jeff wished he was going with his mother instead of Mutt, but that was all settled. Gosh darnit, he sure missed that little wart.

Saturday he slept late and his dad got up early, which was why they went hunting, against Jeff's better judgment. His dad thought he was a crack shot because so far he'd brought a dozen squirrels back from the creek, but in fact he had yet to kill one himself. He was worried about missing some easy shots, but relieved that his dad wanted to hunt west of town because it was much closer than *down* the creek. They took Ranger along, although he was strictly a rabbit dog, and Jeff's dad said he'd bet old Bill would make a good tree dog. Jeff just nodded, because old Bill had treed five squirrels so far when he went along after school, and Jeff had missed all five of them due to buck fever or something.

The country west of town was rolling blackjack hills and tall bottomland timber, including hickory, walnut and cottonwoods. According to Flew-the-Coop, the best way to hunt squirrels during the day was to settle down by a big cottonwood den tree and wait, but Jeff's dad was too restless for still hunting, and Ranger was only interested in hunting rabbits. Also the gnats were bad in the warm September weather, so they kept moving and only saw two squirrels. His dad shot one and Jeff spared the other for fear of missing, and Ranger caught two cottontails, and about a mile west of town Slim McGraw said they might as well give up because there were still too many leaves on the trees and you needed to get out there bright and early. On the way home he tried out Jeff's rifle on some walnuts, and missed, and said the gun threw off to the left—but Jeff knew his eyes weren't what they used to be and he was strictly a shotgun hunter.

Jeff tried his luck and lived up to his unearned reputation because walnuts didn't make him shaky the way squirrels did. Miss a walnut and it just hung there, but miss a squirrel and that baby was long gone.

"I'll hafta admit you shoot good," his dad said, "but the main thing is to use your noodle, be damn sure where you're shooting that thing, and don't hunt with anyone but me."

"Okay," Jeff said. That suited him fine. When it came to hunting and fishing he was a loner. . . .

The next week slid by profitably as far as business was concerned, but he was beginning to miss those little evening get-togethers with Alamo. So Friday he slipped her a succinct one-word note reading: "Tonight"—and she shook her head. Somewhat taken aback, he muttered, "Tomorrow night then?" She shrugged and acted kind of evasive, like how could she promise so far in advance, and said, "I doubt it, Jess."

Suspicious, he went around there Friday night and looked out the back window of the ex-barbershop, and there in the meat market's living quarters, playing cards with Alma and Roy and Mrs. Dexter, was Clarence Olive. Maybe Roy or his mother had invited old Specs for an evening of pitch, but Jeff doubted it. But what the heck—no girl would invite a guy she really *liked* to play cards with her mother.

Saturday was cloudy and he got up feeling depressed about everything except hiring Vern to deliver the papers for fifty cents. He didn't want to hang around home watching people get ready for a train trip, so he went over and got Bill and headed for the creek. He found his lonesome partner in a talkative mood and felt obligated to listen, and just made it back to town in time to wave as the train pulled out.

The house seemed so deserted and lonely that he spent the day at the shack reading, grateful for the companionship of old Bill, who had taken to the shack like it was home. He thought wistfully of having Bill for his own private dog, but figured his mother would take a pretty dim view of the idea.

When he was washing up for supper at home he noticed his cast was getting pretty dirty and thought about asking Doc to put on a new one—but what if Doc said he didn't *need* a cast anymore? After reading the funnies he put the *Times* on the table and lit a lamp, in case he didn't get back before dark. Then after letting Ranger run loose for ten minutes he chained him up again and cautioned him about keeping an eye on the place, since nobody would be home but him. He thought Ranger sort of nodded, but sourly.

The sun was going down when he went in the café, and Arlene smiled and, giving him a menu, said, "Your pappy says you can order anything you want, hero. Also you can give me your expert opinion of my new cook." Jeff looked toward the kitchen and saw Mrs. Strode back there and registered surprise. "I'm trying her out," Arlene told him. "So far so good—nobody has made any cracks yet. Maybe they don't know who she is."

Jeff said probably not many people in town would know Mrs. Strode from Adam if they met her on the street. He was tempted to see how many hamburgers he could eat, but with the supper specials he'd get soup and pie, so he ordered the meatloaf. After eating the tomato soup, meatloaf, mashed spuds and gravy, and so forth, plus the lemon pie, he told Arlene it was the best meal he'd had in a coon's age.

With a put-on scowl, she said, "I don't mind *you* saying it, but I resent my *regular* customers saying it. She cooks so good I'm jealous." She was probably kidding him a little, but he was glad she liked Mrs. Strode's cooking.

He loafed around on the dusky street listening to men discussing the coming Dempsey-Tunney fight for a while, his thoughts straying down toward the butcher shop. He favored Dempsey because his dad did and Mutt didn't— and he sorta wanted to go see Alamo just to let her know how little it bothered him that she was so friendly with Clarence Olive. He was drifting tentatively down the sidewalk when Ranger suddenly materialized, and he said, "Who the heck turned you loose?" Ranger ignored the question, and Jeff figured his dad must have done it. Shrugging about it, he went on down to the empty building next to the meat market and was about to go inside when he heard the music begin. It was too loud and too bad to be a phonograph, so he went around to where he could see into Dexters' living quarters.

It was the first time he ever heard Alamo pick her banjo, and about the fifth time he'd heard old Clarence play his fiddle. As music, it was stuff a person would pay not to listen to, but as people having a good time it gave the lonely watcher a kind of sorrowful envy. Doggone it, she knew he played French harp, but she'd never offered to accompany *him* on her darn banjo.

But what the heck, if *all* she did with Clarence was play cards and her banjo . . .

He wandered disconsolately up to the Teapot Dome and watched Hack Kelso gas up a Model T, but it was a quiet night in Cottonwood, so finally he headed for home.

Turning the corner, he noticed Rileys' porch light was on, and saw Caroline in the porch swing, and heard music—real music. Might go visit with her a few minutes, he decided, noticing that his house was dark. His dad must have turned off the lamp when he let Ranger loose.

He said howdy and asked what she was doing, and she said, "Listening to our new radio that Daddy got so he'll be able to hear the boxing fight. That's Chicago now."

Boxing fight, he thought indulgently, sitting on the edge of the porch. "I can't git over bein' able to hear sumpin' here while it's happenin' away off somewhere."

"Big mystery to me, too," she said. "How's Alma?"

"Well"—he shrugged—"I never was crazy about banjo pickin', so I come on home."

Mrs. Riley heard them talking and came to the door, and seemed pleased that Caroline had a visitor—not like some suspicious mothers he knew—and asked how they would like some popcorn. So he stayed longer than he'd expected to, sitting in the swing with the ugly duckling Kerosene who had somehow been transformed by the miracle of tonsillectomy into a bird of another feather. The pleasure was enhanced by his gloaty feeling of getting even with old Alamo.

But all good things must end, and he finally had to go home. He let Ranger precede him into the dark house, lit the dining-room and kitchen lamps, and checked all the downstairs, although he didn't quite have the courage to go up the narrow stairs to his dad's small bedroom. He started to whistle, but it interfered with his listening, so he quit.

When he tried to read the newspaper he kept yawning, but couldn't decide where to sleep for maximum safety, and finally, mainly to kill a little time, he decided to add the day's profits to his savings and count the total. It was over eleven bucks, but he didn't know the exact amount—and never would know it, he discovered when he got the empty fruit jar out of the bedsprings under his mattress on the back porch. He'd been robbed.

Whoever let Ranger loose did it, he thought, and turned out the lamp I left lit, while I was eating supper! How many people knew he kept his money under his mattress? Alma and Vern, Mutt of course, and no telling who else.

It occurred to him the thief might still be in the house, maybe at the top of those narrow dark stairs. Beating it back into the kitchen, he bolted the wooden door, his heart thumping and his skin twitching, and made a beeline for the closet to get his rifle. And *that* was gone, too, and suddenly his uneasiness about being alone in the house became plain shivering fright, along with the sick feeling of loss. His imagination peopled the night with murderous criminals not yet satisfied, still lurking around waiting to get at him. His urgent yearning to go running over to the shack and stay with his dad was canceled by his fear of the ominous, threatening night, even with Ranger along. He had the feeling evil eyes were watching him through the windows. And Ranger had been in cahoots with the robber, if you looked at it a certain way.

He was scared of the dark but also scared of being in the light, yawningly sleepy but afraid to sleep, wanting to holler for help but still rational enough to know it would be foolish, or seem so to other people. Finally he pulled out the duofold in the parlor and went to bed with a baseball bat, with Ranger beside the bed and both lamps lit in the other rooms. Tense and jumpy, fighting a losing battle with sleep, he wept a little because of the irredeemable loss of what amounted to his entire summer's earnings.

He lay awake for ages before he drifted in and out of bad dreams, and finally awoke all sweaty and tired in the sultry mid-morning, feeling instantly sad. But in daylight he realized there was only one logical suspect, a known thief with a double motive, money and revenge. Old Chink.

He wanted to wake his dad, but his dad always slept late on Sundays and usually got up sort of bad-tempered. So after breakfast he went trudging dispiritedly down to the rendezvous to tell his partner why they were no longer in the squirrel business.

Mr. Strode was outraged. "Dirtiest deal I ever heard of," he growled. "Well, you can kiss the money good-bye, but he can't flash that rifle around here, an' the hardware must have the serial number. So you notify the law, an' in case the buzzard tries to hock it in some other town . . ."

Jeff felt a faint stir of hope, but not much optimism. Chink wasn't dumb enough to get caught that way. To make his misery complete, none of his customers wanted to skin catfish on a muggy Sunday, and neither did he. When he saw Dolittle's auto at the end of the street he went down there, hoping his friend would accept the fish as a present.

Chink's dog and Miss Burns were with Dolittle, who said he was trying to sell her the house and asked how come Jeff looked so down in the dumps. "Couldn't sell those fish?" he inquired, and Jeff said, "Well, that's partly it, I guess, but not mainly." And he told them the whole sad story.

"Well, first things first," Dolittle said. "I'd buy those fish if I knew anyone who could cook 'em properly."

"All right, smarty, buy them and find out," Miss Burns retorted prettily, and Jeff spared a moment to envy Dolittle, who grinned and said, "That takes care of the fish. As for the theft, I only know one bird low enough to pull that kind of deal, and he's not at home now so let's go talk to his uncle, who happens to be a friend of mine nowadays."

He searched the Britton house and Jeff searched all the outbuildings, but found no rifle. As they were leaving, Chink's uncle Ralph said from inside the house: "Wish you'd found it, so I'd have an excuse to get rid of that wiseacre kid."

But if wishes were green apples everybody would have the bellyache. If Chink took the rifle he must have hidden it somewhere else, or, Jeff thought with dull despair, tossed it in the creek or something. But maybe Chink *didn't* do it, in which case it could have been almost anybody. . . .

His dad still wasn't up, so he went to the café to eat an early dinner of chicken-fried steak and peach pie with ice cream on it, but his enjoyment was marred by thinking stuff like: maybe Lex or Von did it as a sort of joke, and they'll bring it back in a few days. But he wasn't fooling himself; he knew it was no joke. The rifle was gone for good, just like his life's savings, and he was destitute. Again. And in a mean enough mood to go give Alamo a piece of his mind, only she wasn't home. Neither was Hud, so he went on home

210

to read the Sunday funnies and wait for people to get back from Kansas.

They came up the street with his mother hurrying on ahead, his dad carrying the suitcase, and Mutt bringing up the rear, and he knew something was wrong. His mother came in the yard and up the steps like she didn't know he was there and sailed past him into the house, and slammed her bedroom door. When he saw his dad's bloodshot eyes and unshaven face he thought maybe that's what she was mad about, but his dad looked kind of sore himself and just shook his head at Jeff and went on inside. So when Mutt finally came through the gate, Jeff said, "What's the matter?"

And Mutt, acting like everything in the world was Jeff's fault, said, "We never even got to see Jody, you sap!" He stalked inside, and Jeff just sat in the porch swing staring at the gloomy street, feeling kind of helpless and hopeless.

Pretty soon his dad came back out with a cup of coffee and told him what had happened. When they got to Kansas yesterday evening his mother had called Uncle Tobe on the phone from the depot, which was her main mistake. She should of just got in a taxi and gone on out there. Uncle Tobe sounded surprised and hemmed and hawed, saying just a minute a couple times like he was holding his hand over the phone and talking to someone else, and he finally said, "Doggonit, Jewel, I wish we'd known you were coming. Gus and Jody left this morning to go visit her folks—they live on a farm forty miles from here with no phone. Stay where you are, I'll be right down."

So he came in his car and took them to a hotel, saying under the circumstances it wouldn't look right to put them up at home, Gus gone and all. He took them to a café for supper, then to a movie, jabbering all the time about how sorry he was he hadn't known they were coming, why didn't she give him advance warning, etc.

211

Then this morning he took them to breakfast, and Jewel said she'd love to see his house, but he said he'd just put his car in the garage for repairs—on a Sunday, mind you—and it was quite a ways out. But she kept after him until he finally took them out to his house in a taxi, and in the kitchen there were two plates with egg yolk on them, and a cup, and a glass with a milk ring, and other evidence that two people had eaten breakfast recently. At first Tobe said it was *yesterday's* breakfast dishes, but she said then there ought to be three plates and two coffee cups. So finally he gave up and admitted he'd lied last night, but this morning his wife had taken Jody to her parents' place in the car, and if Jewel insisted on hanging around he would call Gus and tell her not to return—because goddammit, Jody was giving them a hard enough time without her getting him all worked up, etc. So she finally gave up, and they came home, and that was that.

"I told her it was too soon." Jeff's dad sighed. "That poor little guy hasn't had time to get used to Kansas yet. I guess I woulda done the same thing Tobe did, in his shoes. Goddammit, it's better this way!"

That depended on what he meant by better.

18

An endless autumn rain set in, a cold interminable drizzle, and although he had a slicker and gum boots, going down the creek after school was a miserable deal. He didn't want to, but thinking of Dallas Strode camping down there made him feel sort of honor bound to do it. He could imagine how depressing it must be, how long the gloomy days must seem to his partner.

When Jeff got down there one Wednesday, his partner said, "Let's go where it's dry an' warm." And he took Jeff to his hideout, a sort of cave under a ledge halfway up the steep bluff, hidden from below by bushes and made snug and cozy by stacking rocks and logs across the opening. There was a small fire going, and Mr. Strode gave him a pan of steaming rabbit stew and some coffee.

"I never knew this cave was here," Jeff said, adding politely, "You're about as good a cook as your wife is."

His partner grinned. "Thanks, but I hope not, Jeff. I want her to keep that café job. If she gits hired on a steady basis, I'd wanta turn myself in without any publicity—but if she don't, I'd like to make a deal with someone to take me in an' split that reward. Know someone you can trust, that has a car an' might be willin' to help me out?"

Jeff nodded. "Sure, Dolittle, my dad's assistant. We're good friends, an' he's got an Oldsmobile."

Mr. Strode smoked for a moment. "Well, I trust your judgment, pardner. Tell him the whole thing, an' see if he'd haul me back over to Blackthorn, sometime next month. This place beats jail now, but wouldn't suit me too good when the weather turns cold. Say, I'm runnin' low on coffee an' tobacco. About all I've done these last three days is smoke an' drink coffee."

And eat delicious stews and stuff, Jeff thought.

Thursday it didn't rain much and Friday the clouds began to dissipate, but it still wasn't what you'd call good fighting weather. Too muddy and slick.

Jeff didn't hear about the upcoming showdown until afternoon recess, when Hud said, "You gonna stick around an' watch the fight, or go run your trotlines?" Jeff said what fight, and Hud acted surprised. "Ain't you heard? Ol' Mutton an' Fred Leeks are gonna fight Lumpy Jackson after school." *Fred Leeks!* Jeff said disbelievingly, because Fred, a freshman buddy of Mutt's, medium-sized and mild-mannered, never had a fight in his life.

Hud said Lumpy was picking on Fred at noon and Mutt took it up, so Lumpy said he'd fight them both together. Jeff felt something like alarm, because if those saps fought old Lumpy, Mutt would have to do most of the fighting, and he'd be outweighed maybe forty pounds. He needed some of the sarcastic cockiness knocked out of him, but not by a big mean lummox like Lumpy.

It seemed to Jeff that his brother looked a trifle worried the rest of the day, but he never doubted that Mutt would go through with it. Gritty as a rooster and proud as a peacock, he wouldn't back down from anybody.

It was kind of a nervous afternoon for Jeff, too. He had to go to the pencil sharpener and on the way back Ethel Peck slipped him a note from Alamo that read tersely: I need to talk to you tonight! And he knew what about. She wondered why he'd been acting kind of sore. Well, he'd tell her, don't worry, boy. Get shut of Clarence or else.

But he didn't know what to do about the fight. If he stayed to watch it and Mutt got beat up, his dad might say,

"You mean you just stood there and let that big sonofagun pound on your own brother?" So the sensible thing would be to just go on about his own business like he didn't even know there was going to be a fight.

When the bell rang, Alamo was the first one out of the room, and when he got downstairs and outside she was sailing up the street like she was afraid he'd try to catch up or something. Someone oughta tell her that J. McGraw would never run after any girl. If he seemed to be walking fast it had nothing to do with her, it was a private family matter.

He got all the way home before he changed his mind, put his books on the porch, and headed back to the corner where all after-school fights were held. He wasn't sure why, but he had to go watch it—maybe because he didn't want to be the only guy in town that missed it.

The mob surrounding the principals was milling around between the Methodist church and the lumberyard, and he leaned on a maple tree by the paint shed and watched the confused proceedings. He could see Lumpy's shaggy head but not Mutt or Fred, because of the wall of spectators, and was about to move closer when Hud came over and said excitedly, "Fred never showed up, he skinned out for home."

Jeff sighed, both relieved and disappointed.

"But Mutt's gonna fight 'im anyway," Hud reported.

Jeff couldn't believe his ears. Mutt was spunky, but he wasn't crazy, for gosh sakes! Was he?

Apparently he was. The circle of spectators began to spread out, and through a gap he saw Mutt backing toward him with his dukes up, and big lumbering Lumpy following him—and kicking at his legs! *Kicking!* That was dirty fighting, but it was happening, with Mutt dancing around avoiding Lumpy's big muddy brogans. Jeff started moving in closer, scared for Mutt and feeling very strange.

Lumpy took a few clumsy swings that missed, and Mutt ducked under one of the wild haymakers and hit him on the nose, but Lumpy kicked out at him and caused Mutt to slip on the slick mud and fall. Then Lumpy started to kick him while he was down—which was when, much to his own astonishment, Jeff substituted for the defected Fred Leeks and joined the fray.

Outraged more than angered, and certainly not from any love for his darn brother, Jeff just took a sudden run and jumped on Lumpy's broad back and wrapped his arms around the bull neck, horrified at what he was doing but unable to control his reckless impulse. Lumpy gave an indignant yell and began trying to unlock the strangling arm and plaster cast, and Mutt jumped up and started peppering him with fast punches. Lumpy slipped and fell, so Jeff dismounted, scared silly but also kind of elated.

"You dirty little %&*#%*&!" Lumpy snarled, getting up and coming after Jeff, a tactical mistake allowing Mutt to slug him in the kidneys, and then in the face when he whirled around. But Mutt was a little careless and Lumpy got him by the shirtfront and drew back his big fist—so Jeff mounted up again, hooking the cast under Lumpy's chin and grabbing his wrist so he couldn't pulverize Mutt. But he paid for it, because Lumpy started hitting back over his shoulders with both fists. Before he could slide off and get away Jeff got hit once in the eye, and on the head a million times, it felt like. But meanwhile Mutt was punishing Lumpy worse, one punch hitting him smack in the mouth.

Jeff was groggy and confused after that, but he remembered jumping on Lumpy's back at least once more, with the tiring bully trying to shake him off and protect his face from Mutt. Then suddenly it was all over; Lumpy was backing away from the deadly team of McGraw and McGraw, bleeding from the nose and mouth, and he kept backing away until he got some people between him and Mutt. Then he turned and took off for the school barn in abject retreat. He was outnumbered, outmaneuvered, probably tired from carrying Jeff around, and he'd had enough. He

216

should have had a sore Adam's apple from Jeff's cast, and busted knuckles from hitting Jeff on the skull.

Mutt grinned fiercely after the vanquished foe and blew on his sore knuckles, his only injuries. Jeff had a black eye, a skinned forehead and about fifty welts and knots on his head, plus some of Lumpy's red blood on his plaster cast. So after watching the bully's ignominious retreat, the audience crowded around Mutt and showered him with praise and congratulations. Boy, you sure worked 'im over, Mutton. Man, how many times you reckon you hit 'im, anyway? Musta been a couple hunnert at least.

Hud looked at Jeff with something akin to astonishment and said, "How many times did *you* hit 'im, Jiffer?" Jeff just shook his ringing head and started home, because he hadn't even hit old Lumpy *once*. All he'd done was jump on his back and choke him. Old piggyback Jeff, the terror of the West. If someone said, hey, I hear you had a fight with Lumpy, he'd hafta say, naw, I just rode him a little, choked him and slowed him down so he wouldn't kill my brother, is all I done. Don't give me no credit, boys.

He was almost home when Mutt overtook him and said, "Wot's the rush?" Gotta go run my durn trotlines, Jeff replied, and Mutt heaved a wheezy laugh and said, "How come you jumped in? I thought you didn't like me as much as I didn't like you! For cripe sakes, I don't git it."

It was a big mystery to Jeff, too, so he said, "I was scared he'd lame you up an' I'd hafta carry your papers."

"Anyway, we sure cleaned his plow," Mutt gloated.

We, hell, Jeff thought. In case anyone wanted the straight of it, what happened was Mutt whipped Lumpy and Lumpy whipped Jeff, who still hadn't had a fight; all he'd done was help his brother have one.

Their mother was in mournful seclusion as usual, so they didn't have to explain Jeff's bruises and Mutt's muddy britches. While changing clothes Jeff thought: Well, it just goes to prove blood is thicker than water—and lots harder to wash off. His cast was so dirty he needed to whitewash it or something.

At supper when his mother scolded him for fighting while his arm was still in the cast he said heck, that was his best weapon. And his dad said while they were on the subject, that cast was getting pretty ripe and it was probably time for Doc to remove it.

"Or put on a new one," Jeff said hopefully, because he sure dreaded having to part with the security a cast gave him, the immunity from stuff. Like fights, for example.

There was a beautiful sunset, and as he sauntered toward the butcher shop he felt pretty mellow and decided he wouldn't be too gruff with her if she sort of apologized. He hadn't kissed her in a long time and sorta missed it.

She was so anxious to patch things up that she was waiting for him by the Bull Durham sign, just like the first night, and heck-fire, he was willing to let bygones be bygones. "Howdy," he said amiably.

"This won't take long," she said. "Is it true about you runnin' home after school all last year from Chester what's-his-name?"

Jeff was taken aback, and very embarrassed. "Well," he said, "we had us a few footraces."

"If *you'd* told me," she said, "maybe I woulda—wouldn't —well, you can see my position, no doubt."

"No doubt," he said. "Who told you, Mutt?"

"I'm not tellin'," she said. "I couldn't hardly b'lieve it until I asked some others—anyway, you can see what a peculiar position it puts me in. . . ."

What about *his* position? He felt sick, but tried to act casual, saying, "I guess it's so long then, huh?"

"Well, at least that's how I feel now," she told him, and fled into the butcher shop, leaving him to his shame and sorrow and disgrace and other stuff. *Well,* he thought bitterly, *maybe me and Fred Leeks could organize a coward's club. I guess I didn't prove anything today.* He'd sorta known that sooner or later they'd bust up, but gosh almighty, not like this! If she'd said she didn't love him anymore, okay, fine. But this way she was ashamed to be his girl, and from now on whenever he saw her he'd feel all hot with embarrassment probably. He wished she'd move away to another town.

Saturday, being rifleless and girlless, he didn't know what to do with himself except play his French harp in the barn loft. He even played "Somebody Stole My Gal," although it didn't fit the case. While playing "The Prisoner Song" he remembered about Dallas Strode, so he went around to Dolittle's place to have a secret parley with him.

Dolittle was painting the new addition to his house with the help of Miss Burns, Clara Conners and Lizzie Horn, and they all took time off to admire Jeff's black eye. Miss Burns said normally she didn't approve of fighting but in this case she understood Jeff pitching in to help his brother, etc. Dolittle apparently sensed from Jeff's manner that the visit wasn't social and said, "Let's us withdraw and allow these flappers to get on with their exterior decorating."

"Calling me a flapper is a good way to get your nose painted apple green, sonny boy," Liz Horn called after them.

In the garden, while eating some runty autumn tomatoes, Jeff confessed to his involvement with an escaped criminal and explained the need for a trustworthy accessory. Dolittle was amazed and kind of delighted.

"I thought there was something odd about your flourishing fish business," he said, "but I never woulda guessed you were partners with a wanted man. You tell Vern's dad whenever he's ready to go back I'll drive him over to Blackthorn."

"Another thing is, if somebody tried to accuse him of the bank robbery we could swear it wasn't him," Jeff said, and added, "But I still don't understand about that deal."

Dolittle said the way he figured, Mr. Bradman needed to cover a shortage and hired some guy to fake the bank heist,

219

but everything went wrong and old George found out about it when he helped count the recovered washers. But instead of turning Bradman over to the law he transferred him to the feed mill in Walston so he could dock his wages until the shortage was made up—except that old George might have been in on it, too. "It'll always be a big mystery to me," he said, "but I don't aim to lose any sleep over it."

"Me neither," Jeff said. Ambling homeward, he felt pretty good about Mr. Strode's situation, but then he remembered his own situation and began dreading facing people Monday at school. It was probably all over town by now, how Alamo ditched him, and why. The why of it was the bad part.

The first person to mention his disgrace was Caroline, who was waiting in her front yard with a sort of message for him. "I saw Alma this mornin' an' she told me about bustin' up with you," she said, "but see, she didn't know then about you fightin' that big bully yesterday afternoon yet."

"I didn't fight 'im, I rode him," Jeff said.

She didn't see the humor of it. "Anyway she says what she said last night wasn't necessarily final—I'm spose to tell you that." Her expression was sort of anxious.

Feeling vindicated but bruised, Jeff said, "You tell her even with chewin' gum she always tasted onionish."

Caroline clapped a hand to her mouth, horrified. "Oh, I couldn't!" She giggled. "Did she really?"

"Aw, just sometimes," Jeff said. "But so did I, maybe." Nobody could say he wasn't fair about stuff like that.

Caroline said she seldom ever ate onions herself.

After lunch his sad-eyed mother ordered him to get his spoiled cast removed, so he went reluctantly to Doc Schuman's office in back of the drugstore, and old Doc said: "Phew, you should haff come in sooner." He used vinegar and his pocket knife to remove the cast, examined the arm and said wash it good with soap and water and don't be doing any monkeyshines in trees from now on. Well, but

220

shouldn't he use a sling for a while? Jeff asked, and Doc shrugged and said, "Chust as you please, Cheff, it's your arm."

So he told his mother Doc said it wouldn't hurt to keep his arm in a sling awhile longer, and she made him one out of an old sheet, extending his time of peace and security.

No longer feeling disgraced, he sauntered around to Main Street mentally prepared to face Alamo with studied indifference, and prepared to discuss the Lumpy Jackson brawl if anyone was interested. But he didn't see Alma, and the only fight anyone wanted to discuss was the million-dollar Dempsey-Tunney brawl they'd heard on the radio—which was like being there at ringside, so they were all experts on the subject.

According to Jeff's dad, who had lost money on the fight, it was the biggest gyp of the century; Tunney was kayoed fair and square, coldcocked, but hell almighty, anyone could come to if you gave him that long count the referee gave Tunney. So those were Jeff's sentiments, too, although he didn't really care one way or the other. All the arguments in the world couldn't change the outcome, so the heck with it. And the heck with Alamo, too, who skated past him twice that afternoon without stopping to apologize, although she did say "Hi" both times.

That weekend old Bill resumed his interrupted journey. Dolittle said he and Miss Evans had seen the dog five miles west of town on their way to the Saturday night movie over in Blackthorn. Jeff felt pretty sad about it, but he had to admire Bill for his courage, family loyalty, and for knowing which direction California was. Anyone that would ditch a dog like Bill didn't deserve a dog like Bill.

Sunday at supper Mutt said, "After tomorrow you take back your washday job, Catfish." He didn't deserve a brother like Jeff, so Jeff retorted: "Tomorrow's when Mr. Glass paddles you an' Lumpy for fightin' on the way home from

221

school." Mutt said oh yeah, what about yourself? Jeff grinned. "I come home first." "Oh, yeah?" Mutt repeated. "How you gonna prove it?"

"By me," their mother said from the kitchen. "He put his books on the porch, and I'll give him a note to take to school. It seems he used his noodle for once in his life." It was a left-handed compliment, but Jeff appreciated it.

"But I didn't know I was gonna fight," he said. "An' if I had it to do over I probably wouldn't." He was an honest man.

"Oh, I think you would," his mother said from where she was scraping a pan, and that was a *real* compliment if you looked at it a certain way. It sounded like she thought he had guts and gumption. He only wished he was that certain of it himself, but doggonit, how could you tell in advance?

19

He'd never fully realized what a comfort the plaster cast had been until he tried living without it. A cast needed no alibi, whereas a sling had a dubious character and required vague excuses. But it was better than no protection at all, and you could carry other things in it besides a timid arm. Books and stuff.

"How long you hafta use that hammock?" guys would ask, and he'd reply, "I dunno, Doc didn't say for sure."

He didn't use it during recesses unless Chester was hovering around, but he didn't go in for sports, either. No acrobatics on the pipes and swings, no playing catch, wrestling, or even footracing. Just marbles or spinning tops, because you had to be darn careful long after a green fracture seemed to be healed. It was a wonder he hadn't reinjured it in the fight—but who could say for sure he hadn't?

Monday, after Supt. Virgil Glass paddled Mutt, he came back to class dry-eyed and grinning, making him even more of a hero. Whereas Jeff seemed to lose face a little, like he'd violated an unwritten code by going home before the fight so he wouldn't get paddled. Nobody put it into words, but it was funny how soon they shortened the nickname Piggyback McGraw to just Piggy. Anything that could be shortened usually was, but it rankled to have guys call Mutt "Tooney" and him Piggy, even good-naturedly.

Being a whole man again was a continuing worry, but

for several days after the breakup of his first love affair he felt itchy self-conscious, wondering who all she'd told, and he was extremely uncomfortable in the same room with her. When nobody mentioned the subject, he gradually stopped feeling nervous about it, but he avoided her and tried not to get caught looking at her. He wasn't even sure he'd want to resume that sort of sneak-around romance. He might just prefer the kind of deal where you could sit in a porch swing and eat popcorn with a girl, by gosh.

So the mellow late September days passed, uneventfully on the surface but with an undercurrent of tension, a feeling that the inevitable had only been postponed. He wondered if other guys ever had that uneasy sense of some calamity hanging over their heads. And all the glum self-doubts, the fear that when a real showdown came you just wouldn't be able to stand up to it. How could you tell?

Because of after-school chores and all, he'd cut the fish-selling down to Tuesdays, Thursdays and weekends. He still had as many fish that way but a lot less walking to do, and more time for playing in the street after supper. There was usually a marble game under the corner street-lamp every night, or he'd roll hoops with Caroline and Hud —and wonder what old Alamo was doing, only who cared?

A week after jilting him she smiled at him in the hallway and said, "Hi, Jess, how's your arm?" Fine, he replied, how's yours? And kept going. Maybe later on when it got too cold for night marble games he might take up with her again, but only on a part-time basis, like say two nights a week, weather permitting.

That night at supper his mother announced: "I wrote a letter today notifying your brother and his wife that I'm coming next Saturday to see Jody." At that point she lost her composure and began weeping. "And he-he duh-darn well better buh-be there this time." She looked at her husband with streaming eyes. "I know you cuh-can't get a pass

224

that soon, and we can't afford it, but I've juh-just got to see my baby . . ." As usual she got up and rushed out of there, and as usual the three of them just sat there staring at their food like it was poisoned, and finally their dad said, "Maybe the budget can stand one round-trip ticket, but not two." He sighed. "It would be Jeff's turn, but . . ."

"Let Mutt go," Jeff said. "I'll deliver his papers."

"Dammit, what I'm saying," his father growled, "is I can't afford to send either of you guys . . ."

"Heck, I can," Mutt interrupted. "I'll buy both of the tickets, Dad. Call it a birthday present for Mom."

"Well, I'll pay half of Mom's ticket," Jeff volunteered.

That's when their dad got up and went out on the porch, swearing a little. Mutt went to the bedroom door and called out, "C'mon back to supper, Maw, it's all settled. We're goin'."

It would have been a dandy weekend if he still had his rifle. Sunny but crisp, with the trees turning all shades of green and yellow with splotches of red here and there. Indian summer was a great time of year, but a little sad because it wouldn't last long. Then pow! winter.

Saturday he took his partner some bacon and coffee. Vern kept his dad supplied with eggs, and he was eating a lot of bacon and eggs now. He said they never had fried eggs or good bacon in jail, and he aimed to enjoy stuff like that while he could. Which, he remarked, might not be much longer, because that strutty kid with the opera glasses had been prowling down there yesterday afternoon and had robbed some of the trotlines. But he hadn't found the fish in the spring branch.

Jeff sighed and shook his head. That dang Chink.

Mr. Strode grinned. "I put a hex on 'im, the old Indian sign. If it works he'll break a leg." Jeff figured he was just kidding; only witches could hex people. After sharing his noon meal of smothered swamp rabbit, Mr. Strode said if it could be arranged he'd like to meet the man who was going

225

to help him bust back into jail, and Jeff felt depressed on the way to town, knowing he couldn't keep the fish business going without old Flew-the-Coop. Once a guy got accustomed to having money it would be a calamity to be poor again. He didn't have much to show for his summer's work as it was, after being robbed and all. But at least he had an agate shooting taw.

That evening was balmy and ideal for shooting marbles, but nobody was on the corner when he arrived, and he was standing there debating whether to get up on the paint shed roof and wait, or amble on downtown, when someone made the decision for him. A big crumbly clod came whizzing out of the dark and whapped him in the back. It didn't hurt much but it startled him into explosive action, and as he sprinted toward Main Street he tried putting his own hex on sneaking Chink Britton, wishing he'd just break a finger on his damn throwing hand. Was that asking too much?

About an hour later Earl Yancy—who delivered cobs, among other things—went down across his yard to look at the stars, as he put it, but saw instead the silhouette of someone in the elm tree by the hotel bathroom window, and hollered: "What the hell you think you're doin' over there?"

The guy in the tree started scrambling down, suddenly fell with an audible thump, got up, and tore out around the front of the hotel—where Slim McGraw was coming down the cinder path from the railroad tracks. Slim snapped on his six-cell flashlight and said, "Hold 'er, Newt. What's all the rush?"

"Which way'd he go?" Chink asked excitedly. "I seen a guy lurkin' around yonder an' woulda got clost enough to see who it was if Yancy hadn't yelled an' scairt 'im."

"I didn't see or hear a soul," Slim said. "Except you."

"He musta cut around back, then," Chink said. "Maybe if I hurry I can spot 'im over on Main." Whereupon he went running north, and Jeff's dad shrugged and headed on up the street, and met Earl Yancy at his driveway. They discussed the curious occurrence, and Earl said, whoever it was, the buzzard didn't climb down, he fell a good six feet. A wonder the dang prowler hadn't killed hisself.

Jeff was loitering in front of Arlene's Café waiting for Vern to finish his dishwashing chores, inhaling the delectable aromas wafting out the windows, when he saw old Chink come limping up the sidewalk and turn into the drugstore solicitously clutching his left shoulder with his right hand, too preoccupied to see his enemy there.

It seemed like a good time to go home, knowing Chink wouldn't be lurking somewhere along the way with a supply of clods or slingshot rock. It was darn seldom you could be sure where that guy was at any given time.

Sunday afternoon Dolittle parked his Olds by the gate to Buffalo Wallows and they walked the rest of the way because he didn't want to risk his casings on the rocks and cactus. At the rendezvous the two men shook hands and talked about the war awhile, smoking, and then Mr. Strode said he'd like to be a free man another week or two if the weather stayed nice. Jeff listened soberly, brooding about the impossibility of running the business by himself. Anyway, who'd want to run trotlines in cold weather? Dadgummit, he'd just have to get used to being broke all the time again.

"Sure wish I could see my wife an' kids before I go back," Mr. Strode said. "But Vern says she's at the café 'til ten ever' night. An' the little fellers would be asleep . . ."

"Why, shucks," Dolittle said, "nobody in town would know you with a haircut an' respectable clothes. You could walk right in the café like a customer, durin' a slack time, say a Sunday mornin' while church is goin' on. We'll just sashay in there an' eat before we drive to Blackthorn, Dallas."

"Oh, man, wouldn't that be something?" Mr. Strode said. "Sure make turnin' myself in somewhat easier." He squinted at his cigarette. "Many a night layin' here I made up my mind to cut out for east Texas an' send for the family soon as I got located—an' I reckon I would if she was gonna be takin' in washin' this winter. But she's all set now, gettin' paid good for doin' something she likes . . ." He smiled ruefully. "Seven days a week, with just a couple hours off afternoons. Won't be able to come visit me, for the next long old year, I guess, but we can tough that out some way."

"No problem there," Dolittle said. "I'm free afternoons an' I'll be glad to drive your wife over to see you an' fetch you a sack of hamburgers once a week. Or even oftener."

Dallas Strode winked and blinked for a moment, then went to the cave opening and squinted off into the timber, and used his thumb to blow his nose and shook his head like he couldn't quite believe his good luck, or something.

"I'd forgot about this cave," Dolittle told Jeff. "Use to come here when I was your age." He got up off his rock. "Well, I'm takin' my gal out to dinner this evenin' . . ."

"Hold on," Mr. Strode said. He went over to his bedroll and got the Bible Jeff had loaned him. "I've read a right smart of this good, an' it was slow goin', but maybe it's done me some good." He gave Jeff a sober gaze. "It's just like when you lent it to me, pard. Nothin' missing."

That seemed like an odd thing to say, but Dolittle was ready to leave, so Jeff just nodded uncertainly and they all said their so-longs. "Just notify Jeff when you're ready, Dallas," Dolittle said, and they headed back to town, with Jeff still puzzled by that remark. So when they got in the Oldsmobile he opened the Bible and began turning pages, and the first thing he knew he found a dollar bill. Then another, and another, until he'd found nine one-dollar bills in all.

"So that's where Turkey banked his savings." Dolittle smiled. "Looks like you just inherited a fortune, pard."

"Not me," Jeff protested. "It's really your Bible."

"I gave it to you, so that money is your problem, not

mine," Dolittle said, and abruptly changed the subject. "I was just thinkin', ol' George Rose has a lot of political pull in this county. Suppose I told him we looked in that bank bag and know the robbery was a put-up job. Then I remark that a friend of mine is turnin' himself in to the law an' I sure would appreciate ol' George usin' his influence to see this army buddy doesn't have to do extra time for breakin' out, an' gets treated decent while he's in there." He cocked an eye at Jeff. "Reckon that'd be blackmail?"

Jeff grinned. "I dunno, but it's a keen idea."

The nine unearned, undeserved dollars kept nagging at his conscience until that evening, while pumping wash water, he suddenly knew what to do with the money. Give it to his mother for the railroad tickets and stuff. Maybe that was the way God intended it to be used, he reflected solemnly and a trifle sanctimoniously. Maybe the Lord was trying to give him back part of his lost life savings, even, as a reward for being generous although no longer well-to-do.

So in a way he was thinking of Chink when Hud showed up with the news that old Chink had caught the morning southbound passenger train and left town. For good, he'd said.

Jeff was delighted but puzzled. "How come he went?"

Hud grinned. "On account of his collarbone he claims he fell an' broke chasin' you last night after catchin' you winder-peekin' down at the hotel." When Jeff began sputtering angry denials, he held up a hand. "He only said it looked like you but he couldn't be sure. Anyways, he can't take care of his uncle anymore so he went an' up an' blew town."

"I'm sure gonna miss that sonofagun." Jeff grinned. "Hey, was he carrying anything long an' narrow, like a rifle?"

Hud shook his head. "Funny, though, he did mention your rifle. Said if he hadda stold it he'd of hid it in the last place you'd ever think about lookin' for it."

"That's a lotta help," Jeff said, scowling.

"Ol' Chink announced to all them at the depot to see him off, which was jist me an' the agent, that this here's the sorriest town he ever had to live in," Hud went on. "I was of a mind to say any town he lived in would be sorry about it, but I didden because I was so blue about him leavin' us."

Jeff wondered about Chink's dog, and Hud said Chink told the agent he guessed someone would hafta shoot ol' Killer if they wanted to go inside the Britton yard. That made Jeff laugh, because apparently Chink never did find out how his Killer had been exposed as a big blowhard renamed Wilbur.

"Well, I just thought you'd wanta know he's gone, you an' him bein' such dear pals," Hud said. "I'll let you git back to your favert pastime of pumpin' water." He started to leave, then added: "They painted the bathroom winder, but I wasn't aimin' to use it no more anyhow."

Another temptation removed, Jeff thought.

That night at supper Mutt announced he had a new part-time job, shopping for Major Ralph Britton and helping Granny Hanks look after the house, and taking care of Chink's dog Killer that had miraculously become tame and gentle as soon as his ornery master left town. Jeff let it go at that.

Jeff forgot to wear his sling Monday morning and worried about it until recess, when he found out he wouldn't need it any longer. Hope Cannon, the new third- and fourth-grade teacher, had been noticing Chester chasing Spotty and other guys after school because she liked to look at the view out the north windows, and she finally reported it to Superintendent Glass, who called Chester in that morning and put the fear of Virgil Glass in him. No more chasing kids after school. Great news for all the rabbits, including Jeff McGraw. There was other sort of great news at supper Monday. Jeff's dad said guess who came back to town, and Jeff recoiled, thinking: Oh lord, not Chink! "Old Bill came limping back this afternoon," his dad said. "I expect he finally heard how far it is to California." Then before Jeff could put in his bid for a keen squirrel dog of his very own, his dad added, "I gave him to the Coonrod boys."

Jeff was bitterly disappointed for a moment, but then he thought: Well, heck, the railroad *owed* the Coonrod boys a dog, after running over Prince last summer. They needed Bill worse than he did, probably.

Tuesday he didn't need to make anyone think his arm was still puny, so he had a lot of fun chinning himself and skinning the cat and so forth, pretending not to see Alamo watching him in a kind of friendly, willing way. He also pretended he didn't notice old Chester watching him, too. But shoot, he didn't need to worry about outrunning that ornery sap anymore, so he gave the glowering erstwhile chaser of scared guys a sort of tauntingly nonchalant, somewhat sarcastic grin.

20

There was something contagious about crisp October that made guys feel peppy, reckless and kind of ornery. Like Wednesday, during the noon hour when the teachers, the janitor and the town kids were home eating dinner, some of the country boys got an itch to have a real old-fashioned cob fight. The cob pile was in the girls' side of the basement, so either they trespassed, or else got some of the girls to furnish the ammunition. In wintertime Mr. Bird would sometimes let guys go down there and shoot rats with their slingshots or BB guns, but it was a scandalous offense for a boy to invade that female sanctuary during a school day.

Whoever furnished them, the schoolyard was littered with cobs, mostly water-soaked, when Jeff went back after lunch. Soaked cobs threw better and inflicted more damage, and he sorta wished he'd been there during the battle, but his first thought was: Doggone it, I forgot to tell Dad we need cobs again. And as soon as he got upstairs he wrote a reminder and put it in his shirt pocket, hoping he didn't forget that, too. Then he tried to settle down and concentrate on studies, but it wasn't easy with golden October beckoning outside, the trees aflame with color, the air hazy. Boy, to be out in the woods just rambling around. It was torture to be cooped up inside on a day like this.

Even when recess finally came, his longing was only aggravated by the restricted allowance of freedom, and he tried to work off his fidgets by exercising vigorously. He chinned himself a dozen times, and was skinning the cat when a hard wet corncob whacked him in the back, and it hurt like heck. Upside down and looking the other way, he bellowed: "You dirty stinkin' rotten . . ." Stinging and smarting and reckless with anger, he dropped to the ground and finished: ". . . yeller-bellied buzzard!" Then his enraged vision cleared and he saw who had thrown the damn cob, and got an awful sinking feeling.

Chester acted surprised for a second, then put on his malevolent, intimidating scowl and said ominously, "*Whud you call me?*" Suddenly people were coming from all directions. Rubbing his back, Jeff muttered: "You heard me . . . if you the one threw that cob."

Chester glowered menacingly. "You better take it back."

Jeff tried to scowl and shook his head, aware of all the avid eyes on him. He longed desperately to take back his rash, impetuous words, but something in him just wouldn't let him eat crow with all those people watching, *expecting* him to back down. Hud and Dock, Jake, Windy and Jelly, Lefty, Nate, Spotty; Caroline and Alamo, Eunice Tifferton, Alice Brubaker. Vern Strode. And Mutt McGraw. He would rather die than act the coward in front of such an audience, and he just stood there, his back smarting, dumbly shaking his head. He'd stepped across an invisible line and couldn't go back without losing honor, self-respect, pride, the esteem of friends and ex-girlfriends. Life would be intolerable forevermore if he backed down now.

"If I's you I'd take it back," Hud said. Mutt didn't offer any advice. Vern was mute. Caroline said, "I saw the mean thing you did, Chester Stone!" Alamo remained silent and neutral, and that was her final mistake.

"Gonna take it back?" Chester demanded, and Jeff said in a strange, bleak voice: "Heck no I ain't." Chester blinked, then squinted. "See you after school, then," he said, and went swaggering toughly away.

There was only astonishment and pity in the faces of the

onlookers, and that was pretty much how Jeff felt about himself, too. But he tried to act unconcerned and went back to skinning the cat, sickly aware that at four o'clock he was going to get the stuffing knocked out of him. He hung upside down on the pipe awhile because the world looked a little better that way and made more sense. Some of the bystanders lingered, staring at him with disbelief before they began to drift away looking dazed, troubled, shocked, trying to understand what madness had suddenly possessed normally sensible, good-natured Jeff McGraw. Finally only Caroline remained, gazing at him with worried admiration, and he did ten chin-ups, partly for her benefit but mostly because he couldn't think of anything else to do. Oh man, if he could only stop the clock, so four P.M. would never come . . .

Usually he could forget worries by reading, but not today; not impending disaster. The printed page blurred and shimmered, and he was trapped inside his head, tormented by his dread. The others in the room didn't seem real, for they had nothing to do with this terrible thing, they were safely out of it. He was aware of Mutt's sober, appraising scrutiny, of Hud's concerned glances, of Alma's questioning over-the-shoulder looks, and all the other eyes upon him, and he envied each and every one of them because they weren't *him*.

He wished *he* wasn't him, either. He'd rather be somebody else, or something else, preferably something with a nice secure hole to hide in, faraway and safe from cob-throwing bullies. Thinking of faraway places he'd rather be at the moment, he couldn't think of any place he wouldn't rather be.

"Jeff?" somebody said. A vaguely familiar voice. "Are you all right?" Miss Ewbanks asked solicitously. "Don't you feel well?" She didn't know, of course, why that question caused a few muffled, callous sniggers.

Oh, man! Jeff thought. The perfect excuse. He really was

sick, and all he had to do was admit it, and she would excuse him and let him go on home and escape his doom—for the time being. He wasn't so sick he couldn't see that running out would only postpone the inevitable massacre, and he'd have to suffer this dreadful waiting a whole extra day. And people would think—would know . . .

He managed a lame smile. "I'm okay," he said. I just wish I was dead, is all, he thought with a shuddery sigh. Faintly, from over in the auditorium, he heard people singing, rehearsing for tomorrow's assembly program, and recognized the song. "The Big Rock Candy Mountain"—where the bulldogs all had rubber teeth and the cops had wooden legs, etc. He sorta wished he had rubber teeth. Or Chester had wooden legs. And he kept remembering how it had felt the time Chink bloodied his nose, the time he fell out of the tree, the time . . .

The bell began to ring and his heart leaped into his throat. It couldn't be four o'clock yet!

"Lemmee have your books an' stuff," Hud said. It was four o'clock, all right. Then Mutt was there, saying, "You got your pockets fulla junk, as usual, Jeff?" He hadn't called Jeff by his right name in years. It was four o'clock, doomsday for Jefferson McGraw.

He began unloading his pockets of marbles, knife, whetstone, string, sinkers, matches, a walnut he was carving into a monkey-face ring, and the note to himself. "Give this to Dad," he mumbled. "We're runnin' low on cobs."

They escorted him down the stairs and outside, all the partisan seventh- and eighth-graders, and he went like a condemned man resigned to his fate, silent and obedient, staring east along the street and longing for home and mother, so near but a million miles away. It appeared that only girls and little kids were leaving. The word was out, a crazy sap was going to fight Chester—stick around, boys. Once across the street, his feet had a tendency to keep going, but his well-wishers, or pallbearers or whatever they were, hemmed him in and detained him. "We'll wait for Chester here, then go on up to the corner," Lex Yancy said.

They waited, and Conrad Coonrod said maybe Slapper was keeping Chester in, but a sixth-grader said: No, she ain't. So they waited, and Jeff suspected it was Chester's way of making him more scared, turning him into a nervous wreck.

When Chester finally appeared he seemed preoccupied and absentmindedly headed for the school barn, and for a moment hope of clemency stirred in Jeff's tight chest. But these people didn't mean to be cheated out of their gory spectacle, and they began to call out to the foreordained victor, asking where the heck he thought he was going. "Sumatter, Chesty, you scairta Jiffy?" Dock Ballew yelled. "You runnin' out?" It was the age-old story: Let's you and him fight.

Chester turned and came marching confidently to fulfill his duty to the roused mob, and Von Yancy said, "Less take it up to the lumberyard." Because naturally they didn't want the teachers stopping it before it got interesting, and that was where the big fights were always held—across from the church where all the funerals were held.

Jeff kept reminding himself that it was no disgrace to get whipped, but a coward could never live it down. Don't shame the family name. Even in his desperate plight his subconscious rhymer went on functioning. In a week or two I'll be as good as new . . .

Von appointed himself referee by saying: "Okay, this is far enough. Stand back an' give 'em room." Then Chester was being pushed into position, and Jeff noticed that discrepancy—Chester coming not too eagerly to the fray? Or maybe just not liking to be pushed. Requiring no assistance.

In times of great peril even backsliders may consider the efficacy of prayer, and Jeff suddenly remembered how Jody used to end his bedtime devotion with: "If I should die before I wake, wake me yup." In spite of his tremulous fear and dread he grinned a little, and Chester's scowl slipped a trifle, revealing wary, puzzled uncertainty.

The impatient Romans began to exhort the gladiators. C'mon, wotta you waitin' for? Yess go! We ain't got all night! Start the show, you guys!

"Well, do sumpthin'," Chester growled, but Jeff just blinked at him, unable to make the first hostile move. "Whut yuh waitin' for?" Chester asked him, and he replied: "Wotta you waitin' for yourself?"

Then suddenly they weren't waiting anymore, because Lex Yancy gave Chester a shove, sending him lunging toward Jeff, who struck out in cornered desperation and hit his enemy smack in the eye. The lucky punch caused Chester to reel and clinch to keep from falling down, but Jeff mistook it for an attempt to wrestle and, with the extra strength of panic, flung his lighter opponent to his knees and backed away, holding his fists like pictures of Dempsey. Angered and embarrassed, Chester launched a voluntary attack that fared no better than the involuntary one had, because Jeff wasn't thinking anymore, or scared anymore, but merely obeying a primitive instinct for self-preservation, lashing out with both fists and discovering that without a baseball bat old Chester was only human. Tough and aggressive, but lighter and a bit shorter, the famous Chester Stone was vulnerable, and maybe Jeff had boxed enough, or watched enough boxing, to be much better at fighting than he'd ever dreamed. He was hitting Chester oftener than Chester was hitting him, and kind of amazed at how little it hurt to get hit.

Chester's main asset, belligerent aggressiveness, was also his main weakness—he kept charging into Jeff's pumping, flailing fists. No fancy footwork or feinting, just crude country-style fistfighting, spunky but foolish, even clumsy. He just kept boring in, and Jeff would hit him and get hit in return, then they would clinch, and Jeff would use his superior weight to shove Chester away. The trouble was, Chester kept coming back for more, undiscouraged and tenacious, and Jeff's surprised delight in his hitherto unsuspected fighting ability began to fade a little, crowded out by a growing anxiety. How many times did you have to hit a guy to make him start backing away instead of always attacking?

In the heat of battle he felt no aches or pains, but he was getting tired, arm-weary and short of breath, and maybe that was Chester's sly plan, to just wear him down to a nubbin and then finish him off. And nobody would stop it—all those darn yahoos would let it go on forever. But Chester was tiring too, and by a kind of unspoken agreement the clinches were getting longer, time-outs for resting a little. Brief panting truces, during which Jeff searched among the ringside faces for signs of relenting, for indications that Von or Lex or Charley or someone with a little brains and pity would decide the fight had gone on long enough, but they were ruthless in their astonishment and delight and only urged the fighters on. They wanted a definite winner, a bloodied loser, and so far there was neither. Just a couple of bruised, skinned, weary guys who had worse enemies than each other all around them and took refuge together in the clinches. Jeff wished the highschool guys would separate them and call it a draw—he'd gladly settle for a draw. He didn't even want to whip Chester; all he'd been doing was trying not to get whipped himself. He wasn't mad at Chester; he was mad at the rest of the dang world for making them keep on endlessly hitting each other.

During one of the clinches, while scanning the crowd for a teacher or a preacher or anyone else with sense enough to at least call a time out, his befuddled eyes almost tricked him into believing he saw little Jody peering through a crack in the human circle, but he realized it must be Albert Gronstetter, the kid Miss Burns used to confuse with Jody.

So he pushed Chester away and they wearily pummeled

each other some more and clinched again, and this time he thought he saw Mutt pick Albert up and hug him, and he mumbled, "It can't be him?" Who? Chester panted. "Jody," Jeff wheezed. Oh, Chester said. Thinking out loud, Jeff said, "I wonder wot time it is," and Chester said he didn't know but he was already late getting home. "You wanta quit?" Jeff asked hopefully, but Chester said heck no, do you? So all Jeff could do was say heck no himself, and keep on with it.

So they went through the same old monotonous rigamarole again in a slow, leaden-armed, gasping and grunting parody of fighting, and this time during the blessed clinch Jeff imagined that Mutt was holding Albert up so he could see the burlesque of battle better, and he said, "It *is* Jody, but wot's he doin' here?"

"Search me," Chester panted. "You wanta quit?"

"Not unless you do," Jeff said.

"I ain't quittin' until you give up," Chester said.

Neither of them could quit; it had to be stopped by third parties. They were fellow victims of an implacable and pitiless tribal tradition that all young males had to prove their courage and fortitude on public demand, and although you could lose with honor, you couldn't quit unless grievously wounded, or coldcocked. Quitting was cowardly.

It seemed to Jeff, finally, that the only thing to do was to actually try to *whip* the sonofagun, maybe get him down and get a choke hold on him or something so he'd have to say uncle, and he was getting ready to cut loose with all his remaining strength when at long, long last the slowpoke teachers arrived. The hotel trio of Horn, Ewbanks and Conners, who had painted their bathroom window so he would always have to accept Hud's word for how they looked naked.

"Stop this at once!" snapped Miss Ewbanks, who had the jurisdiction because the brawlers were gradeschoolers. Then Liz Horn said, "You ought to be ashamed of yourselves!" But she meant the highschool guys who hadn't stopped the terrible brawl several hours ago, and probably never would have because nobody liked a no-decision fight.

Lex and Von Yancy pushed the fighters apart, and Miss Conners, who was homely but witty, got a laugh by saying, "Kiss and make up, fellas." Even the fighters had to grin a little, but then Chester said, "Git one thing straight, you never licked me."

"I know it," Jeff panted, happy that it was finally over, amazed that he'd actually fought the legendary bully and come out of it alive—and also no longer afraid of Chester. And, by golly, no longer intimidated by Mutt, either. He felt a kind of fondness for Chester, who had turned out to be much less mean, ornery and vicious than he'd been given credit for being—like old Chink's dog. But Jeff would always believe that Chester would never ever have admitted defeat, and if someone hadn't stopped it the darn fight would have gone on forever.

Chester gave an abrupt, scowly half-grin. "I'll tell you sumpthin' else—I never licked you, neither."

Boy, that made Jeff feel good—it was like getting an A-plus in toughness, spunk, grit, etc. Most guys managed to grow up without ever having a serious fight, and in that case you'd never know for sure whether you were any good at fighting or not, and you'd always wonder. Like Jeff used to, but not anymore—he not only wasn't yellow, he just happened to be pretty nifty with his dukes, too. Ask Chester. Ask anybody who was there that day, boy.

When the suddenly pacifist crowd demanded that they shake hands and carry no grudges, there was none of the customary sullen hesitation. They shook hands firmly, and Chester said wryly, "But tomorrow we'll both git licked— only you'll git licked worse'n I will."

He won that round. The gradeschool teachers had that darn agreement that when guys from different rooms had a fight, the teachers would swap victims—which meant that Miss Ewbanks would paddle Chester and Jeff would get his punishment from old Slapper Hallet, who probably had a few private grudges to settle with him. But she'd better watch out how she messed with J. McGraw, boys.

The crowd was dispersing, still awed and incredulous at having either seen a myth diminished or a new one born, and Chester said with a kind of shy gruffness, "See yuh tomorrow, Jeff." With no menace, no implied threat. And Jeff said cordially, "Yeah, if I ain't too stiff an' sore to make it." Which Chester seemed to take as a compliment, as he was meant to.

After Chester went west, some of the guys came to express their utter amazement at Jeff's unexpected courage and prowess, and Dock Ballew, of all people, said: "Boy, you had 'im purt nearly licked when they went an' stopped it." But Jeff knew better. Chester would never say uncle.

Hud, who had seen the whole thing, got a laugh by saying, "I jist got here, wot happened?" He knew what happened, all right, and looked at Jeff with new respect. And so did Mutt, who said, "Hey, Catfish, look who come alla way from Kansas just to see your first real fight."

And it really was Jody after all, climbing all over Jeff so he had to hug the little wart whether he wanted to or not— only he did. And before he could ask the question, Jody answered it. "Daddy Tobe brought me back," he announced happily. "I git to come back here to stay, Jeffy."

It was all still pretty dreamlike and unreal, but Jeff was beginning to feel the physical effects of being the first person that ever almost practically whipped tough Chester Stone, who used to have the entire gradeschool buffaloed; who not only couldn't outrun Jeff McGraw but couldn't whip him, either, by golly. Or anyway hadn't quite.

He let Jody slide from his weary arms and leaned against the corner maple tree that was butter yellow and aglow in the late afternoon sunshine, and Mutt said: "Wot I don't git is how come you let up on 'im like you did when you coulda finished 'im off if you'da tried. You acted like you didn't wanta hurt 'im, for Pete sakes." There was more bewilderment in his tone than scorn or censure.

Still breathing with difficulty, Jeff gazed benignly upon the elder brother he had for so long been intimidated by. "It was too easy to hit 'im, an' I didn't want to hurt 'im. I never wanted to hurt anybody. Maybe that's why I never wanted to fight you."

Ordinarily that would have got a sneery sarcastic retort from Mutt, but now he just raised his eyebrows and sort of shrugged and said, "Well, I got papers to deliver. Here's your junk." He gave Jeff back his marbles and knife and stuff, including the memorandum about needing cobs, while Jody stood there grinning, happy to be home again for good —if he really was. But instead of going on about his business, Mutt hung around, seemingly reluctant to depart.

Jeff was, too, but the analgesia of excitement and action was wearing off now and his bruises were beginning to sting and burn and ache, so he took a final look at the empty arena and started home. Mutt and Jody gave him an escort, and Caroline Riley was waiting over across the intersection, looking curious and concerned.

"Hud let me hold your books," she said shyly. "But I couldn't see from over here through the crowd. Who won?"

"Nobody won," Jeff said. "It was a draw." Suddenly he felt limber-legged and kind of dizzy, so he cut over to the ditch and sank down on the bank. "I need to rest a minute, is all," he sighed.

Jody came to sit beside him, and after a moment of hesitation Mutt joined them, and Caroline stood in front of the McGraw boys self-consciously, not sure whether to smile or look worried, doing some of both. Jeff blinked at Jody, tickled silly but still confused.

"How come they're lettin' you come back?" he asked.

Jody grinned his sly-sheepish grin and told them. "We didden git along, me an' her. We didden like each other, an' she said I was a spoiled rotten little brat. Also a dickens. It

242

caused them to have fusses. I run away quite a bit of times, an' bawled a lot, an' wooden do wot she tol' me, an' kept tellin' 'em I wanted to come home." Grinning from ear to ear, he added: "So they decided to let me. Boy, Mama sure was glad to see me, I'll bet."

"All of us are, you little wart," Mutt said fondly.

"Besides," Jody said, "they're gonna git a baby."

That struck Mutt funny, and Jeff grinned a little, although his face didn't stretch very good, and Caroline let out a giggle and blushed. They all thought about it for a while, beaming at Jody, and presently Mutt said, "Well, this ain't gittin' the papers delivered." He stood up and eyed Jeff thoughtfully. "The fact is I'm tard of havin' two paper routes. It ties a man down too much. So I'm lookin' for someone to take over the afternoon *Times* route."

Jeff nodded absently, fingers gingerly exploring his scrapes and bruises. "Hud might take it—Vern would if he didn't hafta help around the café after school. Boy, I don't remember Chester hittin' me *here*, but I guess he did." He grinned a tired grin. "Seemed like it lasted a week."

"It's only about four-thirty," Mutt said. "Right now I only make ninety-six cents a week on the *Times*, but a guy could prob'ly pick up a few more customers if he tried."

"What about Clarence Olive?" Caroline suggested in a sly innocent way, and Mutt snorted. "I'd rather give it to Lige Bowzer than that stuck-up, snobberdly fiddler."

"They didn't watch the fight," she said, "but I guess her brother has told 'em about it by now, prob'ly."

Jeff stopped fondling his bruises and grinned at her with unusual perception. She was jealous of Alamo and that was a good sign. It struck him that a first love was like a first fight—fun while it lasted and something to look back on fondly, but when it was over it was finished.

"Don't suppose you'd be innerested," Mutt remarked, and Jeff blinked at him and said, "Who, me?—hey, I never even thoughta that possibility." He thought of it. Ninety-six cents a week was peanuts compared to what he'd been making all summer, but it would be a regular year-round income, and he'd be going out of the fish business soon now anyway. "I couldn't start for a couple weeks yet," he said.

Mutt nodded. "At's okay, I ain't quittin' it until the first of November anyway." He gave his kid brother a long, frowning, rather baffled scrutiny, and shook his head. "Yesterday you're the last guy in town I'da turned it over to," he said, and went loping off toward the depot.

Jeff got up stiffly and thought if he was this sore and banged up, old Chester probably wasn't enjoying his long ride home much, either. Taking his books from Caroline, he said, "Much obliged. Remind me Wednesday an' I'll buy you an ice-cream soda for your birthday."

She gave him a blushing smile and an enthusiastic nod and tore out for home, and it seemed to him that she ran with appealing charm and gracefulness, and he thought: It's sure amazing how much a person can change in just a few months. And thought with surprise: Take me, for instance.

As he went in the yard with Jody he heard his mother singing in the kitchen, and thought with a sudden rush of affection: The layoff didn't improve her voice a heck of a lot. But boy, howdy, it was swell to have that ol' gal happy again. And when he went in the house she gave him the warmest, cheerfulest smile he'd seen on her face in a coon's age. She was all dolled up because Uncle Tobe would be there for supper, and she looked very pretty, but underneath she was still the same Jewel McGraw.

"What kept you?" she asked. "I need some cobs." In the shadowy dining room she couldn't see his battle scars.

"We been havin' a family reunion," he told her. "Say, lissen, Mom, I keep forgettin' to tell Dad. We need a load of cobs." He had to grin, then, at the ironic humor of the situation. One of the biggest days of his life so far, one of the most important events of his life for years to come, probably, and the subject of conversation was corncobs. But even if he told her what happened she wouldn't realize how important it had been, mainly because she had no idea how afraid of Chester he'd been since away back last year. Being an ex-schoolteacher, she would never understand *why* guys had to fight sometimes, and as a mother she wouldn't approve of him fighting with his school clothes on.

She went back to fixing supper and he managed to get the cob bucket and beat it without her noticing his battered and skinned-up features. He stopped at the pump to wash up a little, thinking how lucky he'd been to not get hit in the nose or mouth—or maybe not lucky but just naturally a good shifty fistfighter, by golly.

Ranger was whining dejectedly, so he went to unchain him and then the three of them went on out to the barn and the nearly depleted cob pile. Some dog had been digging in the corner after a mouse or something since yesterday, Jeff noticed. It couldn't have been Ranger. Probably Chink's dog, now that the Britton gate was always open, he thought as he started filling the bucket.

"There's sumpin'," Jody said. "Wot is it?"

Jeff looked where he was pointing and saw the gleam of oiled brown wood down against the wall, and he just stayed crouched there staring, not really trusting his eyes but starting to swell up with excitement. Oboy! Let it be what I think it is! he said to himself, and, like a man stalking a rare and jittery animal, he went over there and took hold of the smooth wood, pulled, and cut loose with a loud yelp of joy. "Hot ziggity! It's my good ol' pump Winchester twenty-two rifle that Chink stole from me," he told Jody. "I thought it was lost forever!" He felt like he was going to bust, he was so happy. So *that's* what Chink meant about hiding it right under his nose.

Hurrying to the house, he felt like kicking up his heels and yelling like an idiot, but was glad he hadn't when he found Mrs. Riley in the kitchen with his mother. She had brought over a cherry pie, knowing they were having unexpected company for supper. "My goodness, where in the world did you find it?" his mother asked. Then, alarmed: "Good heavens! What on earth happened to your face?"

He took the questions in order. "It was buried in our cob pile. I had a fight after school." Meanwhile he thought of something that sort of horrified him. "Gee whiz! What if I'd told Dad we needed cobs an' Mr. Yancy hadda brought a load—I never woulda found this baby."

"With whom?" she demanded, and when he told her she sighed and said to Mrs. Riley, "I guess McGraws will be McGraws. He's a chip off the old block, it would seem."

Feeling flattered, he went out onto the screened porch to clean the dust off his rifle, and his mother resumed her conversation where he'd interrupted it.

"As I was saying, I nearly had heart failure. I heard the afternoon southbound come in and then pull out, and I was ironing in the dining room, thinking about going back to Kansas this Saturday and feeling down in the dumps, believe you me, when I heard someone come up on the porch. I just supposed it was Gabe, but I looked through the screen door and—well, I nearly fainted! I simply couldn't believe my eyes! And naturally I started bawling like a big crybaby . . ."

"Nothing to be ashamed of," Mrs. Riley said.

"Tobe just said, 'Here he is, Jewel—he's all yours. It just didn't work out and never would. Take back your boy that you raised from a baby.' Then I said, 'Let's see now,' I said. 'Do you mean for good?' I said, and he nodded and gave me a funny grin and said, 'Well, hell, you're his maw, aren't you?' Oh, I tell you, I'm still in the clouds about it, I have to keep pinching myself to be sure it's true."

Jeff called out, "Did he tell you they're fixin' to have a baby? Anyway, that's what Jody told me an' Mutt."

"Aha, that explains it, then!" Mrs. Riley said.

"It certainly does," his mother said. "It's perfectly understandable, her wanting a child of her own."

Suddenly Jeff thought hey, now she wouldn't need that nine dollars. Maybe they could use some of it to throw a big weenie-roast party for Jody, a welcome-home party, and invite everybody—including Alamo and Clarence. Even Chester—all the country kids that could make it. Boy, howdy, nine dollars would buy enough weenies and marshmallows to feed an army. . . .

"I always dreaded Tobe's visits," his mother was saying, "because I knew it meant they'd invariably find a bottle and get tooted up, but you know, this time I just don't give a doggone. I can't somehow blame them, especially poor Tobe. If they come home tight I won't say a word."

Jeff put his good old rifle away and finished his chores, and every once in a while he had to let out a yodel of pure joy and exuberance. He felt all shivery good, and the future was suddenly bright—hunting with his rifle, earning a regular income from a paper route, being respected by his fellow men for having fought old Chester to a standstill, having Jody home again, and the great convenience of a rapidly blossoming girlfriend right next door, etc. The only cloud on his horizon was tomorrow's encounter with old Slapper and her painful paddle, but she'd darn well better remember that she lived just across the street and he could get even with her seven days a week if she made him mad. But heck, a smarting bottom wasn't so much when you compared it to the aches and pains he was having right now. The important thing was not to bawl. Walk back into the room afterward just grinning nonchalantly, like Mutt did . . .

When he finished his chores and went inside, his dad and his uncle had come home, already two sheets to the wind, as the saying went, and he wondered if he'd ever be that palsy-walsy with *his* brother. Getting tight together and so forth.

"Sure been nunusual summer so far, few lookitut from a stanpoint of unusual thing sappening," his dad said in a slow and dignified way. "You take f'rinstance ol' Lucky Lindy, the eagle of the U.S.A., flyin' alla way crossa Atlannick to Paris.

France. At never happen be-fore. Nuther zample is ol' Babe Ruth hittin' sixty home runs. *At* never happen be-fore, either. Never happen again, probublee, few want my opinion."

"Yeah, magine at, sixxy home runs," Uncle Tobe marveled.

"Also do' forget thuh Depsey-Tooney fight," Jeff's dad said. "Biggis gyp inna hist'ry of boxin', few ass me."

"F'once in your life you urr right," Uncle Tobe said. "Fir stime I ever knewt to happen, but y're right, Gabe. I loss stwenny bucks on at crooked deal, brudder."

Listening to them from the kitchen, Jeff exchanged sort of tolerantly amused glances with his mother, who shrugged and kept on dropping egg noodles into the bubbling chicken broth. And he thought that it *had* been a pretty darn un-usual year, looked at from almost any angle.

When they sat down to the great supper of chicken and noodles, mashed spuds, turnips, cowpeas, fried apples, bis-cuits and several other things, including strong black coffee for the menfolks, his dad peered at him owlishly for a while and said, "Jeff, whuh happen to your rutherwise han'some face, anyway? You fall outa nuther tree'r sumpthing?"

Before Jeff could reply, Mutt said, "He tried to beat up on a mere fifth-grader." That tickled him, and struck Jeff's funnybone, too. Calling tough Chester a mere fifth-grader was a crazy way to look at it, boy.

"I fail to see anything so terribly amusing about fighting, no matter with whom," their mother said. But she was only a woman, and an ex-schoolmarm to boot, so what could you expect?